the further adventures of

SHERLOCK HOLMES

MURDER AT SORROW'S CROWN

STEVEN SAVILE & ROBERT GREENBERGER

TITAN BOOKS

THE FURTHER ADVENTURES OF SHERLOCK HOLMES:
MURDER AT SORROW'S CROWN
Print edition ISBN: 9781783295128
E-book edition ISBN: 9781783295135

Published by Titan Books
A division of Titan Publishing Group Ltd
144 Southwark Street, London SE1 0UP

First edition: September 2016
10 9 8 7 6 5 4 3 2 1

A CIP catalogue record for this title is available from the British Library.

Printed in the USA.

What did you think of this book? We love to hear from our readers.
Please email us at: readerfeedback@titanemail.com,
or write to Reader Feedback at the above address.

To receive advance information, news, competitions, and exclusive offers
online, please sign up for the Titan newsletter on our website:
www.titanbooks.com

the further adventures of

SHERLOCK HOLMES

MURDER AT SORROW'S CROWN

AVAILABLE NOW FROM TITAN BOOKS
THE FURTHER ADVENTURES OF SHERLOCK HOLMES SERIES:

THE COUNTERFEIT DETECTIVE (October 2016)
Stuart Douglas

THE ALBINO'S TREASURE
Stuart Douglas

THE DEVIL'S PROMISE
David Stuart Davies

THE VEILED DETECTIVE
David Stuart Davies

THE SCROLL OF THE DEAD
David Stuart Davies

THE WHITE WORM
Sam Siciliano

THE ANGEL OF THE OPERA
Sam Siciliano

THE WEB WEAVER
Sam Siciliano

THE GRIMSWELL CURSE
Sam Siciliano

THE ECTOPLASMIC MAN
Daniel Stashower

THE WAR OF THE WORLDS
Manly Wade Wellman & Wade Wellman

THE SEVENTH BULLET
Daniel D. Victor

DR JEKYLL AND MR HOLMES
Loren D. Estleman

THE PEERLESS PEER
Philip José Farmer

THE TITANIC TRAGEDY
William Seil

THE STAR OF INDIA
Carole Buggé

THE GIANT RAT OF SUMATRA
Richard L. Boyer

I would like to dedicate the Great Detective's latest case to Miranda Jewess who made a most excellent Watson to my and Bob's Sherlock—*Sorrow's Crown* would not be half the book it is without her red pen. Scratch that, she's more of a Mycroft, two steps ahead and looking out for us boys. Thank you, boss. We owe you.

STEVEN SAVILE

I would like to dedicate this adventure to Steve, who went from friend to partner. He stepped in to help shape a notion into a novel and did so with verve and patience. And a huge thank you to Miranda who saw to it we had the time and offered us the guidance to make this a worthy read. I owe you both.

ROBERT GREENBERGER

"A sorrow's crown of sorrow is remembering happier times."

Alfred Lord Tennyson

Prologue

As celebrated as Sherlock Holmes was around the cusp of the twentieth century, a number of his investigations were deemed sensitive to national security. The Official Secrets Act of 1889 (52 & 53 Vict. c. 52) denied his companion, Dr. John H. Watson, the opportunity to publish the most fascinating and uncomplimentary details of those investigations in any of the popular magazines that would usually carry the exploits of the great detective, and resulted in a number of his diaries being confiscated by the authorities. There was one such case in the summer of 1881, that was subsequently suppressed by agents of Her Majesty's Government, the ramifications of which were felt the length and breadth of polite society, highlighting the need for a new Act of Parliament.

It is only in recent years that these investigations have been declassified, the secrets contained therein finally deemed safe for consumption by the general public whose appetite for such exploits remains insatiable.

What follows is the unaltered account of one such investigation that is of interest, perhaps, because of the tarnish it adds to the government's reputation during what was a particularly volatile period in our country's history.

One

A Taste for Ash

Being an Account of the Reminiscences of JOHN H. WATSON, M.D., late of the Army Medical Department

Our lodgings reeked of ash. It was a distinctly acrid tang that clung to the air with all the tenacity of a flesh-eating parasite, that is to say—and with an Englishman's natural tendency for understatement—it was quite unpleasant.

While Sherlock Holmes and I got on well from the outset, I must admit that living with him was a series of constant adjustments. Mine, not his. Sherlock was a man very much set in his ways and I was expected to come around to his way of thinking in all matters. Shortly after agreeing to room with him at 221B Baker Street, he had settled in, taking one of the bedrooms for himself while commandeering much of the large, airy sitting room with his boxes and portmanteaus. While it took me the matter of the evening we agreed to lease the space to bring my things around, it took Holmes much of the following day. After that, he took his time setting things up, caring more for his weights and measures, his chemical and microscope slides, than his personal belongings.

During those first few days and weeks he spent the majority of his time at his chemistry table, though increasingly he came to spend more and more time in the sitting room, fussing with one thing or another and taking careful notes with the rigid fascination of an obsessive. Any post that arrived for him tended to be overlooked, tossed into a corner. After several days the stack of letters transformed into a careless heap, and it became increasingly obvious he intended to ignore it until it became a bother to navigate. Not that either of us received much in the way of actual correspondence. I was on the outs with my brother and my parents were long since dead. Most of my acquaintances remained in the armed forces and were busy with their duties to the country. Holmes, however, subscribed to several newspapers, which were cast aside as he lost interest in their grim tales of life outside the window of 221B, and as far as I could tell, he did not seem to engage in much in the way of personal correspondence.

Despite his foibles, as lodgers went he was relatively easy to get along with. His routines were fairly set: he rose early and rarely stayed up beyond ten at night. He did not drink and it was not for some time after we settled in together that I was even aware that he owned a fine violin, he played it so seldom. The music he made when left on his own defied description, but he could, upon request, successfully recreate established works, such as my preference for Mendelssohn. In fact, while I was out trying to build up a viable medical practice for myself, he was either fixed on some scientific study or lying prostrate on our couch, deep in thought, still as a statue for hours. It was at these times that Holmes was at his most enigmatic, barely moving and never explaining himself to me. I will admit that upon returning to our rooms that first time I had thought he was dead. The man had not moved so much as a muscle in the six hours I had been gone. Six hours! I could never begin to guess what thoughts could occupy him so completely and utterly, but invariably he concluded his contemplation and snapped up from the couch to resume his studies without comment.

On other occasions, Holmes would leave 221B without a word or explanation of his plans and be gone for minutes or hours. His comings and goings defied any pattern and upon each return he never disclosed his whereabouts. Occasionally he would return with a package or two, something wrapped in used newspaper, but I never saw the contents, and presumed they were materials for his never-ending experiments.

I knew he was brilliant. That much was obvious, even then. A true one of a kind, and mercifully so. I would not want to imagine a London filled with Sherlocks. When we met he was already building up a reputation with the agencies of the law as a "consulting detective", using his obsessive method of examining the world to assist on seemingly impossible cases. As a result, by July of 1881 he was already making something of a name for himself with Scotland Yard and the good men of the Metropolitan constabulary. Even the newspapers were beginning to acknowledge his existence, although they were yet to fully credit his contributions to the successful conclusion of those cases.

Personally, I was never less than astonished by his studied brilliance, though I must admit that I was becoming increasingly aware that as ferociously intelligent as he was with chemicals and matters of science, he was equally deficient when it came to matters of culture or politics. If the Queen's image was not everywhere,

I think he would have had difficulty coming up with her name, never mind her royal house. His memory was, dare I say, filled with more important things. He was a man without peer, using that intellect and rigorous scientific method to solve puzzles that baffled Scotland Yard's finest. Building his skills through observation and practice, dating back to his brief two-year stay at university, had made him an extraordinary observer of the physical world around him. What he could tell from a smudge of mud or chip of paint never ceased to amaze me or impress those new to his acquaintance. Little wonder inspectors such as Lestrade and Gregson had come to call upon his services with increasing regularity. I'd noticed a pattern developing in those periods between cases when Holmes would manically begin a series of studies, throwing himself into the pursuit of knowledge with a single-mindedness that crossed well over the border of obsessiveness, hence the reek of ash currently wafting out of the sitting room.

I assumed it was a particularly strong cigar, and made a deduction of my own: we had a visitor. I dressed hastily and opened the door to find Holmes bent over a clasp which suspended a thick, dark cigar a bare sixteenth of an inch off the table, a glass dish sat snugly in a recess beneath to catch the ash as it burned merrily away, filling the room with a robust aroma.

We had no visitor.

"What in the world are you doing?" I asked him by way of morning greeting.

"I should think it's perfectly obvious, Watson. I am watching this cigar burn."

"Let me rephrase: *why* are you watching that cigar burn?"

"A better question," he replied. "New cigars are imported all the time and each, quite obviously, has their own unique

characteristics, including aroma and the properties of their ash."
I raised a questioning eyebrow, but didn't say a word. Holmes
continued, "As these new leaves enter circulation and increase in
popularity, I need to know what sets them apart from similar cigars
so as not to be fooled into drawing the wrong conclusion."

"Of course," I said, as though it made perfect sense.

"This latest shipment was just delivered to the docks this
morning. I have one of my street Arabs always on the lookout for
interesting and exotic imports on my behalf. He secured a handful
of these, just in from Honduras, and here we are." He gestured
towards the contraption that held the smouldering cigar. "What
better way to spend a damp, dreary morning than working with
something new?"

"I can think of a few," I offered, but he ignored me. One thing
that we did not share was a sense of humour.

"See here. What do you notice?"

"That it might take some time before the odour leaves our rooms
because the windows need to remain shut," I replied, admittedly
with some annoyance in my voice. I did not smoke cigars and this
was a particularly strong example. The summer's unusual heat
should have meant the windows remained open for ventilation
but Holmes's experiment would have been diluted from whatever
aromas wafted in from the still air outside 221B.

It wasn't the answer he was looking for. Indeed, Holmes
seemed bothered by the flippant remark as if I was not taking his
studies as seriously as he did, which admittedly, I wasn't. "Other
than that, Watson."

To appease him, and to give me something to do now that I
was awake and dressed, I peered at the burning cigar, trying to
understand how the leaves were wrapped and if the burn rate

appeared unusual in some way. I did not know much about the murky world of cigars beyond the most elementary: that the cigar itself consisted of three distinct parts, the wrapper, the binder and the filler, and that if the filler was packed too tightly it blocked the airways through the leaves and if it were packed too loosely the smoke would burn too quickly. As I said, not a lot. Truth be told, dear reader, I doubted I would ever look at the world the way Holmes did and felt I would always be a bit of a disappointment to him. Still, I did my level best to distinguish some sort of anomaly in the ash.

"The ash appears longer than I am accustomed to," I replied, hoping I had made a correct observation. Despite my best efforts and own scientific and medical training, I was always missing some detail that made me a constant inferior to my companion.

"Quite right," he agreed, validating my conclusion for a change. "These are expensive compared with the penny cigars the common man might smoke. The higher quality is found in the leaves for both the wrapper and the contents. As a result it produces a much denser ash, which takes longer to drop."

I could only stare at him, unsure of how this added to his store of knowledge.

"Why is it important? Because ash length changes the flavour of the cigar. A longer column of ash cools and 'softens' the smoke, making for a more pleasant experience, but is also indicative of a purer cigar. Additionally, a longer ash means more mass when it drops. This particular brand appears to drop its ash at the five sixty-fourths of an inch mark, measuring a fifth of an ounce. If that number remains consistent as I burn the remainder, then I can store this reliable information. Couple this with other information, such as whether the leaves were sun grown or shade grown, which can be deduced from the colouration of the wrapper, how the leaves themselves have been cured and fermented, then there is the country of origin, of course. I am sure you are aware, Watson, that tobacco leaves are grown in more than one part of the world?"

"Of course," I lied.

"Significant quantities of the leaf are cultivated in Brazil, Cameroon, Cuba, the Dominican Republic, Honduras, which as I say is where this particular cigar was imported from, Indonesia, Mexico, Nicaragua, the Philippines, Puerto Rico..." The exotic-sounding names all began to blur into one as he reeled them off without taking a breath. "The Canary Islands, even, surprisingly, Italy, and of course the plantations of the Eastern United States. The soil in each of these countries contains different nutrients and a scientific mind could therefore deduce the country of origin if it knew what to look for."

Holmes paused his lecture and watched the greying ash finally tumble from cigar to dish. He scribbled a note in a leather-bound book using an elegant pen. He took one more look at the new heap of ash and continued writing.

"Truly, there is a wealth of knowledge to be gleaned from this humble pile of ash," I said. Holmes appeared to miss the sarcasm in my tone.

He had the remarkable ability to force his mind to empty itself of useless information when he was done with it. That, perhaps, was every bit as impressive as his ability to cram it full of facts. Although there was no science to support his position, he remained convinced that the human brain could only retain so much knowledge, so he regularly created room by "forgetting" facts he considered unimportant. It certainly explained why he knew nothing about particular subjects and cared little for information that did not have a bearing on his detective work. In many ways, he was a simple soul: he just needed to know whether it was raining—which it was on that day—not understand how the clouds absorbed moisture and emitted it under the right and proper circumstances.

I would have preferred a warm summer day, allowing us to air out our rooms, but instead I would have to endure the experiment until it met its desired conclusion. I could only hope that the cigars were the only things that burned down to ash, not the four walls around us.

The ring of the bell at the street door broke the silence. Unsurprisingly, Holmes ignored it, still watching the glowing ember at one end of the cigar with interest. In contrast, I sprang to my feet, knowing who the caller was. Holmes had had few paying clients during the preceding weeks, while our bills remained alarmingly constant. He did not seek out custom, and it was not my place to find individuals with the type of intriguing problems that might interest my companion and help pay for our lodgings in the process. My own practice was frighteningly small and I would not be able to support us both for more than a week or two. It was ever a juggling act. Holmes had an unerring ability to be dismissive of problems I imagined he'd find fascinating, and became utterly absorbed by the minutiae I predicted he'd dismiss as pointless. He could be quite contrary. However, a chance encounter the previous day, while at my bank depositing what little my practice *had* produced in financial gain, had offered a chance of Holmes paying his way.

I opened the door to Mrs. Hudson's knock. She handed me a card, which identified our caller as the man I had been expecting: G. Wilson Waugh, the manager of Shad Sanderson Bank in the city. I asked our landlady to show the gentleman up to our rooms.

The man who stood in our sitting room moments later was more youthful than most in his profession. His side whiskers were a dark brown, giving his face a dire look, and he looked uncomfortable in his damp, light wool suit. I offered our guest a seat on the couch. By this time, Holmes had completed his work with the burning cigar, had made his notes, and was in the process of sweeping the well-weighed remains into a basket. Taking his customary chair, he did not shake hands, but rather sat and looked intently at the visitor, his face a blank mask.

"Holmes, I met Mr. Waugh while I was at the bank. He was most considerate to help me with a matter and we fell into conversation. He mentioned a problem and I told him you might well be the fellow to come to his aid," said I. Turning, I addressed the bank manager who shuffled his feet, a sign of nervousness if ever I saw one.

"Mr. Waugh, when we spoke at the bank, you mentioned there was a problem that mystified you," I began. "Would you be so kind as to elaborate for Mr. Holmes?"

"Of course, Dr. Watson," said he, nodding his head. "I appreciate you seeing me. The truth of the matter is, I remain stumped by the problem and could benefit from a wiser mind."

"That would be mine," Holmes said. "Tell me in as great detail as you can."

"Our banking establishment has been finding various cashier accounts deficient at the end of each day. It is never the same cashier so we cannot begin to accuse any one person."

"How long has this been going on?"

"Two weeks, sir," Waugh said.

"And how much has gone missing each time?"

"By our accounts, we believe the sum total unaccounted for comes to three hundred pounds six pence."

"Is it the same amount each time?" Holmes had barely moved, taking in everything about the speaker, who appeared not to notice, shifting his gaze from Holmes to me and back again.

"No two sums have matched."

"And you say these are all different employees working the cashier windows?"

"Indeed they are; most having worked for us for a number of years. We trust each and every one of them."

Holmes stopped questioning the man and appeared to consider the issue, his gaze taking in the banker, from his brightly polished shoes to his immaculately tailored suit, before focusing somewhere in the middle distance. I could almost hear the cogs whirring as his mind processed every last detail of Waugh's appearance. I tried to apply my own mind in the same fashion, noting the cologne the man wore, deducing from the condition of his footwear that he'd visited the shoeshine boy on the corner—as I often did myself—before his arrival. Waugh fidgeted under the detective's scrutiny and seemed increasingly uncomfortable. I, having had more than a few occasions to see his great mind at work, merely sat by and waited for his conclusions.

The dull early morning light filtered in through the thick curtains and the thin haze of cigar smoke, picking out that familiar aquiline profile, deep in thought.

"I daresay, you are a bold one," Holmes finally said, a small smile cracking his severe face. Waugh looked positively stunned. "Have you noticed, Watson, that Mr. Waugh's shoes are brand new? Italian made, judging by the stitching and suppleness of the leather, and only recently imported." I said nothing, understanding immediately where Holmes was going. "Then, there is the pocket watch chain, new gold, and as of yet showing no signs of wear, suggesting it is a recent addition to his ensemble. One could assume that a bank manager is fastidious when it comes to personal appearance, after all, in order to *be* the part one must first *appear* the part, that is how one engenders trust and encourages fools to part with their money, wouldn't you agree, Mr. Waugh?" The banker said nothing. "We must also consider the cut of his suit, which falls exquisitely on his slender frame, and is of the latest style from Savile Row. Such a suit would exceed the comfortable reach of a manager's salary. I will concede that while bankers must present the most trustworthy of appearances, sometimes it is difficult to discount the obvious when it comes to financial impropriety. Additionally, Watson, I am sure you noted our guest's topcoat when he arrived? Burberry's, new gabardine if I am not mistaken. Also new."

I shook my head, not having perceived any of these facts.

"If the amounts are random as are the days they go missing, I think we may safely rule out the possibility that one of the cashiers is being blackmailed. Equally, if as Mr. Waugh insists, the staff are trustworthy, then someone else must be at fault. Since customers cannot access the money drawers we may rule out the population of Greater London and instead conclude that a single individual is responsible, randomising the funds taken and the burgled drawers simply to cause confusion."

"Sounds altogether reasonable," I conceded.

"But, the bank officials are now growing alarmed and will shortly bring this matter to the police; after all, theft is the one thing in their business that cannot be countenanced. The public give their money to the bank for safekeeping. If the bank cannot be trusted to keep that money safe what is the point of using their services? The shadow of suspicion will cast its pall over the staff and our thief will be among them. That is why he is now worried as to how obvious his crime will be. Isn't that so, Mr. Waugh?"

Waugh bolted upright, a look of terror on his pallid features as every ounce of blood drained from his face. It was immediately obvious he wanted to be anywhere else but 221B, under the scrutiny of Holmes's all-seeing eye. I would have pitied the man, but for the fact that he was a crook.

"You, Mr. Waugh, are the thief. You have endeavoured to make it appear the work of others, but to a trained eye, you have been spending your ill-gotten gains on improving your appearance when not paying off the house. And I am not referring to your home, Mr. Waugh."

Now Holmes had my attention. I swear Waugh thought the detective was consorting with the spirits; how else could he read his guilt so thoroughly? I wondered much the same myself, but knew the question had to have a far more mundane solution, like most spiritualists' tricks.

"How in the world can you tell he owes a gambling debt?"

Holmes offered a wry smile. "You will note the way his hands jostle back and forth when he is nervous? It is a tell, as if his cupped palm still contains dice. In his mind's eye, he is no doubt picturing the rolls that went awry, placing him in debt and precipitating the unfortunate sequence of events that have brought him to our door. No doubt Mr. Waugh here stole when he could no longer afford to cover his gambling debt on his own modest salary, thinking to replace the missing funds when his fortune improved. However, once he realised the checks and balances in place were insufficient to catch a thief in the act, he began stealing in earnest without fear of retribution or recrimination, and continued, exceeding his needs until ultimately guilt set in and made him dispose of it."

"On expensive clothing," I concluded.

"Precisely," Holmes agreed.

"Why would he present you with this as a mystery if he is at fault?" I asked. Waugh remained frozen in his seat between us.

"Ah, my dear Watson, our young banker is merely testing his pretence at innocence and has found it to be useless. Without doubt, he is well aware that his crimes are going to be exposed and is already thinking through the implications. Isn't that so, Mr. Waugh?"

"Are you going to turn me in?" Waugh asked. His voice had shifted its register, the panic clearly evident in his tone. I could see the instinct to run bright in his eyes.

"No. If I am any judge of human nature I should think you will turn yourself in this morning," Holmes said without preamble. "You are clearly feeling the unbearable burden of guilt. Of course, if I do not read of your confession in tomorrow's paper, I will inform the police myself. That should suffice."

The air of agitation quickly left poor Waugh, who sank back into the couch, utterly defeated. "I am through."

"Indeed you are. See him out, Watson."

Holmes was no longer interested in the man. I steered the hapless Waugh back down the stairs and returned to our rooms to an unhappy Holmes.

"You made quick work of that, why do you look so glum?"

"You said it yourself, Watson, and more than once: we need a paying case or we will find ourselves in straits similar to the hapless Waugh. But not just any case: one that will not only pay its way, but one that will challenge my intellect."

I offered a knowing smile. "Then you are in luck, my friend," I replied. "Because I have scheduled a series of such visits today and I daresay at least one of these should prove a worthwhile challenge."

Which, of course, was a bold statement. As the morning progressed Holmes grew less and less interested in the parade of clients and their problems, large or small. He was dismissive of their concerns, blunt in their dismissal, and repeated again and again that he was only interested in a true challenge, which I was rapidly coming to conclude was about as common as a unicorn in this city.

As I had made these appointments over the last several days, I will admit I had been filled with confidence, certain that we should have not one but several cases worthy of the great detective. The word you are looking for, dear reader, is hubris, but in my defence, of late I have increasingly spent time accompanying Holmes on these investigations, taking my notes and recreating the cases to the best of my recollection as yarns for publication. I believe I have become a better raconteur with each such effort, but every time Holmes reads the finished report and dismisses it as exaggeration bordering on outright falsehood. However, not once has he asked me to cease these efforts and the payment for each piece has been sufficient to compensate me for the time not spent practising medicine, keeping a roof over our heads. Indeed, our partnership has become so commonplace that Lestrade has come to expect us as a pair.

What I had not and could not have anticipated was that this July would prove to be one of the wettest in memory, which had turned my injured leg into a throbbing reminder of my time with the Berkshires. The discomfort proved a distraction as the afternoon wore on and potential clients came and went. I should not have been surprised when Holmes managed to solve each "mystery" with the same ease as he did our poor banker's conundrum.

A Mrs. Mary Carrington arrived next, complaining of a missing pearl necklace. Holmes sent a withering look my way, obviously disappointed with the prosaic nature of the crime, but took a deep breath and turned his penetrating attention towards the woman. She was in her late fifties, crow's feet prominent on her otherwise smooth face that suggested a life lived with lots of laughter and gave her an attractive air. As she sat in the guest chair, she fidgeted with her hands, constantly reaching up to her naked neck, no doubt missing the pearls.

"Mrs. Carrington," Holmes said, not wasting time with anything as civil as introductions. "I am going to ask you a few questions. Please be completely honest with your answers."

"Of course."

"First, tell me about your finances," Holmes said, bluntly.

She appeared shocked by such a bold approach, but didn't shirk or seek to deflect the question as she might have done. "We are adequately provided for. My husband works for Shaw Brothers, a trading firm at the London Stock Exchange and has for the last two decades."

"Yes, but that is not what I actually asked, dear lady. Have there been any irregularities in how your husband chooses to spend his money that you have noticed?"

"How so?"

"Are you, perhaps, paying bills later than you would have previously, or buying less expensive cuts of beef?"

"My husband pays our bills, of course, and we have a cook who goes to the market," she said in a defensive tone.

"So, what you are really telling me is that you have no sense of your family's fortunes?"

"I suppose... No, I do not," she stammered, flustered. She couldn't look him in the eye.

"Your perfume is, I believe, French, yes?"

"It is," she replied then looked at me as if Holmes's question marked some kind of madness she couldn't follow. I inclined my head slightly, urging her to go with his line of enquiry.

"Your dress is also of French design, is it not?"

She paused to look down at her attire and nodded to confirm his observation.

"It is my belief your husband has suffered a reversal of fortune," Holmes said. "He has favoured the French which has translated to the lifestyle you enjoy."

"I'm sorry, but favoured how?" the woman asked, earning her a disapproving look from Holmes.

"He was investing in their financial instruments, I suspect. However, in March, a substantial loan was being proposed by the government and I believe he invested thinking the loan would be forthcoming. Instead, the loan was denied by the International Financial Society, the monies diverted to the United States of America to subsidise development of their railways, so your husband's investments turned out poorly. He is now burdened with unexpected debts and I contend has hocked your necklace to cover the family's obligations."

Her jaw dropped in surprise, eyebrows shooting towards the ceiling. "How could he...?" her voice trailed off and I offered her my handkerchief to stem the tears rapidly welling in her eyes. It was not, all things considered, a happy end to her visit. After escorting her out, I returned to the sitting room and confronted my bored companion.

"How the devil can you not know the Earth orbits the sun, but recite by heart some obscure bit of financial business from four months ago?"

"Watson, my job is entirely dependent on what might drive others to commit criminal acts. Among those many causes will be various financial transactions including movements in the financial markets. I do not make a great study of the Stock Exchange, but I do follow it well enough to make such obvious deductions."

"Obvious to you, but not to that poor woman," I said. "How bad do you expect their difficulties to be?"

"If he is keeping the news from his wife and going so far as to pawn jewellery, I would suggest it is quite dire."

Next, we entertained an elderly man who asked for Holmes's help in finding his first love. He wrung his hands as his raspy voice pleaded that he had thought of her every day since they last saw one another when he was but sixteen.

"If you were so much in love, what separated you?" Holmes asked our guest.

"A difference in purpose, I suppose. I was determined to become successful in business, having been apprenticed to a man named Jorkin, and went to London to work. She wanted to raise a family and farm so remained out in the country. I suppose our love was not strong enough."

"No, I daresay it could not have been, otherwise one of you would have joined the other. You are reaching your twilight years, sir, and I suspect you think of the young lady as a life that might have been. Believe me when I say seeking her out will not bring you happiness. It is best you keep her memory and not mar it with a current portrait."

After the man left, I turned to Holmes and smiled. "That may have been the kindest thing I have ever seen you do."

Holmes made a dismissive noise and lit his pipe, which had the virtue of having a far more pleasing aroma than the foul cigar.

A vicar came by seeking help with missing candlesticks but that too was easily solved, a solution so simple that I was fairly close to finding it myself before Holmes determined the conclusion.

With each dismissal my companion grew increasingly sour. I suggested we cancel the remaining appointments but he fortified himself with tea and insisted we not delay the inevitable.

"The sooner we dismiss the superfluous cases, the sooner a true challenge will present itself," he declared. At least that was the plan. But as the morning turned to afternoon even I was beginning to despair. We worked through the potential clients without a single promising problem. By half past two, we had completed the interviews and I was at a loss. I suggested, as the rain had lightened by then, we take a stroll and clear our heads. I privately thought that it would also allow me to open a window and air out our rooms, which still stank of cigar smoke. We were gathering ourselves for a walk through the park when there was a ring at the bell.

"I thought you said we had exhausted your calendar?" Holmes said with some irritation. "I think I have indulged you enough for one day."

"We have," I replied. "I cannot say who this might be."

Mrs. Hudson appeared at our door again, looking distinctly irritated; we had, after all, caused her to ascend the stairs many times already that day. The card she proffered to me was that of a Mrs. Hermione Frances Sara Wynter, with an address in Shoreditch, not the most salubrious of addresses. Holmes joined me in the doorway and took the card.

"She says she has no appointment but seems determined to see you," said Mrs. Hudson to Holmes.

He began to shake his head dismissively when Mrs. Hudson continued boldly. "She's an old woman, sir, and has likely put herself out a considerable bit to be here in this weather. I know you have had a busy day, but surely one more visitor could do you no harm?"

"Oh, very well," Holmes said, spinning on his heel and resuming his place in the chair.

"Would you prepare some tea for her?" I said to Mrs. Hudson.

She smiled. "I already have the kettle on." She withdrew to fetch our visitor. I resumed my own place, curious as to the nature of the visit, but could not resist pointing out to Holmes that our landlady appeared to have taken his measure as carefully as he measured others. He gave a derisive snort but said nothing further, which I chose to interpret as agreement.

Hermione Frances Sara Wynter was at least seventy, perhaps older, as wrinkles softened her features. She had her steel-grey hair tucked neatly under a dark bonnet and her dress was of a similarly dark hue, stern stuff highlighted by a white collar and several pieces of gold jewellery. Even I could tell she had or once had had considerable funds. She was barely five feet tall, the slight stoop of her shoulders robbing her of another two or three inches, and it was obvious that age was not treating her kindly.

"Mrs. Wynter, Sherlock Holmes at your service," he said in tones kinder than any I had heard that day. He was making an effort, most likely for Mrs. Hudson's benefit, but which I certainly appreciated.

"Thank you so much for seeing me without an appointment, Mr. Holmes."

"I will admit I am seeking a case to occupy my mind so I find myself speaking with one and all," Holmes said. "So tell me, how do you believe I can be of assistance?"

The elderly lady wrung her hands, worrying at a silk handkerchief and in the process presenting herself as the very picture of a woman in distress, though what was on her mind had to wait a few moments as Mrs. Hudson arrived and laid out afternoon tea. She poured first for Mrs. Wynter, and through some silent communication knew just how much milk and sugar to use. Holmes let the act play itself out without a word. He did not stir until Mrs. Hudson had closed the door behind her.

"How did you come to find me, Mrs. Wynter?"

"Giles DeVere, a business associate of my deceased husband, made mention of your considerable skills. I understand you helped him with a problem several years ago."

I gave my companion a look with raised eyebrows, but he just nodded in agreement. The name meant nothing to me. I turned to our guest.

"Mr. DeVere is an industrialist up north," she explained. "He and my dear Lyle were associates and we have maintained cordial contact since his passing." I was intrigued as to how Holmes had helped DeVere, but now was not the time to press for details. "I am here about my son, Norbert," she said before taking a sip of tea.

"Is he in some sort of trouble?" Holmes asked eagerly.

"He was due home in June," said she, then trailed off.

"From where?"

"I'm sorry, I should explain. Norbert is with the Royal Navy. He is a lieutenant serving aboard HMS *Dido*."

Being an avid follower of military matters in the press, I knew the *Dido* had seen action during the recent war against the Boers in South Africa, but seemed to recall reading the ship had returned some weeks back.

"And what is your concern?" Holmes prompted.

"I went to the docks to welcome my son home. I waited and I watched, but as our boys disembarked one by one, there was neither hide nor hair of him. Frantic, I asked his shipmates, but many did not know him and those who did said he was not aboard. I had a terrible time finding his superior officers and they refused to say what had become of him, no matter how much I begged. No one would give me any answers. I left with no idea if my boy was alive or dead."

"Did you think to make inquiries at the Admiralty?" asked Holmes.

Mrs. Wynter nodded impatiently. "I have made several trips both to the Admiralty and the War Office—*Dido* sent a naval brigade to fight at Majuba you see, and I thought the army might have the information the navy could not provide. It was most vexing."

It was clear to me that this woman had little understanding of how the different branches of Her Majesty's armed forces worked. There was no need for her to bother the army, losing her precious time.

"People feigned ignorance, offered platitudes, wished me luck in finding him," she went on without pause, "but few seemed genuinely interested in helping me locate Norbert."

Holmes leaned closer, as did I, sensing there was more to this story.

"Finally, I found a secretary who agreed to look through the records after I was refused yet another meeting. He informed me that Norbert was listed on the *Dido*'s manifest as being Missing in Action."

"I'm so sorry," I said. In contrast my companion sat impassively offering nary a word of sympathy.

Mrs. Wynter shook her head. "There's more. He said there was a footnote to the entry and from what he could discern, there was the suggestion that Norbert had deserted during battle." Desertion was one of the most heinous crimes one could commit while in uniform. I could not hold back the wave of revulsion at the very notion, and she could not help but see it.

Holmes and I exchanged looks, mine of surprise, his of something else entirely, then returned our attention to Mrs. Wynter, who dabbed at her eyes with her handkerchief.

"Lyle and I had Norbert late in our married life and maybe we doted on him too much. However, Norbert may not be a war hero," she looked me in the eye then, "but I did not raise my son to be a deserter." I said nothing. "He may have died in battle, his body unrecovered, I can accept that. Too many of our boys are listed as Missing in Action. What I will not accept is his reputation... his memory... being tarnished in this way. I have exhausted all my efforts, Mr. Holmes. I am at the end of my strength. I need someone to take up the baton from me, and am hoping that someone might be you, a man known for his fierce dedication to the truth. I want to know what happened to my son. That is all. That should not be so much, should it?"

Holmes and I sat in silence for several moments as she continued to dab at her eyes. After nearly a full minute, he leaned forward and asked, "Please give me whatever details you have. Leave nothing out."

The relief on Mrs. Wynter's face was deeply affecting. She explained that her son was attached to the *Dido*, which was, in turn, posted to the West Africa Station from '79. According to what the Admiralty revealed to her, young Norbert was part of the naval brigade that went ashore to join the Natal Field Force when the Boers rose up. It was therefore unlikely he would have been

at Majuba Hill in February this year. Still, her boy did not return
with the *Dido* in June.

"I have no idea if he even left Africa, or if something happened
on board during the voyage home. Indeed, it is all a mystery to
me," Mrs. Wynter admitted. "The truth of the matter is that no one
will tell an old woman what has become of her only son. I have
made my appeals at Whitehall and the Admiralty, but as I told you,
all I have learned is that he is classified as Missing in Action. He
cannot be a deserter, Mr. Holmes. Norbert was faithful and loyal
to the Crown. I know my boy; he would never abandon his post.
In his letters, Norbert described his shipmates as if they were his
brothers. Something else *must* have happened."

"When did you last hear from him?" Holmes asked.

She reached into her small handbag and withdrew a well-worn
document. Holmes's long, tapered fingers snatched it from her and
his eyes quickly scanned the contents. He then handed it casually
to me, as if it were nothing of importance. The letter, dated 5th
January, seemed innocuous–reports of shipboard high jinks and
complaints about the food. It contained nothing about the war nor
gave a clue as to Norbert Wynter's disappearance that I could see.

Mrs. Wynter wrung her hands. "It is the not knowing that
haunts me and keeps me awake at night. You can understand that,
can't you, Mr. Holmes? Norbert is no deserter. I know my own son.
Someone is hiding the truth." Her tone was filled with the anguish
of a mother bereft and seemed to be begging Holmes to tell her
she was right.

Holmes seemed far from convinced. His penetrating eyes
remained fixed on hers, revealing nothing. I, however, will admit
that I was moved by her appeal. Having been an Assistant Surgeon
with the Fifth Northumberland Fusiliers, I had seen the horror

of war with my own eyes, albeit in Afghanistan and not Africa. I could imagine just how savagely the lack of knowledge gnawed away at the woman day and night. While my own mother was long gone, I could scarcely imagine what she might have felt had she heard of my injury. Weeks of not knowing how bad it was, if I would ever walk again. Just bringing it to mind caused me to lean forward and massage my knee. Holmes glanced in my direction, and I was sure he had ascertained my train of thought.

"Holmes, surely we can provide Mrs. Wynter with some assistance?"

"Some assistance, yes," he began and in my eagerness to get him to commit, I uncharacteristically cut him off and turned toward Mrs. Wynter.

"Do you have a likeness of Norbert?"

"Yes, I do," said she, and once more dipped into her bag, withdrawing a worn photograph. Norbert, tall, exceedingly thin, stood proudly in his naval uniform. His left hand clutched the sabre while his right thumb was tucked beneath the narrow black belt. To my eye, he appeared maybe twenty-five, certainly under thirty, with dark hair—brown rather than black I suspected—and a moustache that framed his upper lip. His eyes stared fixedly at the camera, filled with pride.

"It was taken when he was promoted to lieutenant," she said with pride.

"A handsome lad," I said politely. Holmes snatched the photograph from my fingers and examined it minutely for some time. He then returned it to Mrs. Wynter and rose to his feet.

"This appears to be a mere missing person case," he said. She began to speak but he cut her off with a raised hand. "However, for the Royal Navy to hint at desertion speaks to something else,

I think, something more than a mere missing seaman. For that reason and that alone I shall accept the case for my normal fee and shall commence work immediately."

Mrs. Wynter rose, her face illuminated by her smile, making the wear of the years briefly fade away.

"I am ever so grateful, Mr. Holmes. If you are half as good as your reputation, I know that you shall find my son."

"I shall find the truth about your son, Mrs. Wynter. Whether the actual man himself materialises along with it remains to be seen," he corrected, hardly comfortingly, as he walked her to the door.

Two

A Bureaucratic Wall

Holmes sat brooding, his disgruntled air a clear indication that he was taking the case against his better judgment, but I could see that the notion of branding a man a "deserter" bothered him. Without sufficient cause such a tarnishing of a young man's life in death was bothersome.

"Watson, my good man, I think it is time for us to make a trip to the Admiralty."

"You mean to start the investigation this very moment?" Our new client had only just departed.

"The sooner we begin, the sooner, inevitably, we conclude the case. Given the financial circumstances you are so keen to remind me of, I feel my time is better used in solving Mrs. Wynter's dilemma than burning more cigars today." I wasn't about to argue with that particular deduction.

The incessant rain had lightened but not desisted altogether, so we dressed in our topcoats despite the summer heat, and descended to Baker Street, where Holmes flagged down a hansom.

We rolled down Regent Street and through Piccadilly Circus. The rain had not kept the city's inhabitants indoors; the shops appeared to be doing a fine trade. Holmes kept his own counsel during the journey, no doubt making many observations, filing away titbits of information for another time. The cab rolled on, steel rims clanking on the hard surface, down past Charing Cross and around until we began to see the first buildings of Whitehall rising before us. The centre of government was both a daunting and an inspiring sight, the true beating heart of this great land of ours.

The Admiralty was housed in a splendid building constructed by the famed architect Thomas Ripley and finished more than a century and a half earlier. It was an imposing structure, sturdy in its white stone and brown brick, with a low wall in front with three entrances, added many years after the main three-storey building.

We passed through the central entrance and across the courtyard, past the two long arms of the building on either side of us, towards the main doors. Despite having served with the army I had never had cause to visit the Admiralty and I admit I was suitably impressed with its serious and sober air. As one would expect, it had gravitas. We passed a variety of senior naval officers, their adjutants hurrying to keep up with them, carrying umbrellas to keep the woollen uniforms dry as the rain continued to fall.

Within, we were greeted by polished wood and marble corridors that led to a warren of offices barren of any appropriate signage, which caused us a momentary confusion.

"Watson, where do you think we should begin?" asked Holmes.

"I suppose we would begin with some sort of records office," I said. "I admit, I would not know where to begin finding such an office without asking for assistance."

"Why start with a lowly clerk?" asked Holmes. My companion

was of a mind to seek a higher authority from the outset. He put himself before a harried-looking officer who was struggling with a stack of books and maps.

"Your pardon, sir, but I am seeking the Board of Admiralty."

That announcement caused the officer and me to gape in surprise. As was typical of my companion, he was beginning at the very top of the organisation whereas I would have naturally begun with the clerks, the ones who always knew what's what, and worked my way up. I could not fathom his reasoning, but watched with curiosity.

"They meet on the top floor," the man said in a rough voice. "Are you expected?"

"No," Holmes said and proceeded toward a staircase without waiting to be challenged.

I followed him in silence, doing my best to keep up as we worked our way to the top floor and there found offices for the Board of Admiralty, the leading advisors to the Admiral of the Fleet. Sir Alexander Milne had only recently been appointed to the post and I very much doubted that Holmes intended to see the man himself but with Holmes one never knew.

Without knocking, my companion swung open a heavy oak door and confronted a startled young man in uniform who sat with a stack of papers on his small, untidy desk.

"Good day, sir, I wish to make an inquiry about a missing naval officer," Holmes began without preamble, putting the clerk immediately at a disadvantage in what was about to become their conversation. The clerk blinked once, then twice, slowly rising and revealing himself to be about a head shorter than Holmes, twenty years of age, if that. There was still some boyish fat to his cheeks and his pale complexion implied he was deskbound and had not been to sea this year, if ever. A quick exchange of names revealed his to be Pegg and he hesitated each time he spoke, displaying a combination of caution and some nervousness.

"You say a missing officer?"

"Quite. He served aboard the *Dido* and did not return with it last month. I'd like to find him."

The clerk was clearly flummoxed, unaccustomed to a civilian walking in and making demands. He seemed uncertain if he should reply or summon help. I almost pitied the man.

"I, ah, well, I certainly have no such information in this room, sir, nor is it the Royal Navy's habit of providing it to anyone other than members of the service," said Pegg, finally finding his voice; one, I might add, that sounded less the able seaman and every bit the bureaucrat.

"Is it also the navy's habit to misplace their lieutenants?"

That gave Pegg pause. I interjected, to try and persuade him as to the correctness of our cause. "I myself have served in Her Majesty's army and while not the same service, as it were, still related to the protection of the empire. I do hope you can be of assistance."

"A lieutenant from the *Dido*?" he repeated.

"Quite right. If you lack such information, who on this floor might be able to provide it?"

"Records are not on this floor," the man said finally, with an audible gulp.

"How good are these records?"

"Her Majesty's Royal Navy has maintained exemplary records for centuries," he said with pride.

"And yet you cannot seem to keep track of a sailor from this very year," Holmes observed, with no trace of humour in his voice.

"I would ask that you redirect your inquiry to the Office of

Records, first floor, left wing," the officer said, addressing me and pointedly averting his gaze from Holmes.

"A moment, sir," Holmes said. Pegg paused and finally looked up again to meet his eyes.

"Yes?" He was clearly trying to sound officious, but his youth undermined him.

"The Board of Admiralty. This is the decision-making body of the Royal Navy?"

"Yes it is."

"Are they always in the habit of wasting the taxpayer's funds?"

The poor man blinked. I myself had no idea what Holmes was getting at.

"The hallways are carpeted."

"Fine Persian rugs, imported decades ago I am told," said he.

"Someone was taken in by fakes, and not very good ones at that," Holmes said.

Poor Pegg looked torn between instinctively defending the fraudulent flooring and wanting to know how Holmes could possibly know they were counterfeit. "What do you mean?"

"If you would be so kind," Holmes said, using a slight gesture to indicate the man was to follow him out of the office. Indeed, the man rose as curiosity got the better of him. He obediently and slowly followed Holmes just past the threshold and turned his attention to the rug he no doubt ignored during his time in the building.

"The Persians are known for their rugs because of the level of craftsmanship, design, and ability to wear for many years," Holmes said. "Even in a building such as this, with a high level of foot traffic, they should hold up. Instead, you will see that this example–" he turned and knelt on the carpet in the corridor "–is in the process of unravelling in certain places. Additionally, true Persian dyes are permanent and these carpets are beginning to fade. Note if you will, the deep blues along the edges are still in reasonable shape, but where the foot treads more frequently, they have grown several shades lighter. Upon closer inspection, you will find other patterns and colours beneath. This was once an entirely different carpet, remade to resemble Persian, and someone in the procurement department was duped."

The speechless young man stared at Holmes who returned the look. "Do keep a better eye on our funds. They are not inexhaustible," Holmes said and turned on his heel. I followed him and we left.

"Really, Holmes, must you be so harsh? He clearly was not responsible," said I.

"While accurate, he still represents an administration that has proven lax on several accounts," Holmes replied.

Having descended the stairs to the Office of Records, we were brought up short by yet another uniformed clerk, this one a veteran, balding and with ruddy cheeks. He clearly was nearing the end of a career, this final station his nominal reward until retirement. He had dark eyes and a rough look about him, one who had served at sea and taken its measure. This was not a man meant to be behind a desk, and resentment radiated from him. He gave us a stern look. It did not discourage Holmes. If something was guaranteed to make the man intractable, it was scorn.

"I was directed by Admiral Milne's office to come see you regarding the whereabouts of a seaman from the *Dido*," Holmes said and I began to see his genius. Having come from the Admiral's office, he now carried a sense of right that went beyond any sort of underling camaraderie and should be enough to convince the clerk of our authority.

"But you are civilians," the man—whose name turned out to be Hampton—said, pointing out the obvious. His very manner indicated he was not here to be of service.

"I can see why you're in records, your observation is most astute," Holmes said drily. Hampton glared in return at the remark.

"Civilians are not permitted to examine the Royal Navy archive," Hampton said.

"Does that extend to the family of your men?"

"We can give them some information," replied he. Retrieving information from this man would be like extracting a cracked tooth.

"Some?"

"That's right. Some of the information is classified and not for the general public. Are you seeking information about a family member, then?" He folded his arms before his ample stomach and stared defiantly at Holmes.

"I am here on behalf of a mother who was given 'some' information but it proved insufficient."

"And you think that by showing up in person you might gain additional information?" the clerk said, taking refuge in the bureaucracy of his position. His beefy arms remained fixed before him, a solid barrier.

"Now see here—" I said. I was ready to cause a mild disturbance, irritated at such treatment from fellow military men, but Holmes waved me into silence and remained calm.

"The Admiral's officer did indicate you would be helpful," Holmes repeated.

"Yes, I can be, but only to a degree. I cannot simply divulge what could be sensitive information. As I am sure you will understand, I will also need documentation identifying the fact that you are as you purport, and actually represent the woman in question." There was little respect in his tone or manner.

"A valid point, Mr. Hampton," Holmes admitted. "Let us do this: please consult your records of the HMS *Dido* and please acknowledge that Lieutenant Norbert Wynter was serving on the ship during its recent posting to the Cape."

"Will you go away then?"

"If you provide me with what we seek, then of course," said Holmes. "If not, I am perfectly willing to wait to speak with your superior officer." Then he placed his arms before him, mirroring Hampton's posture. It was a confrontation that Hampton did not have a prayer of winning.

Sure enough, after several long silent moments, Hampton turned around. The clerk scribbled the name on a sheet of paper, thrust his pencil down, and without a word retreated out of sight. He was gone for several minutes, during which time I fidgeted and worried my cuffs.

"Watson, did you experience this large degree of wastefulness in the army?" Holmes inquired.

"I was in the main preoccupied with trying to stay alive," I said. "I didn't take the time to study the administrative structure. But if pressed, I would admit to a certain number of orders challenging logic."

"Clearly there have to be better ways to run the Admiralty," Holmes said with obvious disdain. I could not argue with my companion but had no solution to offer so stayed silent on the subject.

"I appreciate the size and scale of the operation, but really find much of their organisational structure a most unnecessary waste of manpower. A fairly straightforward request such as ours should not require this many offices and so many more officers."

With that, my companion, unsurprisingly, busied himself by examining our surroundings in microscopic detail.

On his return, Hampton looked smug. It was not a good look on him. "I am sorry, sirs, but I cannot release *any* information without authorisation from the mother or Admiral Milne himself. Good day to you." His rough voice indicated he was done answering questions and I had to wonder if he had even bothered to look or had merely pretended to do his duty as part of some elaborate charade.

Holmes leaned forward. "One more question. Other than those two people, is there anyone else in the Admiralty whose signature would be valid proof to release the records?"

Hampton stared down at him and took his time answering.

"No, sir," the man said, although there was a distinct lack of sincerity in his tone. "But should you wish to pursue the matter I would strongly suggest you go to the Naval Secretary's office on the second floor. His clerk will have current pay records." Before Holmes could reply the man had vanished from sight. He would undoubtedly not reappear until we had removed ourselves.

Holmes appeared to take this failure, consider it, and discard it as a final barrier. He clearly had it in his head to pursue every available resource in this building. His expression had darkened but he wisely held his tongue. We headed back towards the stairs once again.

"Interesting, Watson," he said as we climbed the stairs, his irritation now subdued, replaced with rabid curiosity. "Did you notice he never referred to Wynter by name? Even refused to acknowledge anyone by that name served in Her Majesty's Royal Navy."

"Now that you mention it," said I. "Most curious. I wonder what the next office will tell us."

"Do you truly expect a different response?" asked Holmes. "I do not but we must investigate every avenue available before leaving this building."

After several wrong turns we found the office of the Naval Secretary to the Board of the Admiralty. Holmes gripped the handle, swinging the door open and striding in with great purpose. It was one of his tricks, presenting himself as having the right to be wherever he was, in this case a man who had every right to barge into the office of the Naval Secretary. It was a gambit that worked more often than not.

A young lieutenant, based on the stripes on his uniform jacket, was in the process of putting papers in a cabinet and tidying his desk for the evening when Holmes and I entered. He barely paused in his work as he asked, "May I help you, gentlemen?"

"I am seeking information regarding Norbert Wynter, a lieutenant last seen serving aboard the *Dido* and now currently listed as Missing in Action, specifically the records of his pay," Holmes said.

"And who might you be?"

"My name is Sherlock Holmes and this is Dr. John Watson. We represent the interests of his mother, who is understandably concerned about his whereabouts. Your name, sir?"

"Lieutenant Ward. The *Dido* you say? Let me see if I can be of some assistance," the man said, a smile on his face. This was a pleasant surprise, the first cooperative navy man we had encountered that afternoon.

To my great surprise, he was remarkably accommodating.

"You came to the right place," said Ward. "Civilian questions are handled in this very office and I get so few of those, you know. Some press inquiries now and then, but no, very few civilians such as yourselves."

"We're most happy to provide some variety," said I.

He opened a drawer in the cabinet and withdrew a large book. "Normally I would ask you to speak with our assistant secretary, Edwin Swainson, but he is away from the Admiralty today."

"I am sure you can provide what we need," I said to encourage and speed along the man.

"Just who is the secretary these days?" asked Holmes. I had to admit, even I did not know as there appeared to be several changes in this post over the course of the last year.

Ward placed the book on the desk and opened it. I could see that it was filled with writing in many shades of blue and black ink and in many hands, from unreadable scrawl to elegant penmanship. He began to speak, reciting from memory, "Well, I could see your confusion as we are on our third Secretary in the past year alone. George Shaw-Lefevre just left and the current Secretary is George Trevelyan."

The name was one familiar to me although Holmes's expression indicated the name meant nothing to him. Trevelyan was a man of conscience, actually going so far as to resign as Civil Lord over some bit of legislation about a decade back. That alone earned him my estimation but now Gladstone saw fit as to place him in charge. He was someone I would very much like to meet one day.

The officer continued to thumb through the pages, licking his fingertip after every dozen or so turns, until he found a listing to his liking.

"Wynter, you say?"

"Yes," Holmes said.

"Yes, he shipped out to Africa with the *Dido*, at least according to the pay records. His salary was paid up through July." He closed the book, a look of satisfaction on his face that declared the job done.

"Interesting. So where *is* Wynter then?"

"I'm sorry?"

"His mother was informed he was Missing in Action as of February, now you say he was paid in July. So where is he? Your department is obviously aware of his whereabouts to make the payment, or else how would you reconcile these incongruous pieces of information?"

The man was stumped.

"Navy pay is not particularly good, is it?" Holmes commented.

The man looked confused. "Our wages are quite reasonable…"

"And yet you find yourself in need of additional income."

"I'm sorry?"

"You must be quite exhausted working at a second occupation, no? Hauling coal, if I am not mistaken. Working at the Coal Exchange as a backer or sifter, I presume. Is the navy aware of this?"

"What the devil are you talking about, man?" Ward's ready smile was gone, a look of suspicion in his eyes.

"On the one hand your pallor implies you work mainly indoors, yet a closer scrutiny shows thick callouses on your hands that the repetitious act of filing papers could not cause. So, obviously you are doing some sort of manual labour. Couple that with the fact that the underside of your nails are dark with black smudges of the kind you cannot simply clean away with soap and water. Coal dust."

The man said nothing, avoiding our eyes, but the change in his demeanour was palpable.

"Are you trying to blackmail me?"

"Not at all, merely making conversation while you find the information we seek," Holmes replied. So affable was his tone that I almost believed him, though there was seldom anything "merely" about anything my companion said or did. And while his tone sounded light, the look in his eyes was deadly serious, never leaving Ward.

"As I told you," the lieutenant said, "our records indicate Wynter was paid in March, meaning he was alive to collect and sign for his wages. The records show he was paid through this month so he must not be dead. His mother must have been misinformed about his death in February, or she misremembered." He appeared confident in his response, and clearly hoped that would be the end of it. But Holmes was not satisfied.

"Misremembered..." I began to interrupt this incompetent dolt, but Holmes spoke over me.

"I surmise that Mrs. Wynter was either misinformed or," and he paused slightly, "wilfully told a lie." He let the notion hang for a moment. "I also suspect someone has been collecting Wynter's salary, though whether that is to defraud Her Majesty or complete a fiction that Wynter is here in London despite having failed to disembark the *Dido* remains to be seen. Of course, if that were the case, you would imagine a good son would have been in touch with his mother long before now. Something is most definitely amiss, and if the Admiralty will not facilitate my investigation, it will have to continue regardless."

The man's expression hardened. "Are you accusing me of lying, sir?"

"Not at all, I am sure your book says what you have relayed to me."

"Then are you threatening me, sir?" The "sir" was snapped off, without any courtesy in the tone.

"Not in the slightest. Someone, though, is keeping a secret and I am very good at ferreting out secrets when I set the full force of my mind to it. Good day to you."

Holmes turned his back on the man and strode from the office at a fast pace, stalking down the corridor with single-minded purpose that forced me to hurry to keep up with him.

We left the Admiralty under darkening skies filled with mist. Lights were being lit and the streets were noticeably busier as people began their journeys home.

I was disheartened during our journey back to Baker Street in a hansom. What I could not know then was that our visit spurred Lieutenant Ward into a frenzy of activity, cataloguing our activities at the Admiralty and sending a report bearing Wynter's name to Parliament. We had ruffled a few feathers.

"If Wynter's whereabouts were truly a matter of record keeping, either alive or dead, we would not have needed to be sent to so many offices. While I admit, the Board of the Admiralty may not have contained the precise information we sought, they sent us to the one office that should, that of Records, and yet, they provided no help. And the Naval Secretary, where they are chartered to aid in civilian matters, could tell us nothing."

"You yourself noted there's a certain inefficiency in such a large structure," I said, all too familiar with the workings of the military.

Holmes nodded once.

"I noted in every instance hesitancy," said Holmes. "None were helpful and all went through the motions. While we could not see the documents referenced, it strikes me that there may have been some notation or symbol, some signal that no vital information be revealed."

"Why on earth would they trouble themselves so?" I asked.

Holmes's eyes gleamed with interest. "That is the very question we need answered. It does, though, convince me we have a legitimate case before us."

"This could not be chalked up to coincidence or bad management?"

"While I may not know the full workings of the Admiralty, I recognise deflection when I come up against it. No one, not even the smiling Ward, was genuinely willing to provide us with a service. The mere mention of Wynter's name sent them to scan a list and from there we were sent on our merry way. I dare suggest Wynter is not alone, and an inquiry into the whereabouts of anyone on that list activates a bureaucratic mechanism designed to ultimately frustrate the asker while appearing to present them with an impenetrable wall of *help* that sends them home deflated and defeated. Instead, my dear Watson, it has only served to convince me something foul has happened to young Wynter."

"How can you be certain it is foul and not, as they told his mother, desertion?"

"The notion of desertion is nonsense, Watson. Plain and simple. If that were the case, they would have told her outright rather than it taking her repeated visits and petitions to garner even that piece of questionable information, and it would be a matter of record. No need to hide the fact. But their obfuscation speaks of ill deeds."

I nodded. Clearly there was something sinister at work. My companion peered out of the hansom's window.

"It would appear that Mrs. Wynter has brought us a case that goes far deeper than I originally believed. Something happened to her son, either aboard the *Dido* or before he left South Africa, and the government is hiding the truth." I couldn't argue with that implacable logic. "It is our duty to expose that truth, Watson." I couldn't argue with that sentiment, either.

Three

Rearranging the Attic

At Holmes's request, I did a thorough examination of *The London Gazette* to ascertain if any mention of young Wynter were made in its pages. I scanned the issues from November 1880 until the *Dido*'s return the previous month for mention of anyone named Wynter or an approximation of that spelling, as one could not trust the veracity of many a newsman's word these days. There was no one who came close.

Once that proved fruitless, I spoke to several doctors I knew and found one with an acquaintance who worked for the Royal Navy Medical Service. For the price of a pint I was introduced to Dr. Bartholomew Newkirk, a man of thirty, who I soon discovered loved to tell a bawdy joke rather than relive the horrors of war. I made casual mention of Norbert Wynter, but there was not even a flicker of recognition. He did allow that there were over eighteen thousand men serving in the navy and he could not be expected to know all their names. Still, Newkirk offered to seek out Wynter's medical file to help determine if there was a health reason for his disappearance.

My endeavours proved remarkably time consuming, and yet the spectre of Wynter consumed my thoughts throughout, making me realise I knew nothing about the man beyond what his mother had told Holmes and me. That was something that needed rectifying and I hoped to gain a more objective view once Newkirk obtained the man's medical file. During this time I had absolutely no knowledge of Holmes's activities, but I had no worries about his wellbeing.

I should have worried.

I turned on the corner making my way to 221B where I anticipated meeting with Holmes and ascertaining what he had accomplished to date. Instead, two buildings away from our door, a pair of rough hands grabbed me seemingly out of nowhere. I found my arms restrained from behind and with a tremendous force, I was dragged into the narrow space between buildings, too small to be properly called an alley. The powerful arms held tight despite my struggles and I attempted to plant my heel into the first available shin, but a second figure appeared, blocking the opening and casting a shadow. He was a big fellow and appeared most menacing.

He approached as I continued to struggle, searching for freedom which proved most elusive. All it took was two jabs with piston-precision to force the air from my lungs and cause me to double over, had the iron arms allowed me the luxury of movement. The pain was tremendous and I steeled myself for additional blows.

"What's all this—" was all I managed to say before one of the powerful fists slammed into my cheek, snapping my head around, and my vision clouded for a moment. While I had tried to see details and commit them to memory, information I knew Holmes would need, all I saw now were blotches of colour. I detected a trickle of blood moving down my cheek from my bloodied nose.

My captor hurled me to the ground and landed one booted blow to my side, causing me to roll over. I fully expected these ruffians to help themselves to my possessions but instead, they exchanged a whisper and hurried away.

I remained still, listening to their retreating footfalls while I made certain nothing was seriously damaged. Concluding that I was whole enough, I struggled to regain my feet and patted myself down, making certain nothing had been taken. Then, wincing at the movement, I made my way to our rooms.

To my astonishment, Holmes was already at work, attending to his own wounds, which seemed more severe than my own. There were bandages, tinctures, and gauze scattered about our table and he was completing his work when he finally looked in my direction.

"I see they got to us both, then," he said and gestured to the chair opposite him. As I fell heavily into place, he pushed the medical supplies and a hand mirror in my direction.

"How bad is it?" inquired Holmes.

"Bad enough, but at least I kept ahold of my possessions," I said as I began the process of staunching the blood.

"As I expected," Holmes said.

"Tell me what happened," said I.

"While you were out researching the newspapers, I was verifying the *Dido*'s movements for the last twelve months, using the public resources at the library. I found nothing that did not match what we already knew from Mrs. Wynter. As I was returning here after making some other arrangements, I was grabbed one street over. Two large, powerfully built men took me by surprise and pummelled me for a bit before taking off."

"And likewise, they did not rob you?"

"Of course not," Holmes said as he rose from the chair and began to walk the room. "After all, they were naval men, not common street criminals."

I paused in my ministrations, which were nearly completed, and stared at him. "Naval men?"

"Quite. I never saw them approach and they worked in tandem, making quick work of the business. By the precision of their actions I would judge them men used to working in concert. Then there was the matter of their strength. Hauling equipment, working on a vessel, harden their muscles. There was no fat, and most tellingly, none of the familiar signs of too much drink, common to the street thief.

"Both men had nearly identical haircuts, naval regulation, and were clean-shaven. Their clothing was dark and nondescript with the exception of the trousers which flared at the bottom, allowing a certain freedom of movement. One of the men also had a lanyard around his neck, the very type worn by sailors to hold their seaman's knife."

"Why would this pair attack us?"

"Think on it, Watson."

I did as instructed while cleaning up the first aid supplies and realised the answer was obvious.

"Someone sent them from the Admiralty."

"Not just someone, but Hampton."

"How can you be certain?" I asked, resuming my seat at the table. While presentable, I was also sore and the chair was comfortable enough.

"He's a veteran and knows many men, including a pair who

would likely work in an unofficial capacity. Everything I have learned speaks of Hampton being prone to violence as a means of recourse."

"Did you really rile him so much that he needed to send men to express his displeasure?"

"Not in the slightest," Holmes said. "He sent them because he could. He had the wherewithal and resources but the message could just as easily have come from any of the offices we visited yesterday."

"Because we inquired after Wynter?"

"Precisely. As I suspected there must have been some notation in the ledgers next to his name that stood as a warning against revelation. We have just been warned away from the investigation in a manner the Royal Navy itself could not deliver."

"Did you see their faces? Could you recognise them again?"

Holmes shook his head once. "They were nearly identical in most regards: size, shape and strength. The only discernible feature was a crescent-shaped scar near the left temple of one man."

"For you, that should suffice."

"Quite," said Holmes. "And contrary to their aim, the warning has only served to signal there is something worth hiding here. However deep the concealment, I am now determined to find the truth and with it, the whereabouts of Norbert Wynter."

I sat in the chair and let the events settle in my mind. While my thoughts are not possibly near as orderly as Holmes's, I consider myself a fairly intelligent man, able to connect points into a logical line. There was something bothering me and I had to relax myself after the recent ordeal and see if it would rise to the surface on its own.

Holmes busied himself as I sat, weariness making me groggy, but just before I fell into a sleep, the question nagging at me presented itself and I snapped my eyes open and addressed my companion.

"Holmes, didn't you tell me you have connections in government circles?"

Holmes looked up at that, his eyes narrowing ever so slightly. He gave me a curt nod of the head and returned to whatever it was he was doing.

"Could they not make some form of introduction for us?" I asked. "They might well be able to cut through this blasted bureaucracy and speed our way to finding Wynter."

My companion seemed not to hear me, but after a prolonged silence finally spoke.

"While it is true I have a close relative that works within Her Majesty's Government, he is currently in America on official business and has left no means of contacting him, so no, he won't be of any help in our investigation. Truth be told, he hates to leave the comfort of his club, let alone London, and would happily see out his days within those four walls if he could," said Holmes.

"Sounds like quite the character," I said.

"I would not go that far," Holmes said, and that was his final word on the matter.

It was another day before Newkirk met me in the courtyard at the Admiralty. He carried a leather satchel, which I hoped contained the promised medical file. It was a rare dry day that July and the sun felt good as we shook hands. Even my wounded leg had settled down and was no longer a bother.

He pulled a brown cardboard file from his satchel.

"You may read the papers," he allowed, his voice taking on a more intimate tone, "but I must return them to the office in short order. I already took the liberty of giving it a read and, I must say, found everything pleasantly unremarkable."

I opened the file to reveal a sheaf of papers, clearly an enlisted man's medical record such as I was familiar with from my army days. I flicked through the pages, seeing a series of notations for height and weight, other physical characteristics, and the few times Wynter had reported to the ship's surgeon. There was a broken finger in 1879 but nothing noted for 1881. The last entry had been made in the autumn of 1880; a bout of illness that seemed to resolve itself without intervention.

"He seems like a perfectly healthy chap," Newkirk said brightly.

"At least on paper," I allowed. "I would like to ascertain that for myself, but that is the issue. We cannot seem to find the fellow." I handed the file back to Newkirk.

Newkirk looked at the entries on the top sheet and raised an eyebrow. "According to this, the man is no longer listed as being on active duty. You say you have no idea of Lieutenant Wynter's whereabouts?"

"None, and that is the issue my partner and I are investigating. He appears to have vanished and your fellow officers are being less than forthright about it. At least we can tell from this file that it was nothing related to his health. Eliminating this will be invaluable in our search for a cause for his absence."

Newkirk nodded thoughtfully.

We shook hands and I returned to Baker Street to share these developments, precious little as they were. As I entered our rooms, Holmes was deep in concentration, wrapped up in the study of a map of Africa. His long index finger traced a line across the blue of the ocean. As I settled into my chair, I told him about my meeting with Newkirk. He absorbed the information with a curt nod.

"I am glad you have returned," Holmes said, looking up from the map. "We have a visitor coming at three who should help shed some light on the entire affair."

The news brightened my spirits and I sat straighter in the chair and asked who was calling on us.

"His name is Professor G. Morgan West, a lecturer at the University of London."

"How will Professor West help us with this matter?" I was genuinely confounded. How could a professor help us find a missing sailor?

"As I have explained in the past, I store only the most vital of information and clear mental space as needed. You have on more than one occasion noted that I lack much in the way of awareness of how the world works."

"Quite right. Just the other night I mentioned how I wished to see *Bunthorne's Bride* at the Opera Comique and you had no idea the show existed or that it was by Gilbert and Sullivan."

"And what was that novel you were going on about?"

I thought a moment and then snapped my fingers. "Ah yes, I was talking about an article I was reading concerning Henry James and his forthcoming novel *Portrait of a Lady*, something I hope to find time for once it sees the light of day."

"I am not entirely without culture, Watson. After all, a mere four months ago I consulted with the British Museum, helping them identify several of their recent acquisitions."

That was a surprise. "I had no idea."

"It was when I was doing my chemical work, just before we met," Holmes elucidated. He was clearing some space on our table, presumably for the professor and his belongings. Several maps of Africa remained in place. "I am not in the habit of paying undue attention to global politics, though it would appear I now need to remedy this, hence the good professor coming to teach us about the recent unpleasantness against the Boers."

I nodded in thoughtful agreement, pleased to see that Holmes knew his limitations.

Professor West arrived shortly after three, perspiring in his brown wool suit, his face damp with sweat. He mopped his ruddy brow with a handkerchief that had seen better days as he gratefully accepted a glass of water from Mrs. Hudson. The man was on the wrong side of fifty, rather overweight, with his ample girth straining the buttons of his colourful waistcoat. His receding hairline was limp, badly in need of a brush, and his overall look was that of a man unaccustomed to venturing out of the hallowed halls of academia.

"Gentlemen, I am given to understand that neither one of you have a good working knowledge of the recent war in the Transvaal, the key battles and locations of same. Is that the case?"

"I served in Afghanistan," I said in a defensive tone. That caught his attention and he nodded. Holmes said nothing and waited for our guest to continue.

"I see. Very good then. I assume that you *do* know that we have been aggressively colonising the southern portion of the African continent for some time now? We have been doing this largely to control the trade routes between Britain and India where our interests are stronger than ever." He drained the remainder of his water before continuing his private lecture.

Holmes returned his gaze to the map. Our guest and I followed his gaze; I supposed that Holmes was imagining the trade routes, quickly understanding centuries of development in a matter of seconds.

"At the same time, the African tribes have been trying to find a way to coexist and create a united front; much like the colonies did in North America. After losing America, the Crown decided we needed to tighten our hold and expand elsewhere. Africa became the next continent where we vied for land against other European interests. Fortunately, we were lucky to discover diamonds in the hills of the Transvaal."

"Wasn't there a bit of a gold rush there?" I asked.

"Quite right," said he in the voice he no doubt used with his students. Approving in tone, it also had a very paternal quality to it.

"We had already annexed the Drakensberg Mountains, which put us between two rival tribes: the Boers and the Zulus."

"The Boers are of Dutch extraction," I interjected.

"Yes and they grudgingly accepted our rule," West continued. "The Dutch formed two republics, the Transvaal Republic or *Zuid-Afrikaansche Republiek* and the Orange Free State, which we recognised at conventions nearly thirty years ago. *Boer* is the Afrikaans word for 'farmer' and they led a quiet life. Once diamonds were discovered about fifteen years ago, the fourth Earl of Carnarvon, who was the British Secretary of State for the Colonies at the time, suggested we combine the two republics into a single unit of South African lands. He urged Disraeli to combine the Transvaal states now and the Orange Free State would follow, a position he had been pushing since '76. While we liked the notion, the Boers were less than keen and when we pressed the annexation, they finally rebelled last December."

"I remember reading some of Carnarvon's speeches on the subject," I interjected. "He was not averse to using force to achieve his goal."

West nodded in agreement, pleased with his student. "Men like him seldom are, as shown by our war with the Zulus even before this recent conflict with the Boers."

"We're drifting off topic," said Holmes curtly. His finger traced another point on the map, this time at the bottom tip of the continent, the Cape of Good Hope.

"Quite right. Carnarvon spent the next few years using his political and financial might to sway a weak Transvaal government. Even though Carnarvon told President Burgers–rather bluntly–of his intentions, Burgers' warnings to the people were ignored or at least not taken seriously enough, giving Britain the time to wear away at any resistance such as there was. Annexation was inevitable, but once it became fact, protests arose in Pretoria and throughout the land.

"As so often happens, a single spark can start a great conflagration. In this case it was a single fellow refusing to pay extra duties on his goods wagon. He felt he was paying enough in Transvaal taxes and objected to paying more to the Crown. You would think we would have learned our lessons from the American colonies, but I digress."

"Indeed you do," agreed Holmes. West stiffened at the rebuke but continued with his lecture.

"The wagon was confiscated but a group of men one-hundred strong wrested it from British hands and things rapidly began to spiral out of control. Any hope of a peaceful resistance ended with that action and the contest became a physical one. There were over seven thousand Transvaalians against fewer than two thousand British troops, and the Boer militiamen, fighting in their own country with the British Westley Richards rifle, proved more than a match for our boys.

"We had three decisive defeats. The first was in January at Laing's Nek when Major-General Sir George Pomeroy Colley tried to break through the Boer defensive positions, losing at least one hundred and fifty men. A few weeks later at Schuinshoogte, the Boers and Colley met again and while evenly matched for a time, the Boers proved to be better shots. Nightfall saved Colley, who retreated.

"Then there was Majuba Hill later in February when Colley settled for the night atop the hill with about three hundred and sixty men. The remainder of his force in different positions. The Boers took advantage of the British being above them. They skilfully scaled the sides of the mountain, effectively surrounding Colley. Their movements were protected by marksmen too old to make the climb. It proved disastrous and Colley was killed."

"He sounds like a remarkably ineffectual commanding officer," Holmes observed.

"In my estimation, Colley was ineffectual from the outset," the professor said. "He had already been bested at Laing's Nek and again by Boer riflemen at the Ingogo River. He even reneged on an agreement he made with Brigadier General Evelyn Wood, refusing to remain in place while Wood awaited to reorganise fresh arriving troops. As a result, he proved a most poor choice for leader. Had he waited for reinforcements, the outcome might have been different."

The professor paused to see if Holmes or I had additional questions, then returned to his subject. "I will note several striking parallels between Transvaal and America—"

"What of the *Dido*'s role?" Holmes interrupted, not allowing West to drift into waters we had no interest in.

"I am glad you told me about your interest in that vessel, as it gave me time to look into its service history. The ship was stationed in West Africa and in February was pressed into service, sending fifty men and two field guns as part of a naval brigade. At the Battle of Majuba Hill on 27th February, three men were reported killed, another three wounded. Captain Compton Edward Domvile took charge at the front at that time and the ship saw no further action."

I considered the fact that Mrs. Wynter had said her son's communications ceased in January, a month prior to the battle, but our researches at the Admiralty had revealed that his pay had continued into July. Perhaps Norbert Wynter had died at Majuba but the fact had been missed from the official record?

"When did the fighting end?" Holmes asked.

"Hostilities ceased on 23rd March," the professor replied. "Majuba Hill was the last military embarrassment Parliament could stand; it was decided that it was wiser to give the Transvaal their independence rather than risk turning our armed forces into a laughing stock. A peace treaty is scheduled to be signed in the next few weeks."

"Interesting," I said.

"I would hazard to suggest there might have been a different outcome had Benjamin Disraeli remained Prime Minister," West said. I nodded in agreement. I myself had been saddened by the old man's sudden fall from popular favour. He had resigned in April of the previous year and in January had become Conservative leader in the House of Lords. In March, just as I was first meeting Holmes, Disraeli took ill and suffered a rapid and tragic decline, finally succumbing in April.

"You know," I said, more to West than to Holmes, whom I assumed would care little for such observations, "his demise seemed to build slowly then accelerate with horrific pace over those final days."

"Do not forget that while we lost a great man in Disraeli, at least we still have our Queen," the professor said gravely. "Russia lost their sole leader, Czar Alexander, the month before."

To my surprise, Holmes looked up from his map. "Do you think there might be a connection between these disparate events?"

I was confounded. I could see nothing to link Wynter on the *Dido* and the former prime minister's death, or for that matter, a dead Russian Czar.

"I fail to see how there could possibly be."

"That does not mean one does not exist," Holmes said, clearly warming to the notion of a grand conspiracy. "The threads between nations can be so thin as to be invisible to the naked eye but bind us all."

"This is rapidly getting beyond my field of expertise, gentlemen," West interrupted. "Unless you have other questions, I should like to collect my fee and depart, if that is agreeable?"

Holmes wordlessly reached into his pocket and withdrew a pound note, which he handed to the professor without so much as a thank you. He had a distracted look that I recognised: his keen mind was already at work, weighing and discarding facts, arranging them in various orders of disparate and seemingly unrelated events, seeking patterns within them. More often than not, this was the key phase in an investigation when he would achieve the breakthrough that led to a case's successful conclusion. Today, however, there was no such satisfaction to be had.

Four

Tea with Lord Rowton

Holmes got out his pipe, stuffed it with tobacco, not too tight, not too loose, and lit it. He did not say a word for many minutes, clearly troubled that a solution had yet to present itself. Eventually he turned to me and said, "Disraeli was deeply involved in the Boer conflict and no sooner does it begin than he is out of the House of Commons and into the Lords, only to succumb to a rapid decline in health. This decline means that he is no longer a voice of dissent when the Queen and Gladstone choose to abandon Africa."

"How do the Czar and the American President fit into this? Surely neither country cared one whit about the war?" I asked.

"Intriguing as a global conspiracy might be, I should think this is a mere distraction from the meat of the matter," Holmes said. "Instead, we should focus on Disraeli and to do that, I am of the opinion it would be worthwhile examining his medical records."

I gaped at him, and surely my jaw dropped open at the suggestion. "You cannot be serious?" But he obviously was. "It was one thing getting Wynter's records–they were easily accessible to a man such as Newkirk. But this is a prime minister we are talking about." I shook my head.

"The man is dead and I sincerely doubt he would object to such an invasion of his privacy, especially if our examination turns up evidence that he died from something other than natural causes. In fact, I daresay the British people might want to know if a beloved figure was taken from them earlier than nature intended."

It was an astonishing suggestion. Could Holmes truly believe that Benjamin Disraeli might have been murdered and that our investigation was somehow related? It was absurd, and I said as much.

"As a doctor, I would expect you to want to know the truth and as a British subject I would think that would double your interest." His tone brooked no argument. This was a line of inquiry he was determined to follow no matter where it led him. "How hard will it be for you, a veteran and a member of the medical community, to find some way for us to inspect those records?"

I had to pause and consider. "Damned near impossible, I should say. I will need to determine who treated Disraeli during his final illness, and the identity of the coroner." The most obvious way to find the former was to ask my colleagues in the medical community, but I was reluctant to so soon after a similar series of inquiries into Wynter's records. I did not want to run the risk of having suspicions raised this early in the investigation. After all, my name had been linked to Holmes in the popular press. If it became known that I–and by extension my companion–were trying to lay hands on the former prime minister's medical records, it would raise more than just an eyebrow in certain quarters.

I stoked the fire, and then spent an hour beside the hearth consulting my army medical notes and appointments book in search of the right man to reacquaint myself with. I daresay things would have gone more quickly had I a proper clerk, or even an organised filing system, but my practice had been rather haphazard since my discharge.

After some time, I came across my notes regarding the treatment of Captain Colin Westfall, with whom I had served in Afghanistan. Suddenly I was alert, searching my memory for a piece of information that I knew lay somewhere in my recollections of that time. A passing comment, made under canvas... I had nursed him through a fever brought on by a tarantula bite, and we had spent several days together, the last of them—once Westfall was over the worst of it—playing cards and talking of our lives at home. He was going on about how close he had come to people of importance while doing nothing of the sort himself.

Clearly, he was feeling low, the ravages of war and all that. It may have been merely a spider's bite but it occurred while doing Her Majesty's business far from home. I had inquired about those people he felt were of more importance than himself. He had some sort of connection, but I was confounding myself with not being able to conjure up the exact detail.

Then I had it. Westfall had mentioned a most tenuous connection to the prime minister; he was related to Montagu William Lowry-Corry, who had been Disraeli's private secretary until the latter's death.

In his fevered mind, being a soldier was of less import than secretary to the PM. One risked his life, the other merely avoided paper cuts, so in my mind there was no real comparison and I said as much to encourage his spirits. The little talk seemed to help him in some small way. I hoped he would recall me with kindness.

I resolved to get in touch with Westfall as soon as possible. But first, I needed to find out what the official record had deemed to be Disraeli's cause of death. All I could recall was pneumonia and gout, but I had a vague recollection there was more to it. I left Holmes burning his way through boxes of foreign cigars and filling our rooms with a variety of combative odours.

I made haste to St. James's Square and the London Library, glad the unseasonal rain had abated, intending to seek out an old acquaintance: Lomax, the sub-librarian. The structure, by Thomas Carlyle, was always impressive to my eyes, with the sweeping grandeur of knowledge alive within its brick and mortar shell, but I did not pause to admire it that day. Instead, I hurried within and sought out my friend. As usual, he was rushing about, his spectacles askew on his sweaty face, his thinning hair flying every which way as his heels echoed out a tattoo on the cold stone floor that was a music all of its own. His suit jacket was threadbare around the cuffs and needed mending, I noted, but in his world there was never time for such things.

As he placed two thick volumes on a dusty shelf, he caught sight of me and broke into a weary smile. We only ever tended to meet these days when I needed something.

"Dr. Watson, so good to see you again," he said in a soft voice.

I matched his volume and greeted him in turn, holding out a hand in friendship. He took it, then gestured that I follow him until each book in his care was safely back in its place. Finally, he led me to the tiny desk; at least I think it was a desk. For all I knew, it was merely a surface designed to hold the clutter of papers, journals, and more books in need of attention. There was no place for me to sit so I stood as he took his own small, well-worn wooden chair.

"I assume you need help with some matter of research, and while I am more than happy to avail myself, surely whatever you need would be more easily found at the Royal College? We are just a humble resource here." Indeed, the Royal College of Physicians was to be my next stop, but I felt the anonymity of the London Library would better suit my needs.

"Indeed, but the subject of my enquiry is rather delicate," said I. "I need back issues of all the London newspapers that covered the period when Disraeli died–say from the beginning of March until the end of April." The request earned me a curious look, but when I was not forthcoming he merely nodded and scurried off into the stacks.

Thankfully, it only took him a few minutes to find the relevant periodicals. He returned and placed the thick bundle in my outstretched arms, before leading me to a small cubicle, away from the general traffic of the other patrons. The light from the green-glass banker's lamp was dim, forcing me to hold the papers closer than was comfortable. With my journal at the ready, I proceeded to relive the final tributes to one of the truly great figures of modern history.

Benjamin Disraeli, it appeared, had long suffered from both gout–as I had recalled–and asthma, which was new information to me. Both were chronic conditions and in March, the latter appeared to develop into a nasty case of bronchitis. He took to his bed and on Easter Sunday he began to decline. He was incoherent by the following Monday, finally slipping into a coma from which he did not wake. There was little detail on his final days; his physicians had refused to comment on their patient's condition to reporters.

Reading on, I found it interesting that those in charge of his estate had refused a state funeral. Instead, there was a much more modest service held in his estate's church in Hughenden on 26th April. Despite her grief, Queen Victoria did not attend, sending only primroses, apparently the man's favourite flower. She also preferred to allow his various titles lapse into oblivion rather than pass them on to his surviving relatives.

All of this struck me as most curious for a beloved popular figure. That got me interested, or perhaps my time with Holmes had made me more suspicious about the world within which I lived.

I leant back in my chair, frustrated at the lack of detail concerning Disraeli's condition at the end. I felt a growing desire to read the man's medical files for myself and was now determined to see this through, folly or not. I thanked Lomax in a whisper and hurried out of the London Library. It was time to track down Captain Colin Westfall of the 66th Regiment of Foot.

Finding my former comrade and patient proved to be one of the easiest tasks of the entire affair. The regiment was stationed in London and I was able to send him a note, inviting him for a drink the following evening and he rapidly accepted.

I was at something of a loose end the morning of our meeting; Holmes was off on some errand, the nature of which he had not divulged, so I was left to my own devices. Rather than sit in our stuffy rooms, I decided to hire a cab and pay Mrs. Wynter a visit. With no newspaper reports of her son's death, Holmes and I knew little of his life outside the Royal Navy, his friends or even lovers. Perhaps his mother would be able to paint me a picture of her son, the better to aid our inquiries.

Much of Shoreditch was distinctly middle class, but the streets on the periphery had seen better days. The street where Mrs.

Wynter lived was ill lit and distinctly down at heel. I felt somewhat uncomfortable calling without an appointment; I hoped that as a woman alone she would be glad of my presence.

I rapped on the door and heard it echo through the house. I knew to be patient, having noticed during our interview that she moved slowly, the result no doubt of arthritis or rheumatism. A minute passed but I waited, hearing movement from within. Finally, the footsteps grew louder and then the door opened. Mrs. Wynter squinted in the daylight but her eyes widened when she recognised me.

"Dear me," she said. "Have you found Norbert?" She was wearing old, well-worn clothing, dark in hue, clearly not intended for public view. The grey hair remained in a bun, held with some ornate comb. She was without jewellery, her expensive baubles no doubt tucked away until she next needed to impress someone.

"Not as yet," I replied, with as much confidence as I could muster.

"Oh, do come in," Mrs. Wynter said. She did well to mask her disappointment. She stepped back, pulling the door with her and I entered the hall, which was cool and full of shadows. It spoke of a once prosperous life, now fallen into disuse, surfaces covered by a thin layer of dust. The old woman beckoned for me to follow her into the sitting room.

"Shall I put on some tea, Doctor?"

"You needn't bother, ma'am, I daresay I shall not keep you long," I replied.

"But I do want to hear what you and Mr. Holmes have discovered." Her voice was eager, making her sound younger than her years. I had to couch my words carefully so as not to offer the widow false hope.

"At present, Mr. Holmes and I are pursuing separate avenues of inquiry, gathering up as many facts as we can ascertain. Once gathered, Mr. Holmes will put his keen mind towards deciphering what it all means."

She nodded once, the resignation clear in her dull blue eyes now.

I outlined where we had been and what little we had managed to verify. She nodded at each point and took it all in, seemingly satisfied with our efforts to date.

"If you have nothing new to share, may I ask why you made the journey all the way out here?"

"When we first met, we spoke about Norbert's disappearance as a case but not about Norbert as a person. I would like to know something more about the sort of man he is." I was very careful to refer to the man in the present tense; I did not want her to think that we thought him dead. Mrs. Wynter deserved our facts not our speculation. Even so a large part of me feared we would never find her son alive.

At my words, she brightened considerably and adjusted herself in her seat. I took out my notebook and pencil, gesturing with them in her direction, silently asking permission to take notes. She nodded and then began.

"As I told you and Mr. Holmes, we had Norbert late in life. That did not deter him from having a robust, playful childhood. My husband liked to sail so Norbert grew up as comfortable at sea as he was on land. It seemed inevitable he would enlist. He was just twelve when his father died. We were fortunate that my husband had left provision for his schooling. Norbert went to the Royal Navy College for cadet training until he was fifteen, then spent a further four years training on the *Britannia*."

When she fell silent, I asked her about close friends. She allowed that once he entered Her Majesty's Royal Navy he was rarely at home and whatever friendships there had been fell into disuse.

"Has he a sweetheart?" I ventured.

Mrs. Wynter smiled at the question and turned to the small table beside her lace-covered chair. She reached for a framed photograph and presented it to me. In the frame was a picture of a young, moustache-less Norbert Wynter, not yet a lieutenant but in a midshipman's uniform. Standing beside him was a young, slim girl of perhaps twenty. She had long, curled dark hair and was gazing more at her beau than at the photographer. At a glance, I could see she was in love with him.

"Her name?"

"Caroline Burdett."

I recorded the name, knowing I needed to seek her out to see if she possessed any correspondence from Norbert that might provide us with clues.

"Are they engaged?"

"I know it had been discussed but I do not believe he obtained her father's blessing before shipping out on the *Dido*. They would have made a splendid match." I could see dreams of grandchildren filling her eyes, mixing with the welling tears that were forming.

"Do you remain in contact with Miss Burdett?"

"Not at present," Mrs. Wynter allowed. "Once we were told he was missing, she has not been to visit."

"Is there an address where I may find her?"

I was given an address that I knew to be near the Quaker burial grounds and rose to head directly there. In normal circumstances it was a relatively short walk, no more than thirty minutes from Shoreditch to Islington, but because the air was thick with humidity it made it an uncomfortable one.

I knocked twice on the front door and a servant answered, surprising me, since I expected the family to be of similarly modest means as Mrs. Wynter. She was wiping her hands on a cloth, traces of flour on her cuffs and stray hairs sticking out from a white cap.

"Is Miss Caroline Burdett at home?"

"Who should I say is callin'?" she asked in a thick cockney accent.

I gave her my name and card, which she snatched from my outstretched hand, and led me to wait in the hall. The house was in a far better state than Mrs. Wynter's home and it was clear the Burdett's fortunes were still on a solid footing. Well-oiled older furniture stood side by side with far newer, more expensive pieces. It was a bright and welcoming place, which began to lift my spirits.

Caroline Burdett came down the hall, looking almost the same as she had in Mrs. Wynter's photograph, trim and well appointed in a green frock. She was certainly the most attractive woman I had interviewed in quite some time. She extended a hand in a forthright manner, which I took, and then she led us to a sitting room.

"How may I help you, Dr. Watson?" she asked, her voice soft and pleasant. She would be quite the prize for Norbert Wynter, should he have survived this ordeal.

I briefly outlined how Holmes and I had been engaged by Mrs. Wynter, and as I spoke, I saw her brows knit, eyes clouding over. As I completed my report, she nodded.

"And how do you feel I can be of help?"

"You see, miss, while no one piece of information will solve this mystery, the more details we collect about Norbert, the better our chances of finding his whereabouts. I would like to hear, for example, about the sort of man he is. After all, mothers describe their children with more bias than impartiality."

Miss Burdett laughed knowingly at that and seemed to relax as she settled herself comfortably into her chair. "Norbert was a caring man. He gave most of his pay to his mother and although we had come to an understanding, he could not afford a ring until he was promoted and his salary increased. Being in the navy, he explained, meant I would need plenty of patience."

I nodded, feeling great pity for her situation. She spoke of Norbert Wynter in the past tense, so clearly she, unlike Mrs. Wynter, had come to a fatalistic conclusion regarding her fiancé's fate.

"He loved the sea, and the navy. He had the spirit of adventure and I daresay it began to rub off on me."

"What about his habits?"

She frowned at the question and considered before responding. The servant by then had come in with a small silver tray laden with the makings of a light tea. Miss Burdett poured, clearly stalling to compose her response. I took the proffered cup and saucer and waited her out.

"He was always punctual which I daresay came from his training aboard ship. He knew the bells by heart and was always at the dinner table promptly." Again her laugh filled the room. "He never kept me waiting, more I him. He was maybe a little too casual about his dress when out of uniform but then again, he never had much to spend on his personal attire. He drank no more or less than any other man and was always the model of decorum with me."

At that last, her eyes darted from mine so I suspect that may have been a slight exaggeration of the truth but it was also an indiscretion that did not factor into the case. If anything, it implied he was devoted to her and other women were not likely to be found in London or any other port he visited.

"Money was always a concern for him. He wanted to save for our future and he wanted to provide for his mother but I could tell from his correspondence there were problems."

This was news. Money, or the lack of it, was often the precipitating cause of many of the cases Holmes and I had undertaken. But was it a factor here? Wynter had disappeared while serving, not while on shore leave. Still, I knew that a fact, no matter how seemingly inconsequential, should not be discarded so early in an investigation.

"I knew Norbert was a Navy man through and through," Caroline Burdett said. "My father is a fisherman and I knew we would be parted for long periods of time. I saw his service on the *Dido* as a test of our love and one I believe we would have passed had he... had he returned."

This pronouncement finally caused a break in her composure but she attempted to cover it with a sip of tea.

"What do you think happened to your fiancé?" I asked quietly.

Holding the cup between her pale hands, Miss Burdett shook her head, clearly mystified. She then met my eyes once more and asked, "Do you believe he's still alive? His mother has heard such ghastly things. I cannot believe he would run, so I am forced to admit, I have given him up for dead."

"I cannot make a promise," I began. "I can say that we are doing our utmost to uncover the truth. Dead, wounded, or whole, hero or coward, we will find out which sort of man he truly is or was. Tell me, you mention his correspondence. Did the two of you write one another letters?"

"Of course. It took some time between replies given his ship's movements, but yes, it was regular."

"Did you detect anything amiss?"

"No, nothing except his money worries."

"Did you keep his correspondence?"

"Yes, of course."

"I don't suppose you would consent to let me or Mr. Holmes read his letters? Perhaps there's something of significance that has escaped you."

Again there was a hesitation and a silence. Finally, she shook her head. "There are... private things in those letters," she said in a quiet voice.

"I understand," and I believed I did. "Well, did he mention anyone, any close friend aboard the *Dido*? Maybe he could help our investigation.'

Miss Burdett gave me several names, which I immediately committed to my notebook. I thanked her, and thought to leave, but paused.

"How are you faring, Miss Burdett? I imagine it has been a terrible strain."

"I am well enough, Doctor. As I said, I am accustomed to waiting, although the darkest possibility remains the most likely one and makes the waiting harder."

"Perhaps it is a mercy. You are still young."

She nodded. "My father keeps saying that. He wants me to think no more of Norbert and find another. But it is... difficult after you have given your heart to another."

"Indeed it is," I said softly. "But you do find a way to move forward and welcome new possibilities." I sipped once at my tea to be polite and then rose, as did she, taking my hands into her own.

"Thank you for helping that sweet woman," Caroline Burdett said. "She will be destroyed if Norbert proves to be a coward."

"But you do not believe that to be a possibility?"

Without hesitation, she shook her head and I saw in her eyes conviction. He had given her no reason to think he would have changed from the man she knew. I, however, knew war could change a man.

"I sincerely hope that will *not* prove to be the case," I assured her.

I returned to 221B Baker Street to find that Holmes was out once again. There was no message so my time was my own. I spent the afternoon with my notes, a cup of Mrs. Hudson's tea, and some nagging doubts as to what had become of Lieutenant Norbert Wynter.

I met Captain Colin Westfall that night at a small pub near his posting.

The man still had the same ruddy complexion I remembered, but he had filled out, adding a good two stone to his already thick frame, as well a bushy moustache that hid his thin lips. He still looked good in the uniform; it suited him. We shook hands, his clammy, and I ordered two pints as we caught up on each other's doings. He had an easy laugh and found humour in almost everything.

"Any ill effects from that bite?"

Westfall shook his head. "I was fit and ready to fight within days. I daresay I had hoped to find its lair, but I never saw a spider again my entire tour."

"Mayhap they knew you were looking for them," I said and we both shared a chuckle at the notion.

By the second pint, I thought it was time to get down to business. As much as we were enjoying our reminiscences, he knew I had not reached out to him simply to rehash our shared past. Carefully, I steered the conversation to Gladstone and the current political strife. "It was certainly different when Disraeli was in charge," I offered, dangling the carrot.

"God rest his soul," Westfall said, tipping his glass.

"Indeed," I agreed. "If I recall, weren't you the chap who was related to his secretary?"

"That's right," said he. "Lord Rowton is my mother's second cousin or some such. A distant relation."

"Do you still consider this distant relation of more importance than yourself?"

Westfall gave me a queer look and cocked his head. "What's all that?" he inquired.

"When I was treating you, you were going on about this distant relation who was more important than you were and I tried to point out that it was you risking your life, not him."

"Can't say as I recall any such conversation," he said.

"Well, it could as easily have been said while under the spider's influence," said I. "There's little surprise in you not recalling things said while ill."

He finished his glass and eyed me closely. "And this is why we're talking? Something to do with my family?"

"Yes," I admitted, but he merely laughed.

"I knew it! No one wants to meet up and talk about Afghanistan. I certainly don't. I knew you were slowly getting around to your point. I don't mind even if I have no idea if I really had those thoughts. After all, you pulled me through those days and I survived to come home. So, tell me, what do you want with Cousin Rowton?"

"I am working with a gentleman on something that requires some discretion and I am hoping you might make an introduction for me," I explained.

"Is this about his lordship or his former employer?"

"The latter, I'm afraid," I admitted. Westfall's eyes widened at that.

"The man is dead and buried; what could you possibly want with him? Trying to commune with his spirit?" He broke into a loud peal of laughter at his own weak joke.

"I would really rather not explain in public, but trust me, everything we are doing is with the utmost discretion."

"Who are you working with?"

"His name is Holmes. He is a consulting detective."

"Never heard of that title, 'consulting detective'. Is he with the Yard?"

I shook my head and signalled for a third round of ale. "He is a private citizen, but lends his services to the constabulary, both the City of London Police and the Metropolitan at Scotland Yard. But this is a more private matter as we are trying to locate a missing Royal Navy sailor recently posted to South Africa."

That seemed to get his attention. There's a bond between men in uniform, brothers in arms. We try to never leave a man or his body behind. What we hope is done for us someday we try and do for others.

"And a missing seaman is connected to Disraeli's death? That sounds fishy if you ask me."

"As well it might be," I agreed. "But I can assure you, Mr. Holmes and I are working diligently to track down every lead and one of those avenues of investigation leads to Disraeli's final days, so I am hoping you can vouch for me with Lord Rowton. I would dearly like to hear some details in person."

He considered for a few moments, let the barmaid put the fresh glasses before us, and then took a long pull.

Finally, he put it down and smiled.

"You're not going to tell me more, are you?"

I shook my head.

"I can respect that, Doctor. Let me send his lordship a note. I have to say that we haven't seen one another in at least a year, so I can't make any promises. He made an appearance when I returned from Afghanistan, though, so he is at least aware of who I am."

"I will be forever in your debt," I said, finally taking a taste of the third and final glass of the evening.

"Nonsense, Doctor. You helped me and now you're helping another man in uniform. That's good enough for me. The fact you're keeping mum—that just shows you're a man of your word."

We shook hands to affirm our agreement and I relaxed, knowing that I must soon join Holmes in the unpleasant task of waiting for things to happen.

I have never enjoyed waiting.

The following morning we were both rather irritable. Holmes had exhausted his supply of foreign cigars, although the lingering reek would take several weeks of humid summer air to fade. That would mean enduring more of Mrs. Hudson's complaints about the odour but there was little to be done about it. His notes were carefully filed away for future use although I suspect he wanted someone to smoke an imported cigar before the case played itself out, just so that the folly might prove useful.

He paced our rooms with an increasing tempo, which began to grate on my nerves. He rejected my suggestion of playing his violin and I found it necessary to caution him from criticising Mrs. Hudson when she tried to bring him some unwanted victuals.

For myself, I had done what I could and now had to wait to see if Westfall delivered on his promise. Even if his message reached

Lord Rowton there was no surety the former secretary would consent to a conversation with an unknown doctor about such a delicate matter. In an effort to distract myself, I spent the morning reading more about the Boer conflict from materials left for us by Professor West. It was dry academic stuff in the main, but it made clear that the British military strategy had failed at every turn. If I were in Parliament, I too would have wanted this conflict brought swiftly to a conclusion and brushed under the carpet.

"Confound it, Watson, there *must* be something else we could be doing?" Holmes said in the strained voice of a man slowly going out of his mind.

This was rather an odd set of circumstances. In the normal course of things, it would be Holmes who was out and about, making inquiries and speaking with his growing connections. Instead, he had been forced to wait for me to use my superior network of connections to find us paths to follow. He is a man of action, so sitting idly by, waiting on the happenstance that Lord Rowton acquiesced to his relation's request, was more than he could manage.

His ill mood coloured my own, since, as I noted earlier, waiting is not a strength I possess.

"We have gotten nowhere with the Admiralty so we are now studying his last tour of duty," I said gently, in measured tones. "I am sitting here re-reading about the battles to better understand where young Wynter may have gotten himself. Thankfully, the *Dido*'s whereabouts are well documented."

"Which makes the absence of one man all the more curious," Holmes interjected.

We sat in silence until finally he returned to his feet and reached for his hat. "Carry on with what you are doing; I will use my time more wisely." I offered a raised eyebrow. "I will be out gathering materials for future experiments," Holmes explained.

"Ah," I said. "Very good. But please see that you do not burn down the building should I be out when you return. I am loath to admit it, but I've grown very fond of Baker Street in our short time here."

That was the last I was to see of Holmes for some time.

After supper I received a card from Westfall, delivered by a young soldier, confirming that Lord Rowton would be willing to see me the following day at the House of Lords library. Apparently, he was visiting from his castle in Shropshire, which was providential as it would save our investigation considerable time. I wished Holmes were present to rejoice in the news but his whereabouts remained a mystery to me.

I did not sleep particularly well that night, worrying in no small part as to where Holmes might be, and convinced he had taken refuge in an opium den rather than face the prospect of being bored. But sleep I did, only to wake far from refreshed.

I fussed all morning with my attire, brushing my suit and shining my shoes. I was about to take tea with a baron, a man who stood in the shadow of greatness and remained a confidant of the Queen. It was not every day one found oneself in the presence of such power.

I ensured promptness by taking a cab, leaving an hour to spare, which meant I had to pace the streets a good while before entering the Palace of Westminster. A smartly attired young aide escorted me to the library, a series of attached rooms, each with its own name. There were wooden shelves neatly stacked with leather-clad volumes from floor to ceiling, most with cracked spines, showing they were actually consulted rather than left to gather dust.

We passed through the Queen's Room and Brougham Room on our way to the Truro Room, the smallest and least occupied of the spaces. Two red leather chairs of high-backed chesterfield design were to the right of a large fireplace, and there, reading *The Times*, was Baron Rowton himself. He was not an especially tall man, but his brushed back hair and full, greying beard were immaculately manicured. He was in a suit, complete with waistcoat and bow tie, much as he had appeared when serving Disraeli.

Upon seeing me, he rose and shook hands, placing his left hand around my forearm in a familiar embrace. "A pleasure to make your acquaintance, Doctor. Please, sit."

I took the proffered chair. The leather was supple and had the ingrained aroma of wax. Being summer, the fireplace was empty, and a nearby window was open. We were alone.

"I am to understand you did my family a service," Montagu William Lowry-Corry said.

"Just my duty to a fellow soldier," I said.

"Still, Britain and his mother appreciate your efforts. And now comes the time to repay your service. How may I help you?"

I had been mentally rehearsing the key points I wanted to raise without ruffling his feathers or calling undue attention to the case, but it was difficult to know precisely where to begin. After all, this was a bit of a stretch and on the surface would seem absurd to those with a traditional outlook. I decided to be circumspect at the outset before making what was sure to be seen as an outrageous request. I knew that his lordship had begun his career as a lawyer before his outgoing personality brought him to the attention of influential Conservatives, including a comparatively young Benjamin Disraeli. I would start with flattery.

"First, much as you appreciate my own small service, I have to express my admiration for all that you accomplished, both at the bar and then with Lord Beaconsfield." I deliberately used his title as opposed to the more familiar name, Disraeli.

"It was a pleasure to serve so great a man," Lord Rowton said.

"Quite so, and I read how you rushed back from Algiers to be with him in those final hours."

"It was pell-mell getting there, but it was well worth the effort and I would do it again in a heartbeat. We worked together since 1865, a full year before I was appointed his secretary—can you imagine that, side by side for sixteen years? It would have been wrong not to be with him at the end."

"Did it not strike you as odd how quickly he failed in the end?" I asked carefully.

He eyed me a moment and then broke into a smile, reminding me of his easy-going cousin. "Of course, as a doctor you would be most curious. I lack the medical training, but yes, those last days seemed to move with terrible swiftness."

"While bronchitis is nothing unusual, the delirium and comatose state I read about in the press seemed unusual," I ventured, choosing my words carefully. "Did his personal doctors have any concerns?"

His lordship narrowed his eyes in thought, stroking the length of his fine beard, then shook his head. "Nothing I can recall. If they had concerns, it is safe to say they did not share them with me. Of course, as I intimated, I got there with barely hours to spare and was not much interested in his condition prior to my arrival. All that mattered to me was that I was on hand to say a proper farewell."

"Understandable, my lord. Your loyalty to him, of course, has been well spoken of. After all, few would take no compensation to remain in his lordship's employ." I was referring to the period between the first and second Disraeli administrations. Even now, after his public service was brought to an end with Disraeli's death, Rowton had continued to serve Her Majesty, and his activities had taken a rather philanthropic turn over the last few months.

"I don't mind admitting that I find your questions curious, Doctor," Lord Rowton said. "Is there something about his passing that you wish to learn?"

"Very insightful of you, sir," I said. "Are you familiar with a man named Sherlock Holmes?"

Another pause as he looked over my shoulder, thinking. There were murmurs in the adjacent room, members of the House arriving. Finally, he returned his gaze to me.

"He's some sort of detective, am I right? I believe the phrase my cousin used was 'consulting detective'. A most curious profession."

"Holmes is a most curious man," I said. "I've never known anyone quite like him."

"As you might imagine, I made inquiries into him before agreeing to meet and there are more than a few people in Her Majesty's Government keen on his work."

"Indeed, sir. Holmes has proven rather useful to the police of late," I said with some pride.

"And in my own circles, I seem to recall he has proven useful in more private matters," he added. I nodded. "So let us cease with this beating around the bush. How, pray tell, does this inquiry of yours relate to him?"

I summoned the words to make my request sound as rational as possible. "I have come to assist Mr. Holmes on his investigations and right now we are looking into the disappearance of a sailor who vanished during the Boer conflict."

"I see." He waited patiently for me to explain, his expression placid though perhaps a tad curious.

"There appears to be some question as to his actual whereabouts," I continued. "The Royal Navy has him officially listed as Missing in Action, but we can find no documentation to support that or any witness who can confirm when he was last seen. Admiralty staff have intimated that the MIA designation is an honourable cover for desertion. We are investigating on behalf of the sailor's mother, who is convinced, as mothers are wont, that her boy could not have abandoned his men."

"I appreciate your work on behalf of this man's mother," his lordship said.

"Clearly something is afoot because we are being physically harassed to cease the investigation," I said.

That caught Lord Rowton's attention and his eyes widened. "The Admiralty has been interfering?"

"Not in an overt way, no, sir," said I. "Out of uniform ruffians attacked Holmes and myself, and their meaning was perfectly clear."

"I see. But what on earth could this possibly have to do with Lord Beaconsfield?" asked Rowton.

"I realise that the link may not be apparent. I myself cannot see it. But Mr. Holmes is a man of singular vision and thought. He sees connections that beggar the imagination of normal men like us, and he has seen a thread that he believes if pulled will lead from this young man's disappearance in Africa to the death of the late prime minister."

"That is a preposterous notion, my good man. Impossible."

"A most reasonable sentiment, Lord Rowton," said I. "Holmes suspects the sailor of having been killed in some sort of action that Her Majesty's Government does not want the general public to know. Surely you harbour a few such secrets."

He did not articulate his reply but the brief nod of his head gave me all the confirmation I needed.

"Someone is trying to capitalise on Africa's instability. Holmes believes whoever is behind all this also wanted to blunt Lord Beaconsfield's voice in the House of Lords during much the same period. Mr. Holmes is attempting to find evidence to connect the two events."

"That's quite the assertion, Doctor Watson," he said. "Yes, there was a question or two about his deterioration but not a living soul in attendance suspected any form of foul play."

"They are not trained as Holmes is," said I. "He sees what the rest of us overlook."

"What is it this Holmes wants to see in relation to this matter?"

"We are hoping you might grant us access to Lord Beaconsfield's papers." I took a deep breath and then added, "And perhaps his lordship's medical records."

Lord Rowton did not mask his astonishment. "You do realise, Doctor, how genuinely absurd this request sounds? Gladstone was prime minister when this sailor went missing and Lord Beaconsfield was merely the leader of the loyal opposition for a brief period and had nothing to do with military matters."

His reasoning was perfectly sound and I needed to press my case quickly lest he refuse any assistance. "If you would be so kind, any papers would be useful."

"It really is quite a preposterous request," Rowton said, and then stopped himself and leaned in towards me, fearsome intelligence glittering in his old eyes. There was no hint of world-weariness in them. On the contrary, I saw myself across the table from a daunting foe. Now there were merely inches between our faces. "You have my attention, Doctor."

I shifted uncomfortably in my chair, trying to sound as reasonable as possible. The last thing I wanted was for him to think he was in the company of a delusional fool. "As I said, if you know of Holmes's reputation, sir, then you no doubt know he is quite exceptional in this field, and while he may not confide all in me, I trust him enough to assure you that if he thinks there may be a connection, then there just may be. I will add, quite frankly, sir, that as a physician, I find the manner of Disraeli's passing curious. Access to those records would put my mind at ease and if it also provides us with a clue then that is all for the good."

Lord Rowton sat in contemplative silence and I decided I had made my case, both for Holmes and for myself. I chose to let him consider what had been said and would abide by whatever decision he reached, whether or not Holmes would be satisfied. It was the best that I could do.

"I will admit now that I have had some time to consider those sad days, it does appear to have happened quickly, but excellent physicians and a renowned coroner were at his side both during and after his passing. I cannot believe they were at fault, or that some shadowy assassin's hand was at play. It is quite unthinkable." I braced myself for his refusal. "But he was my friend, and if there is even a shadow of doubt concerning his final days I owe it to him to shine a light upon it. Fresh eyes upon those records could be no bad thing, and one military man to another I appreciate what you are doing for that man's mother. She certainly deserves the truth, whatever it may be."

I sat still, certain if I moved I would break the spell and he would recant everything he seemingly just offered.

"I do not know if you are aware, Doctor, but his Lordship left me all his papers. They do not include the medical notes of his doctors relating to his last days—for those you must look elsewhere—but you may find something pertinent to your inquiry. They are currently at my home. I will make arrangements to have them brought into the city for your examination should you so wish. Now I think of it, I have a copy of an article by Dr. Kidd that you may find illuminating, which I will include with the papers. But for my own peace of mind, I will keep my man nearby to retrieve them."

I nodded. "Of course, sir. That is a wise precaution and I thank you so much for your help."

"Our lot is one of service, Doctor, and I am all too happy to help where I can, knowing that in doing so we may be helping my friend and ultimately, the Crown," Rowton said, rising to his feet, a clear signal our meeting was at an end.

Despite being nearly an hour away on foot I chose to walk back to Baker Street. I immediately regretted it given the heat and humidity. Perspiration ran down my neck, irritating my collar, but something also was pricking at my neck. Slowly, I turned my head and had a sense I was being followed. I could not identify my pursuer but I was certain of it. Holmes would no doubt have determined the man by his footfall and likely what he had for breakfast but I had to accept what my senses were warning me of.

I returned to Baker Street, quite unmolested having never spotted the tracker, feeling both dizzied and ecstatic at having obtained the support of so prestigious a figure. That we were being granted access to the Prime Minister's papers was nothing short of miraculous. In truth I had not allowed myself to contemplate success in this particular endeavour, so as better to avoid the crushing disappointment of failure, but Holmes's growing reputation was paying unexpected dividends.

Such thoughts were quickly swept from my mind as I entered the building only to be assaulted by the rank odour of charred wood.

My feet propelled me up the seventeen steps, my heart beginning to pound, my mind racing. As I opened the door to our sitting room, the smell grew in intensity.

My emotions were in a flux as I saw Holmes carefully sweeping a pile of ash onto a small glass slide before transferring the still-smoking heap to his scales. I could have killed him, which given my fears of only a heartbeat before was the very definition of ironic.

"What the devil are you doing now?" I asked, doing my best to sound calm. My best really wasn't all that convincing, I must admit.

"Supper will not be for a while," Holmes explained, "so I decided to expand my studies from cigars to wood. It is a natural extrapolation after all as arson is one of the many crimes we have to be prepared for." My companion was a very peculiar man. "In this case, I strolled by a nearby construction project and took some measurements. I then acquired a discarded piece of timber and doused it with alcohol, the most common type of accelerant. It was all done under quite controlled circumstances. As you requested, I have endeavoured not to burn down the building."

Speechless, I merely took a seat and watched as he measured and then made some notations and computations in a notebook. He appeared satisfied with his experiment and carefully brushed the now useless ash into a basket. If he were half as meticulous with the cleaning of the sitting room we would have had no call for Mrs. Hudson's tender care.

Finished with his work, Holmes took the seat opposite my own, fixed the makings of a pipe, and lit it, drawing deep on yet another flavour of smoke, before he indicated he was finally ready for my report. Quickly, I outlined my meeting with Lord Rowton, drawing a single nod from Holmes during the entire account. When I concluded, he slowly smiled.

"While the government can be more efficiently run, no doubt, it is good to hear that there are some servants who never stop serving. Lord Rowton will, I hope, provide us with the clues we need to advance this case, for without more information, I fear we may fail Mrs. Wynter." I could not argue with that. "There's a good chap, Watson. We shall dine together and then I shall take an evening constitutional and see what may transpire."

"Speaking of walks, I had the queerest feeling of being followed after my meeting," I said.

Holmes looked up, his brow already furrowed with concern. "That is most curious as I too was shadowed while out earlier."

"The bounders from earlier?" I inquired.

"Not the same men, that is to be certain," he said. "But then again, Hampton must have a large contingent to summon for such extracurricular work."

"Are we in danger?"

"At present, I should think not. We are being followed, that is all. We have given them no reason to think the people responsible for Wynter's disappearance are about to be exposed. Indeed, I should think the man following you had no clue as to who you were meeting with or how it might connect to Wynter's case. No, Watson, I think for now we are merely being observed. However, should we grow closer to an answer, we should be on the alert."

I slumped in my seat, worried he was being the master of understatement. I would have to keep my wits about me until this matter was resolved. For now, though, we were safe in our rooms and the aroma from supper was blessedly beginning to displace that of the charred wood.

At the time it sounded an innocent enough evening, but in truth it was the beginning of the next phase of the investigation. It did not take long for either of us to realise just how deathly serious this matter was about to become.

Five

Rescued by Wiggins

I intended to wait for Holmes's return before turning in, and settled down with a snifter. The day's affairs continued to preoccupy me. I pondered what little we knew against how much more we did not. Between my thinking and the soothing effects of the brandy I must have dozed off because there was a hammering on the street door below that brought me bolt upright in my chair as I awoke, cursing. The sky outside the window hovered between black and blue; it was very early in the morning. I could hear the clip-clop of hooves as delivery carts made their way down Baker Street.

My first sleep-fogged thought was that the men following us had decided to become bold about their intentions but that made little sense given the hour.

Mrs. Hudson, also awoken by the cacophony, was yelling at whoever was doing the pounding to cease right this minute so as not to wake the neighbours, though I am sure her shouts would have done as much to raise them from their slumbers as the banging. I smiled for a moment, almost pitying the person on the receiving end of her dressing down, but that smile withered and died on the vine when I realised what I wasn't hearing: Holmes.

I took a quick look into his room and his bed was still made. It appeared that he had been out all night. So much for an evening constitutional.

A cry of alarm from Mrs. Hudson had me in motion instantly. I was down the stairs quickly, taking them two or three at a time as best my injury would allow, and was brought up short when I saw two figures on the threshold. One was unmistakably that of Holmes, but the other was slighter and younger. He also appeared far dirtier but once I spied the signs of blood on Holmes's clothes, I gave up my observations of the boy.

"Hurry! Get him upstairs. Mrs. Hudson—some hot water and rags if you please."

The youth and I each placed one of Holmes's arms around our necks and awkwardly made our way up the narrow stairs to our rooms. Holmes mumbled a little, his words unintelligible. Frankly, I was glad he was making any sound. We got him to one of the dining chairs and I gingerly held up his head. There was a gash on his forehead, and I brushed away the matted, bloody hair. The cut flesh bled freely, but didn't appear to be a serious wound. I then studied his eyes and noted they were alert if a tad unfocused. He might be concussed, but I needed to check the rest of him. Rotten-smelling refuse clung to his overcoat and both it and his shirt were mud-splattered and ripped in several places. His hands were rubbed raw in places, abrasions that would leave dark bruises as the healing began. All told, he was roughed up but in no serious danger.

I thought again about our shadows and stifled a shiver of dread.

The boy, who could not have been more than twelve or thirteen, appeared to have lived a life some considerable distance from bathwater. He was sturdy and had the hardened look of a street urchin. I looked a little more closely and realised this youth was Wiggins, one of Holmes's "street Arabs", as he called them. At that moment, I had no idea how he had found himself mixed up in this, but a second look showed he was unmolested and therefore it was unlikely he had been involved in whatever befell my companion.

By then, Mrs. Hudson had arrived with a steaming jug of water and several rags draped over one arm.

"Oh my! Is he all right?" she asked, panic in her voice.

"I will not die," Holmes said in a croaking voice. This evidence of alertness was most welcome, even if it did little to set our landlady's mind at rest. I sent Wiggins for cool water for Holmes to drink as I began dabbing at the grime and blood so I could better see the full extent of his wounds.

"Holmes," said I, "how do you feel?"

"I am in pain, to be honest," said he.

I worked with practised hands, reminded once more of performing similar ministrations to those wounded in Afghanistan. Those horrid memories were rarely far from my mind and here they were made manifest in my companion, though mercifully his injuries were less severe than many I had tended, though with head wounds it was always a concern that what you didn't see was so much worse than what you did. Holmes remained silent as I worked, no doubt recovering his strength and his remarkable wits. Wiggins brought him a small tumbler of water, which Holmes took from him and slowly sipped. The young boy stepped back and watched in fascination.

I turned to him and asked, "What happened, Wiggins?"

"Well, Doctor, I was out and about when I came across Mr. 'olmes. I saw he was out the night before and thought he was on a case, so I follows 'im to be on hand should he need my… 'elp." The boy grinned then. I nodded for him to go on. "He were movin' fairly quickly, so I had trouble keeping up and I lost 'im at one point, but he walks a reg'lar pattern, you know, so I found him quick enough, but by then he was fighting off some fellow."

"I think your timely arrival saved my life," Holmes said.

I paused my work and looked at him in great alarm.

"You were very rambunctious," Wiggins added, though I was not sure he knew what the word meant. "I reckon you had 'im."

"He was a skilled fighter," Holmes said, his voice low and serious.

"Skilled like a sailor," I said obliquely so as not to give Wiggins or Mrs. Hudson any ideas.

"Not at all similar, no," said Holmes which came as a surprise. I continued to minister to him.

"What did you see?" I asked Wiggins.

"It were a man for starters, a good bit shorter than Mr. 'olmes. He was all covered up so I couldn't see much of his face. But he moved liked a dandy."

"No," Holmes corrected, trying to move beneath my care, but I was having none of it. "He was trained in the Far East, perhaps India. He smelled of coriander, possibly a Sikh; he punched with his left hand and had some sort of weapon in his right. I believe you will find evidence of it on my coat."

"Allow me to tend to you first," I said, and resumed cleaning his wounds. None appeared to need suturing, which was a good sign. He would be terribly bruised and no doubt stiff and sore for some days to come, but he had been through worse during our brief partnership. As I completed dressing his injuries, Holmes carefully sipped his water and handed the tumbler back to Wiggins, who placed it on the table. Mrs. Hudson had retreated to the kitchen.

"Holmes, please begin your story from the moment you left," I instructed.

"I left here for my walk as I had told you. And as young Wiggins here has noted, I do have set patterns. I have calculated several paths that enable me to establish in my own mind the state of the neighbourhood, which I can then extrapolate into what might be the current temperament of London. Last night, I began my walk on Baker Street and proceeded down Melcombe Street and through Dorset Square where I spent some time speaking with the local vagrants. From there I headed northwest and explored the streets in that direction.

"I was walking down Harewood Avenue when it became clear I was being followed. Yes, Watson, like you I assumed it was our pursuer from earlier in the day. I led my shadow back to Melcombe Street and then stepped into an alley intending to surprise him. He was a sly one, though, and understood my feint. He was prepared for me. We grappled, he getting the better of me with alarming ease, and I daresay he would have finished me had Wiggins not arrived and scared him off."

"I could have chased 'im," the urchin said. "But Mr. 'olmes had his bellows emptied so I figured he needed me more."

"Quite right," I said, reaching out to pat him in a fatherly way, but Wiggins was having none of it.

Holmes, though, reached into a pocket, wincing a bit in the process, and withdrew several coins. "Our rate is a shilling, but your rescue earns you a gold sovereign, I think." Wiggins snatched the coin with speed, pocketing it in a blink. Given the state of our expenses, it was a most extravagant gesture.

"You might consider using that for a bath," I said with a distinct sniff.

Wiggins grinned at me but didn't agree or disagree with the suggestion. He tipped his cap and turned to leave.

"Thank you," Holmes said to the lad. It was obvious how sincerely he meant it. "Be alert, there's every chance he got a good look at you. I wouldn't travel the streets alone for some time."

"Ain't that the truth," Wiggins said and saw himself out. A few seconds later we heard the street door bang closed.

"Holmes," I said, turning to my friend, "I know you; you will want to think about what all this means. And I do, too, but first you need to be whole. And that means taking the time to heal. As your physician I am recommending you take to your bed and sleep."

"As you wish, Watson," Holmes said.

I will admit there was a dual purpose to my prescription. As I prepared a syringe with a sedative and rolled up his sleeve, I looked for evidence of recent drug activity. None of the marks appeared fresh, which I took to mean his system was clean of any other narcotics. Holmes said nothing as I administered the injection.

Once completed, I helped Holmes out of his coat and examined it carefully.

"The rips in the cloth are uniformly spaced apart and pierced the fabric with ease," said he. "Five slices. This bears further study. Do not dispose of the garment." His voice began to show the drug taking effect so I silenced him and eased him to his bed. He fell in a heap while I removed his shoes and then closed the door.

Left alone, the dawn shone through the windows as I began to put away my medical supplies.

First, there were the sailors attacking us. But now a foreign attacker was added to the mix. Two attacks on Holmes, the death of a former prime minister, a missing sailor—was there a red thread running through these seemingly disparate events? Something was most certainly astir, but as the sun rose redly and a new day began, I could not for the life of me fathom what it all meant. For that, I would need Holmes healthy and alert once more. As I waited for that to happen, I helped myself to the day's first cup of tea.

Six

Cutting to the Chase

I was not surprised in the slightest that even though I gave Holmes a mild dose of the sedative, he slept straight through the day and that evening. While he recovered, I took care of routine matters, which included sending out notes to the sailors who had been close to Norbert Wynter on the *Dido*, names given to me by Miss Caroline Burdett. I then began chronicling the events of the case thus far, taking the opportunity to get things down on paper while they were still fresh in my mind. I was already convinced that the investigation would be well worth reading when all was done and dusted. It had all the elements of a penny dreadful potboiler.

Mrs. Hudson would stop by every now and then to check on the patient, and I expected Wiggins to do the same, but he had apparently taken one of our suggestions to heart, either to stay out of sight or to bathe. My money was on the one that did not involve a rendezvous with water.

It was the following morning, as I was completing my perusal of

The Times, when Holmes finally emerged from his room. His eyes were a little unfocused but I could tell he was feeling better. His right cheek and hands were covered in dark purple bruises and he moved stiffly. I got him some water and asked Mrs. Hudson to prepare a large breakfast.

"How are you feeling?"

"Both sore and stiff, as you might imagine, but on the whole I feel better than I have any right to," he replied. "Where is my coat?"

"Rather than get right back to work, Holmes, take some time to loosen your limbs and eat something. The coat is right here and we may examine it together after you have some sustenance. It will certainly make you feel better."

"If you insist," he said and looked about with impatience for the food.

"Mrs. Hudson will have it along momentarily," said I. "In the meantime, go wash and put on some fresh clothes. Those, I think, are done for."

We ate in passable silence, but I could tell he was humouring me more than actually hungry. His eyes were constantly darting towards the coat, which hung on the back of the couch. When we had finished the meal, he rose from the table, took up the coat, and sat in his armchair by the fire. He fingered the five identical tears in the fabric.

"The weapon was in his hand, almost as if it was an extension of himself," Holmes mused. "I have read of such weapons, but will need to refresh my mind." He rattled his fingertips across the pad of his thumb as though drumming out an inaudible tune.

"Before you do that, let us review the other night. Exactly when did all this happen?"

"Wiggins brought me here at what time?"

"It was early, maybe half past five in the morning. He was making quite the racket given the hour. It is a surprise half the street haven't been banging on our door to see what all the fuss was about."

"He took time to walk with me and the fight lasted only a few minutes. But the actual stalking took over an hour, so…"

"Were you intending to walk all evening?"

"Not at first," Holmes admitted. "But once I began walking and thinking and speaking with people, always looking for more resources much like Wiggins and his urchin brethren, I admit I allowed myself to get carried away."

"Let us address why this might have happened. Why would an Indian, if that is what he was, attack you?"

"We have bothered someone, that much is obvious, and they want us to cease our investigation into poor Wynter. I have no other case so that is the only possible answer, which makes me all the more determined to press on with our investigation."

"But so far the only people we have made inquiries of are the Admiralty. Surely they would not hire an Indian to assault you?" I observed. "After all, they have already sent their own men to dissuade us from proceeding."

"Quite right, Watson, but all that means is someone else knows."

"Someone other than the Admiralty?"

"Watson, at present we know the Admiralty wants us to cease seeking Wynter's whereabouts or fate. We have no conclusive evidence to show it was the Admiralty behind this. They could, after all, be following orders from a different quarter of the government."

"A fair point," said I. "So the Admiralty knows and… someone, some other party is involved?"

"There is a drain of information, leaking out of the Admiralty, and to someone with the resources to hire a foreign assassin. Interesting, but that word derives from the Arabic *hashishiyyin* or 'hashish-users'. It was a sect that would dose themselves and then kill their opponents."

"Are you suggesting your attacker was under some narcotic influence?"

He allowed himself a broad smile. "Not at all, but there is something very ritualistic about the way my attacker worked, and it made me think of that group. His moves were quite precise and well practised. Given your far more thorough knowledge of human anatomy, please confirm whether the following is consistent with my injuries." With that, Holmes rose from his seat and began walking the length of our sitting room. He paused and pantomimed ducking into the alleyway. Then he took a large step from that space and turned on his heel. Now he was the attacker and walked towards the alley, paused, and tensed himself.

For the next few minutes I was given a performance the likes of which I had never seen before. Holmes was his assailant, moving in approximation of how the other man might have moved, striking measured blows into thin air. With each blow, I was mentally filling in Holmes's figure, and I was impressed, as each one seemed likely to have resulted in a wound my friend had indeed suffered. It was a violent ballet. As he finished, a final attack interrupted by the well-timed arrival of Wiggins, Holmes appeared spent. He would never admit to being fatigued by such efforts, but he was still recovering.

"I daresay you have recreated the fight most carefully and yes, each blow you demonstrated would indeed have resulted in your bruises. The sweeping motion of your right hand suggests that he held five blades in his hand. And from your recreation, I can conclude he left more lasting marks than you managed."

"Five blades in one hand, you say," Holmes mused, breathing hard. "That does sound familiar. I will consult my books, but for now that gives us a starting point."

"How on earth did young Wiggins manage to get you away from so deadly an opponent?"

He stopped his pacing and looked at me, as if my question had thrust right into the heart of the matter.

"A most excellent question. As I recall, the mere act of discovery slowed down my assailant. No doubt he feared the boy would summon the police. We'll have to ask him to verify that piece of the story."

"I say we go looking for this man."

"I should like to find him, yes," Holmes said. "But first, I want to know who he is and why he sought me out. The imperative being to learn for sure that he was sent to kill me because of our current investigation as opposed to a grudge held over from some previous case." Holmes steepled his fingers together and considered, no doubt thinking back to the few cases we had worked together since the spring when our unlikely collaboration began.

For myself, I could certainly think of none that would result in an Indian assassin tracking us down.

"To review then," he said, "once we began making inquiries at the Admiralty, no one would confirm to us that Norbert Wynter is alive, dead, Missing in Action, or a deserter. We cannot obtain his military records. But something is going on, something that began this spring, first with Wynter's disappearance in Africa and the near-concurrent rapid decline and death of Benjamin Disraeli. Which reminds me, while I slept, were we fortunate enough to obtain the latter's papers from Lord Rowton?"

"They are expected today, as a matter of fact."

"Excellent. Now, given that Disraeli's death is a somewhat tenuous avenue of inquiry, we must also pursue a more linear one, and track down the commander of the *Dido*. He may well have information concerning Wynter's fate. The ship may well be out at sea, but I think the Admiralty can tell us that much without obfuscation."

"What if there *is* a connection, however tenuous, between Wynter and Disraeli?"

"Watson, we need facts before we can make suppositions. Anything else would be guesswork and I dislike guesswork. Instead, while you read the papers, I will learn more about my would-be assassin's weapon. I am certain I have read something about it."

"I would think importing a killer speaks of a certain desperation," I offered. "As do two different agencies sending men after us."

"I agree, but we have not been about this investigation long, which leads me to think this Indian was already in Britain. The attack suggests that you and I might well have been followed by one or both sources since we left the Admiralty."

"For asking questions?"

"For asking the kinds of questions someone does not want answered," he replied. He paused to massage his temples and despite his lengthy sleep, he still struck me as deeply fatigued. Holmes appeared to draw the same conclusion and rose to his feet, testing his limbs. "I need to take a walk and stretch my mind while we wait."

I rose in alarm. "The last walk you took did not turn out so well," I said. "Allow me to accompany you."

"You should be here to receive the papers from Lord Rowton. We do not know when it will arrive and I would hate to waste any more time than absolutely necessary."

"For once, I disagree with your assessment, Holmes. This is not time sensitive. Wynter is gone and shall remain gone if we walk an hour or a day. Disraeli's papers may well prove fascinating reading, but in all honesty I doubt we will learn much from them pertinent to our case, and certainly even less regarding Wynter. Besides, Mrs. Hudson will be here to take delivery, so hardly any time will be wasted."

I expected him to argue with me, but for once he ceded to my reasoning and we began our descent to the street. As we strolled along Baker Street, I continued to express my doubts that Disraeli's papers would prove to be anything other than sad reading. The connection between the two matters remained elusive to me.

The air was warm but fortunately not brutal enough to roast us as we strolled the nearby streets. I forced myself to count between ten and twenty steps before daring to look over my shoulder so as not to appear to have a nervous habit. Thankfully, no one gave us any notice nor did anyone look out of place. Perhaps the attackers determined Holmes's injuries meant they could be quit of us.

Our walk tired him out after a few streets, so I steered him back to our rooms, poured him some tea, and watched as he drifted off to sleep in his chair. While he napped, there was a soft chime of the doorbell. I opened it to see a man in a livery suit, carrying a large box tied with string. As I took it from him, I noted how heavy it was and wished to offer the man something for his trouble. Instead, he merely tipped his hat and said he would return to collect the box in the morning. I was glad of this, as I had expected him to stay and keep watch on my researches after Lord Rowton's words that his man would be close by.

Holmes slept on as I untied the box and began removing ledgers, notebooks and loose sheaves of paper. Much of the latter was covered in what I took to be Lord Rowton's handwriting–correspondence between the Prime Minister and Parliament, the Queen, and subjects of the realm. It was a treasure trove, no doubt. I quickly sorted the materials into easily digestible piles: domestic affairs, military matters, and politics. It was also clear Lord Rowton was circumspect with Disraeli's effects, letting me see only materials dating from 1879 to 1881, anything that might be connected to the South African affair, but nothing more.

With a fresh cup of tea beside me, I began reading the international dispatches. In time, I realised there was less there about the Boer conflict than I had imagined. Instead, I turned my attention to the general correspondence, amongst which I found a letter between Lord Rowton and Lord Barrington, the latter having attended Disraeli while Rowton was in the south of France. It seemed to show evidence of the beginning of Disraeli's illness, Barrington reporting having to physically support the great man about the house. He also mentioned a walk taken in the countryside, during which the great man said, "I have no strength left, let us return." Soon after, the bronchitis set in.

Finally I found the copy of the article by Dr. Joseph Kidd, Disraeli's personal physician, to which Rowton had referred at our meeting. I knew Kidd only by reputation, apparently a cold, dislikeable fellow. He was a homeopath, no true doctor as far as I was concerned, but a favourite of Her Majesty. His article purported to be an account of Disraeli's death, but did not tell me much that I did not already know. Disraeli had previously suffered from Bright's disease, bronchitis and asthma, meaning their recurrence at the end was not surprising. If Kidd were to be believed, Disraeli began deteriorating during the winter and his condition became severe one particularly cold night in March. "Bronchitis developed the next morning with distressing asthma, loss of appetite, fever and congestion of the kidneys. Notwithstanding prompt treatment he began to lose ground," Kidd wrote. In fact, he was wasting away until the final fortnight, when things gained speed. To me, that was a curiosity that bore further investigation, but clearly Kidd had merely seen a seventy-six-year-old man succumbing to a variety of illnesses, powered by unremitting gout. Kidd was clearly little more than a quack, prescribing claret for Disraeli's gout and arsenic for his cough.

Kidd had treated Disraeli until the end, and had been reluctant to allow anyone else to tend to the great man despite his quickening condition. It took the Queen's own influence to allow Dr. Richard Quain and Dr. John Mitchell Bruce, traditional physicians and not homeopaths, to examine the former prime minister. These little irregularities chimed distant alarm bells in my mind. There was room for mischief in closed circles, and the lack of any sort of post-mortem examination concerned me. I wanted to believe it was purely due to the routine manner of Disraeli's passing—notwithstanding his sudden decline—but Holmes had me doubting my instincts.

As I continued reading, letting my tea go untouched, Holmes began to stir.

"Have you found something useful?"

It was a good question. Had I? I placed the final sheet down on a stack and shook my head. "No. Disraeli succumbed fast and given his chronic gout and other conditions, it did not rouse suspicion. He was attended by three physicians, and none of them seem to have made a thorough examination of his corpse or performed an autopsy."

"Would an autopsy be usually warranted for bronchitis?"

"Of course not," I said. "However, were any of his doctors to suspect a sinister cause for his rapid deterioration, it would have been proper to call for one. You might not know this, but the study of autopsies has dramatically improved in the last decade or so, thanks to the work of Rudolf Ludwig Karl Virchow, a German who developed a systematic procedure to be used, studying the entire body in detail. Had Disraeli been so studied, we might have learned something, if there was something to be learned, of course."

"We still might, Watson. I take it there is no death certificate or detailed medical reports in that box?" I shook my head. "Curious."

"Indeed it is," I agreed. There was more to this. Perhaps the answers we were looking for lay in Disraeli's medical files? But I also felt we were moving further away from our primary goal: finding Norbert Wynter. I said as much to Holmes who shook his head in disagreement.

"Not at all, Watson. We are exploring an avenue of investigation, ascertaining whether or not the timing of Disraeli's death is mere coincidence or suggests a larger, more sinister reason, one which also claimed Wynter's life."

"Can there truly be a connection between the death of so important a man as Disraeli and so unimportant a man as Wynter?"

Holmes seemingly dismissed me as he refilled his pipe and set to thinking on some unspoken problem. No doubt an aspect of this current case he would not share with me for a week or more, by which time my input would be little more than to nod and look impressed.

As he turned inward, I began to think about whom else I might be able to contact in order to access Disraeli's medical files.

"Is there no one in your circle of acquaintances who might be able to support our cause?"

"I have given that consideration, Watson, but frankly, my work has usually not involved these tiers of Her Majesty's Government," said Holmes.

"More's the pity," said I.

I could not go back to Rowton, but perhaps a sitting member of the House of Commons might have the influence to produce that which I needed. It was my last chance. I wrote a telegram to Alexander Macdonald—a representative from Stafford and a man I had been introduced to at several parties over the last year—and called for Mrs. Hudson to take it to the nearest telegraph office. If fortune favoured me, he would remember me and do as I asked.

I continued to review Kidd's article while Holmes, who had roused himself from his brown study, rose and began pulling volumes off a bookshelf. I presumed he was beginning his research into the origins of the weapon that had so nearly shredded him alive.

Being followed, Holmes being attacked—this was taking on a most peculiar and potentially deadly turn of events. What the devil had Wynter stumbled into?

Some time later, Mrs. Hudson rang the bell. She brought with her a telegram, which informed me that Macdonald requested a meeting at five that very evening. I washed, changed my jacket, and took a cab to Parliament, hoping I was not becoming a regular enough visitor to be recognised. Upon entering the Westminster Palace I was taken to a set of small offices where I found Macdonald signing letters. He put his pen down and rose to shake my hand, then offered me a seat across from him.

He was sixty and had a ragged look to his monkish tonsure and a ruddy complexion to his loose jowls. His suit was well worn and in need of repair, but he didn't seem to take notice, much as he paid little mind to the ink stains on his thick fingers. Instead, he sat back and appraised me in his own open manner.

"When was the last time we met?" he inquired.

"It was at a charity ball for the Irish cause, I believe," I replied. That seemed to awaken pleasant memories since he was a major proponent of Irish Home Rule, so much so that it earned him more than a few enemies in both Houses. Other charges levelled against him came from the likes of Karl Marx and Friedrich Engels, the Communist philosophers. Amongst other things, they felt he was too close to Disraeli, although that was the very reason I found myself in his presence.

He did not look terribly well, and to my practised eye, I noticed a slight discolouration in his corneas that might well have been indicative of an underlying medical condition. It dawned on me that I was increasingly replicating Holmes's habits of observation. I was uncertain if that was for the best or not. Today though, I ignored such thoughts and allowed Macdonald to wax lyrical about the latest issues with Ireland. He then moved on to the plight of miners, an issue that had propelled him to re-election the previous year.

"But you didn't ask to meet just so I could prattle on about miner safety," said he.

"As a doctor, I am always interested in the safety of others. But as you will have gathered from my telegram, my interest today is regarding one whose safety is beyond the control of men," I said.

"You piqued my curiosity, I admit. It was a most bizarre request, but given your profession I presumed you had your reasons. It is no small thing to dig into a prime minister's medical reports. Luckily for you, they are now official parliamentary record."

"Were you able to obtain them?"

He opened a drawer in his desk and withdrew a thick folder. He tapped it, then laid a hand atop it. "They are right here, but tell me the truth, Doctor: why on earth do you want to look at Lord Beaconsfield's medical history? No lies, or this goes back in the archive to gather dust."

Once more I felt the need to invoke Holmes's name, although this time it lacked the desired effect. He was unfamiliar with my collaborator so I endeavoured to briefly explain who he was and his value to the government. I then sketched out for him Wynter's sad story and the suspicion that Disraeli's death was somehow connected, which still felt like a stretch of logic that required the listener to take a leap of faith with me. The one thing I omitted was the attack on Holmes since we had yet to determine if there was a genuine connection between this and the other events.

Macdonald looked as perplexed by my story as Rowton had done. "I would not do this for a man I did not know, you understand?" I allowed that I did. "Yet perhaps it will do no harm, and maybe some good." He raised his hand and opened the folder. "I will only show you those documents that relate to the period prior to his death. That should ease my conscience." He shuffled through several pages before finding the ones from March and April. Withdrawing them, he invited me to come to his side of the desk and review them.

"I must admit, Kidd's scrawl is not easy to decipher," Macdonald said with a bark of a laugh. "The man was born to be a doctor."

I scanned Dr. Joseph Kidd's notes regarding Disraeli's deteriorating condition including drafts of the nightly bulletins that were released to quell the concerns of the public. He had recorded Disraeli's move to his home at 19 Curzon Street where his asthma appeared to improve, and the frequency and dosage of various "cures". I was concerned at the increased reliance on powder of saltpetre and stramonium, which was burned and the vapours fed to Disraeli. They apparently helped at first but the efficacy of each treatment seemed to diminish. Despite this, Kidd continued to employ this treatment until the end.

I remembered Kidd's article on the death of Disraeli, which Rowton had supplied. It had made no note of the patient slipping into a comatose state, but his handwritten notes made that clear. And there were a series of other notations, the substance of which had also been omitted from the article, and made me quite alarmed.

"Something wrong, Doctor?"

"I am not certain," I said, not entirely truthfully. "I want to check these notes against my own medical texts before I say anything. May I use some paper?"

He withdrew a fresh sheet from the desk and I hastily copied out Kidd's notations, each stroke confirming to me that my initial suspicions were correct. I thanked him for his help and he rose to escort me out. As he walked, I noticed him wince with every third or fourth step. That clue, combined with the colouring of his eyes, led me to a concerning diagnosis, although I decided to keep my thoughts to myself.

When he bade me goodbye, I suggested he looked tired and might want to visit his own physician. He assured me he would, but the tone of his voice told me that it was unlikely.

I lost myself in thought as I took a cab back to 221B Baker Street. Before I could ascend the stairs, Mrs. Hudson handed me a note, which turned out to be from an engineer from the *Dido*–one of Wynter's fellows whom I had contacted—who was willing to see me the next day. Entering our rooms, I was most pleased to see Holmes at his violin and not creating another pile of ash. A melancholy melody filled the air, but faded as he became aware that he was no longer alone. Holmes put the instrument away, his impatience palpable.

"Was Macdonald of help?" he asked before I had sat myself down.

"Quite. He is also, I am of the belief, suffering from the early stage of jaundice. I have to say, Holmes, I've become a far more astute observer of such minutiae now that I have made your acquaintance."

He sniffed. "You are a trained doctor and therefore would be expected to notice such things. Had you *not* noticed those symptoms I should have been far more alarmed."

I had not thought of it in that manner and realised he was quite right. My association with him was merely making me a better physician. I swallowed his comments and proceeded with my own narrative.

"He had the records and allowed me to read those from March and April. Dr. Kidd's notes were most thorough and it's interesting he kept many of his observations out of the public accounts." That got Holmes's attention. He sat upright in his chair, not taking his eyes from me, his gaze intent. "Disraeli suffered from gout, which affects the kidneys, so his urine output was already diminished. As a result, Kidd and the other doctors in attendance didn't realise that the more rapid decrease in volume in his final days was due to some other cause. A cause that also led to the drop in his blood pressure, and likely explains his comatose state. And there is another symptom that does not fit in with either Disraeli's gout or bronchitis—acute abdominal pain. Presumably his doctors dismissed this as of no importance, given his more clear-cut symptoms. Yet if one puts it together with the diminished urination and lowered blood pressure, one can reach a more sinister diagnosis."

Holmes smiled at the confirmation that something was indeed amiss. Leaning forward in the chair, he asked, "What could have caused this?"

I raised a hand to stay his line of questioning. I rose and went to my medical texts and selected one volume. Holmes settled himself in his chair, allowing me to confirm my theory before speaking. Such caution and dedication to fact certainly earned his admiration. I found the entry I had sought, read it once, twice, then closed the book. As the covers softly sounded, Holmes came alert and leaned forward, anxious to hear the next clue to our case.

"I am of the belief that these are symptoms of an overdose of castor bean extract. The oil of the castor bean is used to treat liver and gall bladder ailments, and is harmless, but a deadly poison can also be distilled by those who know the method. It only occurred to me because a fellow army doctor made a study of it and had me read the paper he wrote on the subject."

Holmes nodded impatiently. "I am well aware of the toxic properties of the castor bean, Watson. I have made a study of hundreds of poisons at great length. Although I admit, it is unlikely that I would have been able to identify the culprit without your medical knowledge." I smiled at this. "Tell me, how do you think it was administered?"

"It was probably delivered orally, smuggled in with his other medications. It would have been no mean feat; he had three different doctors attending him night and day."

"Would he have survived the bronchitis otherwise?"

"Based on Kidd's notes, it is a possibility. Disraeli was quite ill and could have died regardless, but his death was most certainly hastened."

"Watson, do you know where the world's supply of castor beans comes from?"

"I daresay I do not, but clearly you do."

"I do," he said with triumph. "The beans are most plentiful in India."

Seven

Recruiting Wiggins

Holmes's revelation offered a clear link between his attacker and Disraeli, which set my mind to racing. I truly had not expected anything of the sort. Indeed, right up until that moment, I had been of a mind that Holmes was seeking clues where none existed. But here we were, with evidence that not only had Disraeli been killed before his time by a poison, but one that hailed from India.

What I could not puzzle out was how Disraeli and the Indian assassin were connected to Norbert Wynter and the Boer conflict. India was, after all, in Asia, while the Boer conflict was strictly in South Africa. Surely there could be no overt connection between the two territories? Had we stumbled on two completely different crimes? I posed this question to Holmes. He admitted he had yet to piece everything together, but much as a spider spins one thin strand of silk after another until a web is formed, so would this case present itself. Given what we had learned, I conceded his point.

"Should we report our findings about Lord Beaconsfield? It

seems the ethical thing to do," I said.

"What good would come of that? The very first question would be who poisoned him. The next question would be why. After all, he was no longer in power and could not influence trade with India or the Boer conflict."

"Why indeed," I repeated, feeling somewhat dejected despite the previous moment's elation at making our first significant connection.

"I remain somewhat fatigued, Watson," said Holmes. "Let us have supper and retire early. In the morning, I want you to become an expert on the castor bean. I daresay such information now appears vital."

Feeling my own gripping fatigue, I agreed. A summons to Mrs. Hudson resulted in a light meal, which we ate in relative silence, both of us lost in thought.

The following morning I felt properly refreshed and as I emerged from my bedroom into the sitting room, Holmes was already heading down the stairs to the street. I called to him but he either did not hear me or more likely deliberately paid me no heed. After breakfast and my ritual reading of *The Times*, I headed out to keep two appointments, starting with the *Dido*'s engineer and then a visit to the Royal Society of Medicine on Berners Street and their well-appointed library. Being a splendidly sunny morning I decided to walk and half an hour later, I arrived at a small restaurant.

I was fortunate to learn that Raskill had left the *Dido* and was awaiting his next posting. He was in London visiting relatives, which is where my note found him.

George Raskill was a large man in both height and girth. He was the largest object in the restaurant, dwarfing my sight of its rear, and seemed to be straining against his woollen clothing. The engineer had thick hands like ham hocks and a wide, flat nose, red-veined cheeks, and thinning dark hair. Despite his size, there was no loose fat on his frame; he was quite muscular and clearly not one to trifle with. He rose, filling the space ever more, easily topping six feet. As he extended a hand, I was afraid of cracking a bone as we shook.

"Have we met, Doctor?" Raskill's voice was surprisingly high, almost a tenor.

"I daresay we have not, sir," I replied as I took my seat opposite him. A waitress came to take our order and we both had pots of tea.

"Then I am most curious as to your note," he said. "You mentioned Wynter. Are you related?"

I briefly spoke of my connection to Mrs. Wynter and he relaxed his posture, which I had not quite noticed was that of a coiled spring, waiting to explode. "I am trying to build a portrait of this man, which may assist Mr. Holmes and myself in finding him."

"Good enough," Raskill said. "Bert was a good man."

"When did you last see him?" I opened my notebook.

His face crumpled in concentration. "It was while we were in Africa…" After several tense moments, his features relaxed and he said, "It was just before he went ashore. He was one of us sent to join the Naval Brigade. I last saw him the night before he disembarked."

"And he did not return with the dead or wounded?"

"No, and we were so busy below deck I never stopped to inquire of his whereabouts. To be honest, Doctor, I didn't think about the chap for a few days and by then, it was clear he was gone."

I made a note of this, trying to find a blank page where I could begin a proper chronology of events from January.

"What's funny is that he should have been at the forefront of my thoughts when you asked to meet me. The man owed me three quid."

I looked up sharply from my notebook and studied the man, raising my eyebrows in question. Was this the same lack of funds that Miss Burdett had mentioned? Three pounds was no small sum.

"He was a great man to break bread with, have a few drinks, but he was the worst card player I ever saw. Owed me three, owed the ship's doctor another two, and probably a few bob here and there to others."

"All from cards? That is a substantial sum of money."

He accepted his tea from the waitress with a wink. "Bert was good company, but it was getting clear to one and all he had a bit of a problem. Always took long odds, always tried to bluff his way through a bad hand and we could tell. To tell the truth, Doctor, I think he was in a deeper hole than most of us knew. He was beginning to complain he was short of funds to send home to his mother."

I nodded and kept adding notes. I had initially pictured Norbert Wynter as the model seaman, the perfect son, but clearly he was far more ordinary, which I oddly found to be a disappointment.

"What do you think happened to him?"

"By the time I realised he hadn't come back on board, alive or dead, I asked around but no one seemed to know. Eventually the Chief Engineer told me to stop asking so I suspected it was something bad and knew enough not to ask again."

Now that was odd. Could it be they were covering up Wynter's desertion? No, it would be something the men talked about, ordered to avoid the subject or not. But why not ask about Wynter's whereabouts? And of course it wasn't just one man we were talking about, even if Wynter was the focus of our investigation. Twenty men had been listed as deserters along with him. There should have been more people asking questions.

"There was definitely something strange going on, Doctor. Something bad happened ashore and we were never given a report. Lots of unanswered questions came back to England with the *Dido*."

I shot him a questioning glance and he elaborated. "How on earth could we be beaten so badly? We weren't fighting a trained army but a pack of locals, mostly farmers. As far as I'm concerned, that means our commanders were at fault. Perhaps something happened, something even worse than the defeats reported in the papers, that they are trying to hide. That would mean forbidding us to speak of it, even amongst ourselves. Never experienced anything like it in all my days at sea and I was on three tours before that one."

That made sense to me, given the order and rigid code of conduct expected aboard Her Majesty's vessels.

We talked a little more but it was clear Raskill could not tell me anything of further use. I paid for both drinks, which earned me a thunderclap of a thump on the back, and we parted company. Working out the pain of his parting gift, I walked east, heading for the library of the Royal Society of Medicine and more solitary studies.

I sat down with several volumes and lost myself in reading and note taking, letting myself be distracted by the joys of medical research. I was interested to note that there had been an increasing number of cases involving death from the castor bean extract, known as ricin. In 1870, a small child named Francis Murray died after eating a few castor beans in San Francisco. Two miners had died in Africa only a few years before, a bizarre-sounding case in which it appeared that the men had committed suicide by eating the beans. They apparently were at outs with their foreman and were constantly being whipped for slovenly work habits. The two men were starved in addition to the physical abuse and grew increasingly miserable. The beans were on hand and the men somehow knew that it could provide a permanent relief from their deprivations. They smuggled enough to be a lethal dose for the two of them into the mine one day, consumed them and soon after dropped dead, actually stiffening and blocking the mine shaft, a final act of revenge against their abuser.

I wanted to read more about it, see if they were examined by a doctor, but could never find more than the one reference. I admit to having allowed myself to be easily distracted by other topics, not all of them remotely related to the case at hand. For a change, there was no sense of danger, no threat to life or limb, and it felt like a marvellous respite from the previous few days. As it was, by the time I looked up, I realised I had read my way well past my normal lunchtime. Once I reached that conclusion, my stomach confirmed the news and demanded attention.

I made my way in the direction of Baker Street, but an odd sound caused me to quickly look over my shoulder. I saw the usual assortment of tradesmen and servants out doing the daily shopping, but a little further back was a silhouette of a figure that most certainly did not belong. It looked alarmingly very much like one of the men who accosted me just days before. Having avoided the Admiralty since our first and only visit, this was of some concern and made me wonder if I had been followed ever since?

I hurried my pace, seeking a place to avoid confrontation and still address my growing hunger. A few buildings down the street, I stopped off at the Horse and Hounds, a public house I frequented. As a place where I was known to the staff, I felt a level of protection from my pursuer should I be proven correct. I ordered a pint and a kidney pie from the barman, an older man with a rough accent and demeanour, and took a seat. I continually stared at the entrance, scanning each patron who entered. My follower had not bothered to enter but could easily be lurking outside on the street.

The barman brought over my pint, sloshing the suds on the table without apology, which was all part of the tavern's rough charm. Soon after he appeared with my pie, and the man seemed barely able to manage the hot dish without it threatening to find its way onto my stomach, rather than inside it.

"I say, are you new to this profession?" I asked in an irritated voice. I had not seen the man before, and hoped I would not again.

"Not at all, guv'nor," he replied.

"Well, you should be far more careful," I told him.

"Right you are. If you don't mind my saying, guv'nor, I'm thinkin' you should be careful yourself."

"Is that a fact?"

"It is, it is," he said, and I grew bewildered at his words. "Men such as yerself 'ave to be careful. You spend all day writin' notes, you're bound to make your hand sore."

"How the devil could you...?" I began then stopped myself. Only one man could look at me and know what I had been doing all day. "Holmes?"

"Quite right, guv'nor," he confirmed, a smile cracking his wrinkled face. "You see, you have fresh callouses developing on the fingers you use to grip your pencil. The only way you could have developed them so quickly was to spend the entire day at work. Which also explains you having such a late meal, my friend, especially for a man of such steady and predictable habits as yourself."

"Why the devil are you in disguise?" Much as I desired to eat my kidney pie, I needed to understand what Holmes was playing at. I had the distinct impression he was up to no good.

Suddenly, he was seated opposite me, wiping at the spilled beer. "Given the week's activity, it appeared the time had come to resume my practice with disguises. You just so happened to wander in here while I was on my very first shift as Bertram, the new hire."

"Do you mean to say you intend on remaining in the tavern's employ?"

"Not for long, although it should have occurred to me to adopt another persona and practise my disguises while bringing in the necessary income to cover my expenses. On the other hand, had we not needed the income, we never would have embarked upon so interesting a case, so it is a case of hardship leading to good fortune."

"Well, I suppose that is one way of looking at the matter."

"Please try the pie; I need to know if I should be recommending it. I watched the chef earlier and I believe he used the appropriate kind of kidney."

"That is *most* reassuring." I sniffed the air above my plate and everything appeared in order.

"Holmes, I do believe I am being followed. I spotted a large hulk of a figure on my way down the street," I said. Holmes narrowed his eyes in concern.

"People that size would be more of Hampton's men," he said, contempt coming through his accented speech.

"How was your day? You certainly left early enough," I asked.

"No one was following me. I first sought out Wiggins," Holmes explained. "I wanted to hire him and his gang for some work."

I risked a bite of the pie, which tasted fine if a bit hot, and not at all of cat or unlucky customer, so I let it cool and cautiously inquired, "What sort of work?"

"The usual sort of errand running and the like," said he.

"Don't you think the presence of an assassin makes this too dangerous for children?"

"Watson, despite appearances, believe me, that gang is perfectly capable of taking care of themselves. In fact, I might wonder if the Indian gentleman is not the one who should be worried. If it makes you feel any better about my intentions, I am merely tasking the boys to go down to the docks and keep an eye out for vessels that might be importing castor beans. Now that we know what hastened Disraeli's death, we need to find the source and see if we can trace it back to someone with a motive. Wiggins accepted the assignment without fear or hesitation. No doubt he and his companions will be perfectly safe with the usual ruffians and mud larks down by the water. If the Indian is still around, he will be stalking *me*, not them."

"I don't like it," I repeated, but he ignored me, brightening at a fresh thought.

"Speaking of the Indian, I was right, I had read about his weapon before. I had never seen one, just a drawing, so it took some time before I could properly identify it. The device is called a *panja*, or more commonly a *bagh naka*. It is placed over one's knuckles with the blades attached to a crossbar. What's interesting is that it was first used by assassins, but was also used in a form of wrestling they call *naki ka kusti*."

"What on earth does that translate to?"

"Claw wrestling," Holmes said. "As recently as two decades ago, it remained one of the most popular forms of entertainment on the subcontinent. The sharp blades are designed to tear through skin and rend muscle and sinew."

"Holmes, you were lucky. You could have easily been killed. This most certainly should prove to you that Wiggins and the others should *not* be involved in this matter."

"As you say, guv'nor," said he, resuming his role. He rose, a dirty rag in one hand. Then he caught my attention and with a flick of his eyes, directed me to look towards a corner of the tavern. In the shadows, lit by a flickering candle on the table, the hulking man in old, worn clothing sat, hunched over a glass of beer. He had on a bowler hat, dented on one side, and appeared totally out of place. How he had entered and been served without my notice was concerning.

I nodded just once to confirm that I had spotted this man and tried to silently communicate my confusion. Who was this man and was he truly sent by Hampton? Holmes ignored the signals and hurried off to the kitchen. As a result, I was left to self-consciously complete my meal, certain the man was watching me. I wanted to look in his direction but dared not for fear of tipping my hand. Unlike Holmes, who blended in perfectly with the tavern staff, this man was entirely out of place and most conspicuous if one knew where to look.

Maybe he had some sixth sense, for the man suddenly rose, placed some coins on his table and began to leave the tavern. He studiously avoided coming anywhere near me, but the course he took was awkward and actually attracted my attention rather than deflecting it; but again I was looking for it. The other patrons took no notice of him, presumably because of his slovenly appearance, but I took note of his attire to be sure that if I saw him on the street I would know him again. I had little doubt he would be waiting outside in order to follow me or Holmes, depending on which of us was his quarry.

I stood, leaving payment for my meal on the table. I did not leave a tip for Holmes; we needed the extra coin to pay Mrs.

Hudson and it was better served in my pocket than his. As I passed him en route to the door, he whispered, "I will be leaving shortly. Let him follow you, but lead him nowhere. I shall follow and observe."

Stepping into the cooling early evening air, I took a few paces to my right to orientate myself and to scan for the vagabond spy. Sure enough, he was peering through the window of a tobacconist, able to use the reflection in the dirty glass to spot people leaving the Horse and Hounds. I needed to busy myself before Holmes emerged so I stopped to admire the goods of a confectioner, their pastel colours and rich chocolates proving rather tempting, but the pie sat heavily in my stomach, putting me off any added indulgence. Finally the tavern door opened and Holmes, still in disguise, emerged. The moment I saw him, I turned to my left and began walking.

Had I not known I was being followed, not just by the unknown man, but by my companion, I do not think my instincts would have informed me—they were both adequate if not adept at the art of surveillance. I had to think quickly and go nowhere near Baker Street, but also appear as if I had a destination in mind. I turned onto New Oxford Street, walking in the shadows of The Bowery before turning onto Bloomsbury Way, nearing the Gardens. The streets were crowded given both the hour and the people leaving the recently closed British Museum just a few streets north. I then made a hasty left onto Bury Place, a less crowded street, giving my pursuer a clearer line of sight, and therefore, I hoped, giving Holmes a chance to see just how skilled he was when it came to concealing himself. No doubt my partner would see this as some grand sport while to me it was a nuisance. I would have given anything to be at home in Baker Street with a good book.

I could not look over my shoulder to see whether my pursuer was still on my tail without giving myself away, so I adopted one of Holmes's strategies. I began listening for distinct footfalls so I would recognise any that followed me on my next turn. I went left onto Gilbert Place, heading back towards the closed museum. I slowed my gait and listened, picking up several patterns of sound, but I needed to winnow down the options further so I followed the road's curve and turned onto Great Russell Street directly before the museum. A few familiar patterns were now more easily heard, so I continued on my way, figuring the challenge was to keep moving long enough for Holmes to get his fill and then disappear so I could go home. I turned left onto Montague Street, beginning to work my way back to Baker Street and hoping to lose my devoted follower in the crowds of Russell Square.

I was fortunate to accomplish that very thing by ducking behind some overgrown bushes and watched with delight as the legs of my pursuer went by me in one direction and then another. I had to stifle back a laugh when I then saw Holmes's legs pass me by. He could now track the man to his heart's content. My work was done.

It was two hours later when a well-satisfied Holmes finally returned to Baker Street. He wearily took his seat and told me what I had missed.

"You did a splendid job of leading him on a merry dance, Watson. I had ample time to study him and deduce who his employer might be."

"I gather this new development is related to the Wynter case and not the Disraeli matter?" I ventured.

"Quite right. But first, allow me to share my deductions. While your shadow was adequately skilled, he was not particularly gifted. His clothing was unsuitable; too poor to blend into his surroundings. Additionally, he did a bad job of choosing his shoes, which as I am sure you noticed, were highly polished boots, the very type worn by sailors in Her Majesty's Navy. Your suspicion Hampton sent him to watch you was an accurate one. The Admiralty have been watching us every step of the way. He was similarly inexperienced in the act of surveillance, altering his pacing erratically rather than hanging back, from which one can infer that he was unaccustomed to this sort of business. Such frequent changes of speed actually called attention to his activities. Finally, when you gave him the slip, he stopped and turned in a complete circle, signalling to anyone who wished to notice that he was seeking you out."

"Did you follow him?"

"I did, for long enough to confirm that whoever sent him on this errand did so after our visit to the Admiralty."

"That's a given by now, Holmes, surely? My question remains, what might his intentions be? Merely to follow me or to cause me some harm? And if it is the latter, then we have two shadows, which doubles the risk of injury to Wiggins and his lot. I must again object to involving children in this matter."

"And I state again that Wiggins and his street Arabs are fine and may prove more useful to your safety than you imagine. They know these streets better than you and certainly better than anyone Hampton could send.

"Watson, we have ruffled some important feathers. It is still a leap of logic to say we know beyond all reasonable doubt that the former prime minister was killed, but it is looking like a very real possibility. We know one trail leads to India. We know another leads to Africa, but not if the two combine. We know there are people clearly troubled at our investigation of both threads. What comes next may help us solidify exactly who they may be and why they have gone to such lengths."

Eight

The East India Company

We were just sitting down to breakfast the next morning when there was a pounding of feet coming up the stairs. Wiggins came bursting through the door without waiting for an invitation. He was dressed as he had been the last time I saw him, and every bit as filthy. The boy was breathless from his headlong flight. He wiped a hand from his brow to the back of his head, sweeping his matted forelock over his scalp as he struggled to catch his breath. Urgency was writ bright across the boy's ruddy features. Holmes merely gestured for him to take a seat at our table. The youth settled himself, chest still rising and falling rapidly as he struggled to bring his breathing under control. The lad grabbed for a crumpet, but Holmes raised a finger, stopping him dead in the act of pilfering from my plate.

"First your report," Holmes instructed, "then you may eat to your heart's content."

"Right you are," Wiggins said, making no effort to mask his desire for my breakfast. "Me an' the boys spent the early morning down at the docks like you asked, lookin' for anything out of the ordinary, chattin' up the dockers. I wanted to get me 'ands on the customs dockets, but you know how it is, they just won't show those to anyone." He noticed my expression, which was one of disbelief. "I can read, Doctor, leastways nuff for this business. Anyway, I don't exactly look like no official." The boy looked down at his filthy rags. It was impossible to argue that point with him.

"Did you offer bribes?" Holmes questioned. "You recall our agreement includes expenses and that would have most certainly qualified."

I gave Holmes an exaggeratedly scandalised look to express my displeasure at the lessons being taught this boy, but my companion ignored me entirely. I rather think he enjoyed playing with my sensibilities at times.

"Well, I would have tried that approach had I the funds," Wiggins said, all but turning his scruffy pockets out.

"And just what did you do with the gold sovereign I gave you?"

"A boy's got to eat, sir." And with that Wiggins snatched the crumpet from my plate and took a huge bite from it. He chewed noisily, gulping it down.

"Your report," Holmes instructed once more, his tone growing severe. The lad did not need telling a third time.

"Those beans you asked about didn't arrive in London. Leastways, if they did, it weren't in the last year."

I found that report disturbing because castor beans, like any organic material, have a finite lifespan. Those beans would not have kept more than a few weeks. Holmes, though, seemed unmoved by the news. No doubt his mind was already on other things, like where else and by what other means they might have entered the country. This time he allowed Wiggins to wolf down the rest of my crumpet.

"As I assume you know, Wiggins, much of the trade from India was directed by the East India Company."

"I've heard of them," he said, morsels of crumpet falling from his mouth. He scooped them up with a dirt-encrusted finger and licked them down. "Dunno more than that."

"The East India Company dates back to Queen Elizabeth. It was primarily responsible for establishing trade routes between England and the Far East. Although the title suggests it was limited to the Indian subcontinent, in point of fact the company's reach extended as far as China." Clearly Holmes was intent on giving the street Arab a history lecture. "Tea, foodstuffs, fabrics, jewellery and more was imported across the Empire until the Crown saw fit to terminate their charter, putting them out of business in '74."

"Where do you learn so much?" the boy asked, unable to hide his surprise.

"I read, young Wiggins. All the knowledge in the world is there to be found if you have a mind to look for it. I suggest you begin doing the same for yourself if you hope to rise above the rank of street Arab."

While I appreciated his efforts to encourage the boy, I suspected the words were falling on deaf ears. Wiggins's world was concerned with daily survival on the streets as opposed to mastering complex history texts and the lessons of life therein. Perhaps Holmes had reached the same conclusion, as he swiftly returned to the matter in hand.

"You have been invaluable in ruling out a London point of entry for the castor beans. I will now dedicate the day to researching other locations. After all, castor oil continues to be sold so the product must be entering the country on a regular basis."

Wiggins, now done with my crumpet and hungrily eyeing two

rashers of bacon I intended to consume myself, looked about the sitting room and waved his hands in the air. "Is that why you have all these maps out?"

"Indeed," Holmes confirmed.

I felt I needed to remind my companion of our true purpose, for what little good it might do. "Holmes, pray tell, how does the exact route the castor beans came from India have any bearing on poor Wynter's disappearance? Or have we cast aside our true investigation to chase grand conspiracies? I will admit it feels to me that every fresh question we ask and lead we follow takes us further and further from investigating his fate, and Mrs. Wynter is awaiting our report. I trust you are aware we have nothing of substance to share with her. Our focus has moved from Africa to India, and I cannot believe for a moment that is where the bodies are buried, metaphorical or otherwise."

"Your protests make a certain sense, Watson, I will concede that, but if we follow the threads of the story, which like a tapestry appear unremarkable until they are combined to create a vivid image, we will find satisfaction, I am sure of it. Wynter's disappearance was the beginning of the path and by looking under every stone, we will find the clues to refine the direction and determine what became of the man, because something most assuredly has happened to him, and it is a something worthy of covering up and killing for, no less. Our investigations have stirred up a veritable beehive and I was nearly stung once. That attack alone confirms we are moving in the right direction. It is my intention to draw out the stinger without getting stung again."

I confess I must have looked horrified at the notion because Holmes smiled that knowing smile of his. "Now, don't look so alarmed. I have no intention of letting the tiger claw have its fill of me."

"A real tiger? Here? In London?" Wiggins asked, jaw dropping at the prospect of what to him must have seemed like a mythical beast doing for the detective.

"Not at all," I corrected and noted that during Holmes's speech, the boy had made off with my bacon, even though I hadn't seen his hands move. That was an interesting skill.

"My attacker that night you came to my aid used a weapon shaped to resemble the outstretched paw of a tiger. Your arrival was most fortuitous," Holmes said. He rose and rummaged through a stack of books on the other side of the sitting room, his long finger tracing a few spines before he found the desired volume, and returned to show a drawing of the wretched device. Wiggins's eyes grew wide, both out of fear and I daresay some envy.

"You know, Watson, the mention of bees reminds me that I have had them on my mind of late. When this case is done, I want to look into them at length. Would you mind?"

Whether I minded or not made no difference to Holmes, of course, he was merely informing me what form his next obsession would take. Once he made up his mind, he was set on a course of action. No doubt there would be a hive in the garden of 221B before the month was out.

"As we have noted, whilst castor beans are indigenous to three regions, East Africa, the Mediterranean Basin and India, a confluence of seeming coincidences, including the fact that my attacker also originates from the Indian subcontinent would have me willing to wager that the now defunct East India Company played some part in this."

This deduction puzzled me, given that the company had paid out the final dividend on its stock seven years ago and dissolved. I could not see how it could possibly have any bearing on our case. I said as much. "Consider this, Watson: amongst other duties, Benjamin Disraeli was a member of a select committee that in 1852 was tasked with considering how best to rule the subcontinent, and Disraeli himself proposed eliminating the governing role of the East India Company." He rose from his seat. "While you muse on that, I must go out for a time, but I will return later," he promised.

Without another word, Holmes tossed a shilling to Wiggins for the previous day's work, insisted he be more circumspect with his spending this time, and hastened to his bedroom. Minutes later, clad in a fresh disguise, he departed.

Left with no instructions, it fell to me to tend the fire and update my account of this most curious case. In other words, I was left to wait and wonder.

Nine

A Visit to the Club

"I have your tea, sir," a voice said in the darkness, both gentle, soothing, and not a little hypnotic, or so it seemed to my waking mind.

My eyelids fluttered and the aroma of fresh and strongly brewed tea greeted me. Leaning over me was a footman in the finest livery. The man had a slight hook to his nose and his hair was slicked back, revealing hair blacker than black and a widow's peak. He was tall and thin, maybe forty from his complexion. But as I gained full wakefulness, I realised I was sitting in my own chair in my own sitting room, having fallen asleep in Baker Street, not some gentlemen's club.

My bewilderment rapidly vanished and I exclaimed, "Holmes!" earning a chuckle as he poured out two cups of tea with a polished manner that he rarely exhibited in his true persona. Once the teapot was placed on a tray, he stepped out of shoes designed to raise his height by an inch. He then relaxed his tie and unbuttoned his waistcoat before settling down in his chair.

"How did I do, Watson?" My companion appeared to be in high spirits, and I grew eager to hear the full account of his most recent exploits, but saw he awaited a genuine reply.

"I confess you are a far better footman than barman," I offered, stirring my tea.

Sipping from his own cup, the steam corkscrewing before his face and obscuring his distinctly Roman nose, he laughed and sat back. "Quite so."

"Where did you rush off to?"

"I had a theory I wanted to test immediately. I left the building through a rear window, accessing the street from an oblique angle. Sure enough, a man who could only have been your shadow's thinner brother was waiting several doors down. He tried to hide behind a newspaper, but being two days old, it was an obvious feint. Instead, I took up a spot in an alley and it was my turn to observe him.

"Around half past eleven, he was relieved by a different fellow. Neither made any real attempt at being discreet, clearly bored with the task. As the first left, I took up the trail and followed him."

I sipped the tea and nodded, certain where this trail would lead. "The Admiralty?"

"Quite so. Now we know we have Her Majesty's Navy keeping watch. Thankfully, we are more adept at our work on land than they are."

"But why would Hampton keep us under watch? We've gone nowhere near the Admiralty or inquired anything further about Wynter."

"Ah, Watson, Hampton is a man following orders. My question now becomes: under whose command does he serve? I suspect this answer will not be found in any official charter."

"You have your suspicions, of course," said I.

"A few, but nothing with proof so they are useless to mention," he said, finally taking a seat by me, all pretence of service coming to an end.

"Why on earth are you dressed as a footman?" I asked.

"When one trail grows cold, we pick up the next likely thread. What did we learn this morning?"

"The beans did not arrive via London," I said.

"True, but what else did we learn?"

I gave that some thought, reviewing the lessons imparted to young Wiggins. "The East India Trading Company."

"Quite so," he said.

"But if they are no longer in the business, where did you take off to in that outfit?"

"That first costume was merely to leave without any obvious fellow following along. I wore it as I went to the library. There I did some rather tedious research into the East India Company's final years, compiling a listing of its final corporate officers. I then spent some time cross-referencing the names with current corporate boards, seeing if someone may have wound up in a position of still importing from India."

"Were you successful?"

Holmes shook his head and his shoulders sagged a bit in his chair.

"It all felt like such wasted time, but then I realised that the company had investors, shareholders and the like. I wondered what became of these men once they were cashiered after the East India Stock Dividend Redemption Act was passed in 1873. By that point, the last vestiges of the once grand company were merely dealing with tea. Their other commodities, including castor beans, were taken over by other companies.

"Further research led me to a series of ledgers that appear to have been among the last the company maintained before its ultimate dissolution. I admit there were arcane symbols or notations next to some of the transactions. I have copied them into my notebook for further research. There was also a list of their shareholders present, allowing me to copy their names down for research. What most had in common, though, was that these men all were members of what is now the East India Club."

"The East India Club," I repeated.

"The East India Club, of course," said he, as if I should have divined his comings and goings through mindreading or some such arcane practice.

"So, you just happened to have a footman's outfit at your disposal and managed to make your way into the club?"

"I made a visit to a tailor friend who owed me a favour," Holmes explained.

"Why did you think that infiltrating the EIC would help us find out where and how the castor beans came into the country?"

"Watson, just because the East India Company is defunct, does not mean that the members of its club have no information to offer. The same business is done, albeit under a different name. It was the obvious place to investigate the trade in Indian commodities."

Although I had never had the pleasure of dining there, the East India Club was known by all London gentlemen, the last surviving vestige of the defunct trading concern. It had opened its doors mid-century and rapidly became a fixture of the city. While it had initially been a London hub solely for members of the East India Company, after the latter's dissolution the club survived by relaxing its membership requirements. More than a few peers of the realm, including Prince Albert himself, routinely visited 16 St. James's Square for meals and deal making, making it a popular meeting place for commerce and political interest where palms could be greased and wheels set in motion. The club had a library, a gymnasium, as well as a variety of meeting rooms, each with a specific ambiance from smoking to gaming. No doubt Holmes knew all this so I kept my own counsel and allowed him to continue his narrative uninterrupted.

"Wiggins having discovered nothing at the docks, and lacking time to research every coming and going of every ship at every port in England, I thought it best to insinuate myself where those who *own* those ships discuss their business affairs. As you know, servants are invariably invisible to people of a certain social strata, making the guise of a footman the perfect camouflage. As chance would have it, I managed to serve William Francis Frobisher, one of the last vested shareholders of the East India Company, and a retired army general. The general was taking luncheon with Edward Haldaine, a shipping magnate, and Patrick Chatterton-Smythe, a Member of Parliament."

"Those names mean nothing to me," I admitted.

"I did not know them myself before today," Holmes said. "But now I am convinced I need to study them most vigorously."

"Good god, you mean to say in a single casual visit you have managed to ascertain vital information on the case?"

He chuckled again, so good was his mood.

"The other staff treated me with suspicion, no doubt not recognising me, but as luck would have it one of their number, a man named Pennyworth, was absent so they were short a footman and assumed I had been hired by the management. I said nothing to the contrary, knowing well when fortune was smiling upon me, and my silence allowed them to fill in the blanks to their own satisfaction.

"After some inquiries as to the identities of those members present, Frobisher was pointed out to me by one of the other footmen and I decided to focus my efforts on him, endeavouring to be at his side for the rest of the day. He sat by himself at first, reading the newspapers and making conversation with other members of the club, though nothing of note was said. No doubt due to his time in the army, that long-standing family wealth and his position with the EIC, he knew most of the other members by sight and recalled most of their names, which is a skill of note as it suggests a certain recollection and memory for faces. When he was alone, I made efforts to attend to his every whim, and was therefore in a position to exchange polite conversation, earning a measure of trust.

"The other two men I mentioned—the magnate Haldaine and Patrick Chatterton-Smythe the MP—arrived together late in the day. Through careful observation I was able to assess what manner of men they were.

"Chatterton-Smythe is haughty and overly confident of his skills, much to the perturbation of the other two," Holmes noted. I suspected there was more to this, but knew he would come to it in good time. "He comes from Leeds and is serving a second term, largely on a platform of increased international trade and further consolidation of the Crown's authority. The softening of his accent, plus some curious inflections suggests he has spent a considerable time abroad and is quite impressionable.

"Haldaine is a self-made man, rich beyond the comprehension of mere mortals, going from one fishing vessel to a fleet of international traders in two decades. Although I doubt he's done a hard day's work in years, his hands are still rough and he has kept his vigour, which suggested to me that he maintains his physique.

His clothing was functional but not expensive, from which I inferred that he cares little what others think of him. His money has given him the freedom not to care about the opinions of others and he is proud of that to a fault."

"That's all very interesting, Holmes," I said, "but what do any of the three men have to do with our investigation?"

"For a beginning, we have Frobisher with ties to India and Haldaine who ships goods around the world. A little research, I think, should turn up that among the goods he ferries here and there are castor beans."

"Accessing a ready supply of the beans, then, would provide a means for the overdose," said I.

"Precisely. As their meeting was concluding, an argument of sorts broke out. You know the kind: words exchanged in harsh whispered tones. There was an undercurrent to it, suggesting, I think, cracks in their unlikely alliance. I could not make out all the words, just the tenor of the discussion. One word did catch my attention, however."

"A word?"

"Yes, Watson. A single word: 'mystic'."

"And mystics come from India," I concluded, following his tenuous line of reasoning.

"Exactly!" he said in a triumphant tone and held his teacup under his nose, savouring the aroma as if it were his reward. "And there is more."

I waited expectantly, knowing he was enjoying making me tease the facts out of him.

"Fortunately I was summoned to clear their plates—which allowed me to clear away scraps of papers including handwriting samples from two of the three men—just as Haldaine said something even more interesting. Something about being glad they would be rid of 'them' when his tour ended in Newcastle."

"Rid of whom?" I asked.

"The mystic and his accomplice, I believe," said Holmes. "As the word 'tour' suggests he is some sort of performer and he is currently or soon to be treading the boards in Newcastle. If my surmise is correct he is our link between the castor beans, Disraeli's death, and the attempt on my life."

"Holmes, there are many Indians living and working in England, many of whom no doubt tour with performing troupes. Are you not making a series of connections that will only fall apart when a single one of your suppositions proves to be wrong?"

"Perhaps, but there is one other clue that convinces me that those three men were discussing the same Indian who nearly took my life, and that he is the link that ties our various threads together to form the solution we seek, and that is the final stage of his tour."

"How so?"

"Do you not see the significance of Newcastle?"

I sat stumped, unable to summon a useful detail about the city. Given its full title, Newcastle upon Tyne was a long established settlement to the north of the country first settled by the Romans. I seemed to recall that the city had a remarkable library and a history of industrial innovation, notably the work of George and Robert Stephenson, the fathers of the railway.

My silence was taken as permission to conclude his report and Holmes said, "Watson, according to what I overheard at the club, Newcastle is where the formal treaty to end the Boer conflict is currently being drafted."

Ten

A Trip to Newcastle upon Tyne

I admit that I must have gaped at Holmes as he made that revelation.

While I knew a treaty was in the process of being written, I had read as much in the papers, the location had not been publicly announced. Now that I knew it was to be in Newcastle, I too began to see how everything was starting to fit together. Still, there were some gaps, some connections that still confused me, and I said so to Holmes, trusting that he was not magicking these lines of investigation from thin air.

"I contend that these three men have a vested interest in the outcome of the treaty; whether that is it being signed or not, I cannot yet divine," Holmes began. "Presumably they have business dealings in South Africa which will suffer as a result. They have treated with some Indian assassin—likely a contact made by Frobisher, given his time in India—the man they call the 'mystic', to do their dirty work, including carrying out the attack on my person."

"But why would they send this man after you?"

"That, my dear friend, is where I believe the Wynter connection comes into play. I believe that it was our visit to the Admiralty, inquiring into South African affairs, that led to these men ordering the 'mystic' to attack me. We were public in our questioning, and no doubt a report was made, probably to Chatterton-Smythe. As an MP he is the most likely of the three to have contacts at the Admiralty. I was to be dissuaded from investigating Wynter's disappearance, or perhaps they intended my death. Wiggins's intervention means we do not know either way."

"Now wait just a minute, Holmes," interjected I. "We were both certain that Hampton had sent men after us. Are you now suggesting the Admiralty hired an Indian assassin as well? That stretches belief too far."

"Indeed it does," he said rather calmly. "Hampton was under orders from someone–perhaps Chatterton-Smythe–to keep us away from Wynter's trail. That is as close as we have to a fact in this sordid affair. Someone *else* also wants us away from Wynter's case and it is my belief that man is Edward Haldaine, who could easily have transported an Indian here and unleashed him."

"And you are suggesting Haldaine brought in a mystic to do away with you?"

"The title 'mystic' would suggest he is accomplished at several things, not merely parlour tricks," he observed. "For instance a knowledge of chemistry, including how to extract the toxins from castor beans. Could this man possibly have been their agent in Disraeli's death? Retribution for his role in the dissolution of the East India Company?"

"But that was years ago, surely?"

Holmes cocked an eyebrow. "If these three are involved in some criminal activity in South Africa, it has to be something large enough to force them to see off Disraeli before he did something that could have a negative impact on their affairs."

"Not retribution?"

"I think not. They have had several years to seek revenge for his push to shut down the company's initiatives in India and the subcontinent, so their motivations must be something entirely different. But we do not know what, or for that matter the roles Wynter and the Boer conflict play in their schemes."

This was all getting to be too much. The search for Wynter's whereabouts had taken us to locations that were at the height of the government. We had been researching conspiracies, murder, and something to do with India and now South Africa. Two of the men Holmes just observed, may or may not have been involved in having us followed. The extraordinary circumstances to date had been staggering in their implications. I could not believe these to be true.

"But, Holmes, do we have any substantive evidence to take to any authority who can either produce Wynter or arrest the mystic?"

"Not as yet, Watson. We do not yet have all the facts and need to go about gathering them. Drink up so we may be on our way. The trail has grown more obvious, but if we delay we risk it going cold. I feel the need to act."

Holmes's logic was less clear to me, but his argument was compelling if far-fetched. I was ready to follow where he led, wherever that might be. The enormity of the matter was not lost on me, or I confess, the danger. However, this affair, whatever its exact nature, might threaten the Empire itself.

"What is our next move?" I asked.

"We need to learn where the treaty is being drafted in Newcastle. We also need to determine possible venues in that city where our

Indian mystic may be performing, and divine how much longer he will be in the country. Once he leaves our shores, apprehending him becomes problematic to say the least. That is an eventuality we can ill afford."

"I suppose we are off to the library, then," I ventured. This was becoming a bit of a habit and I hoped my friend there would not feel put upon.

He nodded in agreement, then looked down at his footman's attire. "But first, I must change."

We managed to get to the London Library just before it closed for the day and I persuaded Lomax to allow us to stay after hours. Much as I might have found the lengthy history of Newcastle interesting reading in other circumstances, I needed to focus on its most immediate condition. Much of what I read confirmed what I already knew: references to its past as a mining town and a major site of industrial manufacture.

In reading on more recent history I came across an item that made me shudder as pieces continued to fall into place, creating a picture I liked not in the least. "Holmes," I said in a voice appropriate for a library despite us being the sole patrons, "the ports do take in trade from India and Newcastle is in fact the entry port for shipments of castor beans. In fact, their volume seems to grow by the year."

He paused his own reading to absorb the information, his keen mind matching it with what we had learned so far. A curt nod of his head meant he accepted the fact, added it to his limited repository of information and resumed his research.

The volumes he was perusing were not related to the recent

periodicals but were older works, dark leather-bound and reeking of age. "What are you studying?" I asked.

"Those symbols I copied down. I am trying to ascertain what they mean, where they came from. The notations were always next to property not financial transactions. But I cannot fathom what they mean."

"Might we need to consult a real estate expert?"

"I would hope not because I believe we are pressed for time and finding someone versed in arcane symbology will be difficult to come by. However, I see where knowing of such a fellow might actually come in handy in the future."

I merely grunted in assent and refocused my attention on the newspapers. Holmes made his own sound of frustration and with a loud thump, turned aside from the ancient tomes to assist me in our contemporary research.

Holmes sat beside me, working his way through back issues of various newspapers, searching for articles related to the peace treaty with the Boers. At one point, he thrust a newspaper just below my nose and stabbed a finger at an article. "Watson, the treaty is scheduled to be signed in a week, on 3rd August!" A date not too far away, I noted. Closer, indeed, than I would have liked.

"You think something will happen to stop the signing?"

"A mystic assassin who just happens to currently be in Newcastle as the British preparations for treaty are being finalised? I should say that is more than mere coincidence, wouldn't you?"

"You say that, but we still have no evidence of any connection between the men at the club and the treaty," I protested. "You are looking for coincidences that conform to your bias, rather than letting the facts form the basis for your deductions. This is most unlike you, my friend. You are usually far more rigorous, but I fear you are allowing the grand conspiracy to run away with you. We need incontrovertible proof." Holmes took this with good grace.

"Quite right. We need more evidence, and we cannot find it in London. We must make haste to Newcastle first thing in the morning."

"Holmes," I said, not entirely sure how to broach the subject, "not to be indelicate, old man, but do you have the funds for the fare?"

Holmes took out his wallet and did a fast count. "I should have just enough, I believe. My time at the Horse and Hounds was certainly providential. But you are correct, my parsimonious friend, we should be careful with our spending."

"Even if we solve this case, we will be fortunate if Mrs. Wynter pays her bill promptly. Our rent is due on 1st August," I added. Holmes was silent, leaving me to presume we were tapping the last of our finances. He rose from his chair and headed for the door.

"Where are you going now?"

Holmes glanced back over his shoulder. "To find the Baker Street Irregulars."

I left the London Library shortly after, returning to Baker Street. As was my wont, I was up a good part of the night, reading and contemplating the case. Holmes himself returned well after dark, but we were both up as the sun rose. Upon exiting 221B, I was not at all surprised to see Wiggins's grubby face and several of his gang loitering on the street corner.

"Mornin', guv'nor," said he to Holmes, tipping his battered cap. The other boys, in similar states of grime, silently saluted. "Is it time?"

Holmes nodded. "I should think so." He turned to me. "Let us find a cab."

He stuck out his arm and a passing hansom began to slow for us. The boys scattered as if on some silent cue.

"What are they up to?" I inquired.

"General mayhem," Holmes said with a slight smile. "I also had one of the Arabs play postman, delivering a letter of inquiry regarding those symbols. In reviewing the handwriting samples I obtained at the East India Club, one included a random sketch with some numbers. It looked remarkably like one of those symbols so its identity has risen in importance.

"I admit I cannot fathom of the numbers. 33, 27, 50, 20, 59, 10. It may be a cypher, it may be some bank account. This leaves me at a loss."

My eyebrows raised in surprise at such an extraordinary finding but such is the way with Holmes and his investigations, of that I have learned more than once. I glanced out the cab once more and saw the final three urchins bolt. As they did so, I spotted our old friend, the man who had followed me from the Horse and Hounds. His idea of a change in disguise was a fresh coat; otherwise he looked just as he had when I'd led him a merry dance. As Holmes and I climbed into the cab, three of the boys gathered around him and proceeded to make a racket. I presumed they were making certain there was no possibility of him overhearing our instructions to the driver. I looked out of the window and smiled with delight. The hapless man could only watch as our cab rolled out of sight.

We arrived at King's Cross Station at eight, but as it turned out, the next train to Newcastle would not leave until past ten so we had time to spare. We secured our tickets and then passed much of the two hours before departure with the morning newspapers and a breakfast bought in the small station café. Holmes took it upon himself to study the comings and goings of our fellow passengers. When he finally settled into a seat opposite me, I presumed the boys had done their job well and that there was no sign of our pursuer, but I was still concerned as to whether the man had spotted our bags. They offered him a clue that we were about to travel. Of course, there were several stations the cab could have taken us to, on all sides of the city. Would he possibly know that we had discovered the Newcastle link? It seemed unlikely. Holmes had not been unmasked while eavesdropping on Frobisher, Haldaine and Chatterton-Smythe.

That Hampton would continue to have men following us even as our investigations took us further and further from the Admiralty was cause for concern.

"Holmes," I said, interrupting whatever private musing he was undertaking. "What on earth could Wynter have gotten himself mixed up in if Hampton still has people following us?"

"Do not forget that apart from the naval men enjoying some extracurricular activity, we also have the Indian assassin to contend with. Our movements are of interest to a good many people it would seem. Something is afoot, that is for sure, but beyond that, Watson, I would not hazard to conjecture without more information. After all, that is the purpose of this trip."

We took the East Coast Main Line, a conglomeration of smaller lines that had merged through the years, and resulted in the sleek, speedy Flying Scotsman. Its ultimate destination, some nine hours later, was to be Edinburgh, but first we would have to endure stops in Peterborough, Grantham, and Doncaster before a half-hour stop for lunch in York.

Holmes and I settled into our compartment, with me taking a window seat while he sat close to the door in order to study the other passengers as they moved up and down the corridor outside. On the platform, the guard blew his whistle and the engine responded with a lurch as the brake was released, then we were underway. Steam streamed past my window as we gathered our head and powered away from the platform. As we began the journey, Holmes had withdrawn a notebook and was working out various combinations, trying to find a meaning in the jumble of numbers he had obtained from the gentlemen at the East India Club. After a quarter hour, he appeared to have given up.

We were perhaps an hour outside of London when Holmes—who had satisfied himself that none of our fellow passengers posed a threat and had been reading my copy of *The Times*—stiffened and asked for the other newspapers. Something had obviously caught his eye.

I had also picked up the latest editions of the *Standard* and *Daily News* and offered them to Holmes. He paged through them, scanning the dense columns of text carefully and without saying a word. His focus alarmed me, but I held my tongue, waiting for his conclusion.

"Watson, did you see this thimble of a report from South Africa?" He thrust a finger at a story on page fourteen of *The Times*, one I had missed when I thumbed through the papers at King's Cross. It was a report of the death of Charles Lewis, a solicitor, who had passed away suddenly after a short, mysterious illness. While details of the single column inch report were scant, the piece did contain a single gem that sparked my interest: he would now be unable to complete the work he had begun on "a treaty of great significance". I understood Holmes's alarm immediately. The news of Lewis's death only made it as far as the British papers because of his relative status in the Boer community, I was sure.

"It is possible that this man Lewis did not die from natural causes," Holmes said, voicing my own thoughts. "The coincidence of this undiagnosed illness so close to the signing of the treaty has me convinced there was foul play involved."

"Holmes, surely there can be no connection between Lewis and our case," I said.

"No," he asked in a tone that I had come to recognise as being one of disapproval. "Wynter was in South Africa and has disappeared. We already have one suspicious case of death with the former PM, and now this lawyer working on the very treaty that might be the catalyst to everything we're investigating. This is far more than coincidence."

I reread the story then read a similar account in the *Standard,* although the *Daily News* carried no mention of the death. Based on the few details presented in the reports, both of a similar paucity, a proper diagnosis was impossible; Lewis had suffered from gastrointestinal symptoms and slipped into a coma in the course of only three days. But Holmes had been teaching me to think more deductively over the previous few months.

"The man's rapid decline strikes me as markedly similar to that of Disraeli," I said, slowly conceding the point. I couldn't help but think that we were missing some detail, some finer point that would change our perceptions of everything, but it was thus far elusive.

"I concur, Watson," Holmes said. "And if as I believe, Lewis was poisoned with the same castor extract as the prime minister, we can further conclude our original hypothesis was indeed correct and we are on the right track. What alarms me is that we may have a problem on two continents linked by poison from the castor bean, but if they are truly connected as seems to be the case, it serves to shed light on our main investigation."

"Wynter," I said. However, the global implications of these deaths and what could possibly be gained by stalling the treaty struck me as something far beyond the remit of our adventures to date. Even prior to my meeting Holmes, he had never taken on a case of such a scale or sensitive a nature.

"Quite right. We do owe Mrs. Wynter an answer," he said. "But it cannot be denied that this has grown beyond a poor old woman's missing son. The Indian assassin is an agent for powerful men who I believe are trying to disrupt a peace that has been hard won, and seek to rule the world with their greed. They must be exposed and brought to justice. Along the way, I do hope we can find answers for Mrs. Wynter, but she can no longer be our primary concern. The game has changed. This is bigger than one missing sailor, Watson. And that only serves to make me all the more determined."

Holmes sounded resolutely defiant, and I was glad to see the fire lit under him. However, his dismissive attitude towards the fate of Norbert Wynter concerned me. His mother was our client, not to mention the answer to our financial straits.

Holmes snatched up *The Times* once more. "I had almost forgot. Did you also notice the item of significance?" he asked, taking me by surprise.

"I read both accounts and saw nothing else regarding the death of Charles Lewis," said I, shaking my head.

He turned to a back page and handed me the paper, a finger tapping a small notice. This announced that Nayar was concluding a year-long tour of England with a two-week appearance at the Theatre Royal in Newcastle before returning to his home on the subcontinent. It was headed LAST CHANCE TO SEE THE GREAT INDIAN FAKIR!

"Ships travel to and from India out of the port of Newcastle," Holmes said. "Not only do they import castor beans, but I daresay they now export murderers. And see here—" he pointed to a list of performance dates "–he was in Exeter at the end of March, then Oxford, and was performing in London at the Adelphi from the 10th to the 20th of April." Holmes looked exultant. "Disraeli's health truly failed on the 17th, while at his home on Curzon Street. And Nayar was only two miles away!"

"How did an Indian fakir gain access to his residence, to Disraeli?" I asked, thinking that such a man would be somewhat conspicuous.

Holmes snorted. "He didn't need to feed it to Disraeli on a spoon. I imagine a man of his talents would be well able to slip in at night, gain access to the kitchen, or perhaps Dr. Kidd's own medical bag. That man was feeding his patient all sorts of pills and potions. Easy enough to exchange one quackery for another."

"That sounds awfully tenuous to me, Holmes."

"The truth will make itself known in good time," he said.

I had nothing to disprove this, and my instincts told me that Holmes was correct in thinking this stage performer was the man who had attacked and nearly killed him, but his extrapolations were dizzying to my mind.

"Holmes, you are still healing from the beating he already gave you. Do be careful before you engage him again," I warned, knowing he would not heed my words if it came to a physical brawl.

"I will do my utmost to avoid further injury, rest assured. This will more likely be a match of words and wit, not fisticuffs. It is my intention should things go that far, though, to give him the sound thrashing he so richly deserves." I sighed at that.

There was some comfort that came with each new piece of information, each clue fitting in with the general picture Holmes had first created out of little more than wisps of fact, but I will admit it was cold. But now that the mysterious poisoner had a name, Nayar, we had new focus.

A sudden noise broke my reverie. It was the door at the end of the carriage, and I moved to the other end of our compartment and peered out into the corridor. A clergyman was approaching, wearing the vestments of his office, complete with the Canterbury cap and double-breasted cassock, not to mention a large, ornate wooden cross around his neck. He looked to be in his sixties and had grey hair clipped close to his broad head. His gait appeared unsteady, rolling with the lurch of the train, and he frequently clutched at the wall to steady himself.

Something about his movement seemed awry. Unnatural. No, not unnatural, I realised—practised. "Curious. Do you believe the good father to be inebriated so early in the day?" I asked Holmes.

Holmes watched him for a moment and shook his head. "I do not believe him to be a man of faith at all."

"A thief perhaps, working the train?" I ventured.

"Perhaps," said Holmes.

We watched in fascination as he ambled and stumbled and finally fell over one gentleman who was trying to pass, all apologies and blessings as he patted him down, confirming, I believed, my suspicion that I was watching a conman in action. When he came level with our compartment he nearly fell in. A bony hand reached out, clutching on to my shoulder for support. I revised my impression immediately as his warm breath was tainted with the tang of alcohol. He quickly straightened himself and waved his hand, forming a cross in the air just above my head, mayhap warning the evil spirits of whiskey, cognac and other temptations away.

Holmes coughed, attracting the priest's attention.

"What is the trouble, my son," the man said, in a practised voice pitched at the level of confidant and confessor. He paused, meeting

Holmes's eyes for the first time, and then the most remarkable thing happened. His entire character changed as his shoulders slumped and eyes wrinkled. He appeared more disappointed than anything and I was most confused.

"Damn it all, Holmes," the man said, much to my astonishment. "You take the fun out of everything."

"Watson, I would like to introduce you to Charles Bennett, imitation priest and full-time pickpocket. Please return the wallet to my companion, Dr. Watson, there's a good chap."

Bennett sat on the seat beside me and reached into his coat pocket, withdrawing my wallet. Somehow, even with my suspicions, I had completely missed the lift. He seemed a trifle reluctant to hand it over.

"He's not a priest," I said, stating the obvious as was often my wont.

"Indeed not. Bennett is as much an Anglican as I am a cricketer," Holmes said before turning his attention to the man. "You are wearing the detachable collar the Anglican clergy abandoned some time ago, Charles. But you maintain its use to make it easier for you to slip in and out of costume. Most clergy today no longer wear the complete vestments away from the pulpit and I am also given to understand the cap is going out of style, but it is a familiar picture of piety so helps complete the illusion. The double-breasted cassock is useful as it allows you to secrete your stolen goods. Now, if you would be so kind?"

"Didn't mean to bother a friend of Mr. Holmes," Bennett said, then turned his attention back to my companion. "Whatever are you going north for? It's godforsaken country up there, man. No one gets out of there alive." This last he said with a grin.

"The doctor and I are headed to Newcastle on a case."

"Is that a fact? Well, Holmes, if you don't mind, I intend on continuing my occupation, but out of deference to your presence, I shall move on to the next car, if you are agreeable?" He rose to leave.

I expected Holmes to put an end to this nonsense immediately and summon the guard to have the man locked up on the spot, but he didn't. Instead he called out, "A moment, Bennett. You no doubt trade the wallets to someone back in London, yes? You hear things, so tell us, what news travels in your circles?"

Bennett stroked a well-manicured finger under his chin, deep in thought. Then he shook his head. "I am sorry to say I really have not heard anything that strikes me as out of the ordinary, Holmes."

"You don't happen to keep up with international affairs do you?"

The thief stared at my friend. I tried to judge his expression but could not read faces as well as Holmes. He covered his mouth, seemingly to hide a yawn. "Apologies, I do not. I have enough to occupy my attention on these fair shores." He stretched. "I'll be damned but I could use some fresh air."

With a look from Holmes, I reached to the window of the compartment to open it, but to my surprise, I could not make it budge. I rose and left the compartment, and tried the nearest window in the corridor. It too was stuck fast.

"What the devil," Bennett asked, once more staggering, but this time my practised eye showed he was not pretending.

I walked down the corridor and peered into the other compartments, Holmes at my heels. Several of their occupants were asleep, others yawning, and at least two others were attempting to pry open their windows in vain. Holmes turned to me, concern clouding his features. "I have read of this, Watson. Criminals will tape up the windows and the air vents, pumping gas into the carriage to knock their victims unconscious, then pillage their belongings." He tried the handle of the door that led to the next carriage. It would not budge. "See here, the door has been bound shut. Do you have a knife?"

"No. This is monstrous," I said, already beginning to feel sleepy, confirmation that Holmes was correct. He reached into my coat's outer pocket and withdrew my handkerchief and rapidly tied it around his face. I understood, despite my hazy condition, that he was attempting to filter out the gas and remain alert to thwart the thieves, although I was somewhat put out that he had used my only handkerchief.

We hurried back down the corridor and I peered into our compartment. Bennett was already asleep and would be of little use. Suddenly a figure appeared from a compartment at the other end of the carriage. A man, his head entirely covered with a complex gas mask. His nightmarish countenance was constructed from glass eyepieces, a rubber-coated hood with a short hose connected to a canister strapped to his chest.

At first, I feared it was one of the navy men, sent by Hampton to escalate matters from merely following us to ending us. His silhouette was wrong, however. He was shorter and slighter, not at all built for the rigours of the sea. I could only ascertain so much given the peculiar picture he made.

As bizarre as his appearance was, the knife in his right hand was downright deadly.

I struggled to remain alert, determined to bear witness to what was to come next. The nightmare man began stalking down the corridor towards us. All I could think was that despite our best efforts, we must have been seen and followed, allowing this assassin to gain access to the train complete with this diabolical scheme to eliminate one or both of us. That, or we were the victims of the most appalling luck and had stumbled into a train robbery.

I knew that Holmes had not travelled with a weapon but he would not simply allow the man to take his life. He darted towards him, but abruptly ducked into the carriage next to ours, which housed an elderly lady, now asleep. He returned with a large carpet bag under one arm, a skein of wool and a pair of knitting needles protruding from the opening. I could not imagine how this would help our defence. I pounded on our compartment window, willing it to shatter, but I felt the strength ebb from my arms. Beyond the glass the landscape became a hazy blur, my eyes no longer able to focus, the unseen gas stinging and drawing tears. I watched, helpless, as Holmes stood in the corridor, the carpet bag in hand, as the masked man closed in.

The man approached to within striking distance. Facing him, Holmes held up the carpet bag. As his attacker's arm swung in an arc, the sharp blade pointed at Holmes's heart, my companion hefted the bag in an upward counter, deflecting the blow. Holmes was lucky; his opponent's mask apparatus clearly impeded his vision and motion, and it made his gait stiff from its weight. Even so, he swung again, though this time Holmes opened up the bag and caught his attacker's arm between the handles. He slammed it shut, both immobilising the arm and preventing it from bending at the elbow.

Clasping the bag with one hand, it was Holmes's turn to strike and he thrust a knitting needle, not at the man, but at the hose that connected the mask to the canister. His aim was true and the wooden point punctured the hose, making a deep tear, but the thin needle also broke in two. Holmes tossed his end away, but the other remained in the hose, defeating its intended purpose as it effectively plugged the hole. The man's struggles though did not permit more damage as a leg kicked out, forcing Holmes to disengage. With the rasping sound of his breathing as it filtered through the mask's vent filling my ears, I watched as the nightmare man flexed the once-trapped arm. Holmes took advantage of that moment and braced himself against the walls of the compartment and the corridor. He hoisted himself up, swinging his long legs with great force, and kicked out at the attacker's mask and canister, stopping the man in his tracks. Holmes pressed his advantage and rushed the man. They both fell to the floor, bodies entangled in a frantic fight.

As they grappled, I gave up on pounding at the glass and instead, used what little of my strength remained to grab the large wooden cross hanging from around Bennett's neck. Tightening my grip so it would not slip away, I smashed it against the window and was rewarded with a loud cracking sound as the glass splintered. One more strike, although in honesty it was no more than a tap given my dwindling strength, shattered the window. Glass went flying as summer air rushed in.

I braced myself on the frame, inhaling deeply albeit slowly, and as the fresh air filled my lungs I could already feel myself growing more alert. No doubt the gas in the carriage was being pumped in from some hidden canister and would soon run out, defeated by the endless supply of air.

My mind clearer, I turned back to the battle in the corridor. Holmes was now atop the assassin, and as I watched, he ripped at the man's mask. A brown face was revealed confirming my earlier thought he was not from the Admiralty. Was this Nayar, the mystic we were hunting? Had he found us first?

The man snarled with rage, the sound mixing with the susurrus of rushing air, and he rose to a kneeling position. Holmes was no stranger to fisticuffs and landed two quick right jabs and even from where I was I could hear the man's nose snap. The second blow also sent his head back at such an angle that it collided with the wall, stunning him. Holmes took up the man's knife, which had skittered from his grasp. He then paused long enough to remove his makeshift mask and breathed deeply.

"Are you alert, Watson?" he called to me.

"I am feeling better, yes," I replied.

He handed the knife, hilt-first, to me. "Cut through the bindings around the door handles at both ends of the car. Keep the doors open. That will help revive our fellow passengers more quickly. Then go to the guard's carriage and find a conductor. We will need help securing this villain until we reach York."

He stood erect and tested his arms and neck, assessing himself for damage. I wanted to check him over, but our priority was to free the other passengers from this deadly carriage and arrange for our Indian attacker to be taken into custody.

I worked my way down the carriage, looking at the passengers slumped in their seats and was all too aware of just how terrible this day might have been if not for Holmes. I do not mind admitting that I shivered at the prospect, a chill chasing down my spine.

By the time I returned with a conductor, most of my fellow passengers were waking, disorientated and frightened. Bennett, to his credit, was playing the role of priest to perfection, calming down as many people as he could. His very appearance among the passengers went a long way to restoring calm. Order was soon reinstated once our fellow passengers realised they were sleepy but unharmed. That is, of course, the remarkable resilience of the English people in the face of adversity.

Holmes helped the conductor haul away the assassin to the

guard's van at the front of the train near the coal supply. By the time he returned a short while later, our shattered compartment window was the only evidence that the journey had been anything other than smooth. He took his seat beside me.

"Our assailant is not Nayar, of that I am sure," he began. "He did not say so much as his name, he bore no more than a passing resemblance to the fakir. A cousin or brother perhaps." I knew better than to question Holmes about it now, but determined to ask him later. "The respirator he wore was most interesting. That was Samuel Barton's design, introduced in 1874, and while I have read about its operation, using lime, glycerine-soaked cotton wool and charcoal to filter the noxious air, I have not had the opportunity for an up-close examination before this moment."

"If the contraption was of English design, how would an Indian come in possession of it?"

"A very good question," said Holmes. "One to add to our lengthening list, I'm afraid. Now, I can only presume someone learned of our whereabouts and must have sent a signal, which was no easy undertaking. We should be flattered, Watson, we have our enemies worried. Consider the logistics of this attack, assuming we were the intended victims. The car would need to be mostly sealed before passengers boarded at King's Cross—whilst we were at breakfast in the station café. They had almost two hours between our securing the tickets to Newcastle, so were able to discover our destination with old-fashioned bribery or simple subterfuge at the ticket office. What we can be sure of is this man had accomplices. Nayar and his kin may not be their only operatives. It would explain how they evaded my street Arabs. They were trying to free us of one tail, not multiple shadows. I now fear that there might well be a cadre of Indian agents working for our friends at the

East India Club. Obviously we were mistaken and the boys didn't succeed, but even so they had less than two hours to accomplish this while we waited for our departure. That shows not just an ability to act quickly, but a level of influence."

"That all makes good sense, Holmes, but at the risk of seeming like an idiot, I cannot fathom *why* this is happening. I see that it *is*, obviously, but I am at a loss to understand the whys and wherefores that would normally draw the strands of a case together. It feels like we are no closer to a solution than we were before and yet you have been attacked not once but twice, which would suggest we are close to our ultimate goal, surely? So how can I not see it?"

Holmes's smile was almost indulgent. "All will become clear, I believe, now that the distraction has passed. We begin by determining the motivation."

"And how, pray tell, do we do that?"

"The question starts with: who would benefit from all this madness? If Wynter was indeed mixed up in all this, as it would seem on the most superficial level, did he see something in South Africa he should not have and was killed for it? There are more questions of course: why kill Disraeli? Why kill the solicitor in South Africa? I daresay, at present, we are no closer to answering any of these questions than we were a few days ago, but our enemy does not know that. They see our actions and believe them to be reactions, I think."

"Then let us examine these questions one at a time," I suggested.

"Very good. It will help pass the hours productively. Perhaps we shall even deduce something. Let's start with *The Times* article on the solicitor, Charles Lewis. It mentioned that he was working on a treaty, presumably assisting in a legal capacity. Could it be our treaty, which is currently being worked on in Newcastle even as we hasten our way there? Was Lewis brought in by the Boer government to prepare their demands? Perhaps his death, if it were the first of several, could sow seeds of fear among the international delegation gathering for the signing? For all we know, others have died the same way. It is only our luck that one such death merited reporting in an English newspaper."

I nodded in agreement, following my companion's reasoning, terrified at the thought that others might die. It was possible.

"Now that we know that there are at least two Indian assassins in play," Holmes began, but I had to interrupt.

"Holmes, could this be one of those death cults I have heard about?" I inquired.

He chuckled mirthlessly and shook his head. "Actually, Watson, history shows there were only two organisations that might possibly be considered death cults. The lesser known of the two is the Aghori ascetics, worshippers of Shiva the Destroyer. They believe that contact with the dead will enable them to better understand the true nature of the universe. They trace their origins to Kina Ram, who left the mortal realm a century ago, having lived for some one hundred and fifty years. Whilst active very little knowledge of them has filtered west.

"The popular literature, though, has glorified the Thuggee cult, which is now considered extinct. One of the better things the East India Company and Her Majesty's army did was eradicate these killers from Indian society. They faded from sight in the last century and once they were considered gone for good, the Criminal Tribes Act was passed in 1871. Therefore, a cult of killers is not a practical answer to the question of the Indians. It is far more likely they were independently contracted."

"How on earth do you know all this?" I asked.

"Obviously, I have read up on such options once I identified the weapon that nearly dismembered me," he said.

I merely nodded at that, knowing he would immediately forget this information at the case's conclusion.

Holmes continued to say, "We do not need to assume that the first, Nayar, was responsible both for Disraeli's death in England and Lewis's death in South Africa. There are likely several, one of whom killed Lewis, while Nayar himself hastened Disraeli's death. That is my current hypothesis. Now, ask yourself who would gain from his passing? He was out of office and was little more than an irritant as Conservative leader."

"But before that, he was vehemently in favour of peace," said I.

"Which someone did *not* want to happen, for their own purposes," Holmes added, a smile on his lips.

"How did his death influence the peace treaty with the Boers?" asked Holmes. "The fighting had ended by the time he took ill."

"I daresay I have no clue, Holmes," I admitted.

"Think, Watson. If this conspiracy is as large as it appears, money is being expended. One spends money in the expectation of making more. This leads me back to the men of means."

"You mean Frobisher, Haldaine, and that MP fellow, Chatterton-Smythe?"

"They seem the most likely candidates, given the current limits of our knowledge. After all, they were the ones to mention an Indian mystic and we have one in the same town where the castor beans arrive. All very convenient."

When we finally disembarked at York for a hasty lunch, we caught sight of the local constabulary taking charge of our would-be murderer. I suspected they had not had his like to deal with before.

Eleven

A Rematch with a Killer

The sun was long past the horizon when we crossed the Tyne, no glow to glimmer welcome across the tightly packed rooftops of the miners' cottages and endless terraces. I was not sure what to expect as we disembarked in Newcastle. We followed a path through what can only be described as one of the seedier districts I have ever had the displeasure of visiting that led, incredibly, to one of the most beautiful streets I have ever seen. The buildings were predominately four storeys, with vertical dormers, domes, turrets and spikes, designed by the architect Richard Grainger. We were in Grainger Town, within which stood the Theatre Royal where Nayar was said to be performing his final shows as the entertaining mystic.

Holmes suggested that I find us rooms while he went to the theatre, where I would join him. I secured us temporary lodging at a small inn and was strolling towards the theatre on Grey Street, when Holmes appeared around a corner.

I could tell from his hunched shoulders that something

was amiss. "He cancelled this evening's performance," said he without preamble.

"Can we not wait until tomorrow's?" I asked.

"No. It appears the notice we saw in *The Times* was out of date. Tonight was to be a final curtain call. Word reached him of our coming and he refuses to make himself a target."

"No doubt the same ones who arranged for the attack on the train," I surmised. "A telegram would have outpaced us, even if the people orchestrating this are back in London."

"Most likely true," said he, his frustration palpable. "I believe our next destination is the quayside where, if I have judged this right, he may well be trying to leave on an earlier boat." He set off to marching down the steep hill of Grey Street.

"Holmes!" I called after him. "You've been through much these last few days. Should we not go to bed and start afresh in the morning?"

His eyes were blazing with intent. "Nonsense, Watson. How will we feel in the morning if we go to the docks and learn he has fled? We must go *now*."

I could not argue with his point so accompanied him, assuming he intended to take a cab to the Port of Tyne, which was in point of fact some considerable distance outside of the city proper. Not so. He led me a hurried chase down Grey Street, which turned into Dean Street as it curved around to the bonded warehouses on the waterfront. This was where the Keelmen operated, hauling coal from both sides of the river onto tugs that would take them down to the mouth of the great river where they would in turn be loaded onto colliers and shipped to destinations all across the country. Holmes announced that we would catch a ride with one of the keel crews to the port, which would be considerably faster than a carriage, though much less comfortable. Given that we would be sailing with twenty chaldrons of coal, it would be much dirtier, too. It meant parting with a few coins, but we found a skipper willing to transport us, and kept company with his two crewmen and a boy they called a *pee dee*, although I must confess I have no idea what this rather peculiar title implied.

When we arrived at the Port of Tyne, it was fairly dark with few people visible, though the sound of activity was near constant, the loading and unloading of coal going on apace. It was likely that while there were ships scheduled to depart that evening, none would carry commercial passengers. Still, Holmes wanted to verify that information so we found the harbourmaster, a man in a thick sweater, despite the summer temperature, and inquired about outbound ships. As expected, he confirmed that the next departure was not until eight the following morning and no, it was not scheduled to carry any passengers.

"Now, Holmes, I insist we go to the inn and you get some sleep," I said, knowing that it would take us a good hour to get back to our lodging house, and he readily agreed. This time we were forced to travel by carriage. It was the very height of luxury in contrast to the outward journey.

As it neared our inn in Grainger Town, we heard a tumult of cries and ringing bells on the streets. Then we saw the yellow flickers of light dancing up and down the stone facades of the nearby buildings.

As we drew closer, I gasped in astonishment as I spied that it was our very inn that was burning! The flames roared high, out of control, as a makeshift fire brigade of men and women passed buckets back and forth, tossing water through the downstairs windows in a futile effort to fight back the flames before they could consume the buildings on either side. A wagon approached and with it a pump to help extinguish the blaze.

Bystanders clustered on the street, and we could hear the words spreading: was there anyone inside? I hadn't even considered that eventuality. My heart sank. Could someone have died because of us? It did not bear thinking of.

I hastened to see if anyone was in need of my medical skill, leaving Holmes to scan the crowds, seeking out Nayar or one of his potential compatriots in their number. When I returned, he shook his head. We did not need to speak for me to know his thoughts. Clearly Nayar had yet to flee the city and while we had been hunting him, he had been hunting us. But it also meant we had every opportunity to find and apprehend him. I was relishing the thought of clapping him in irons, but had to temper that with the collateral damage he had caused. Thankfully, no one was in need of a doctor, but I stayed close to see if the firemen needed my assistance when the first of them finally emerged from the building.

I watched as they worked quickly and saw to it the nearby structures would remain sound. The inn itself, I judged, would survive although it would be in need of extensive repair. The fire was contained and the police began clearing away the crowds. As things settled down, Holmes beckoned for me to join him as he approached a large, older man who was clearly in charge, police sergeant by his stripes. He initially ignored my companion, barking out orders and waving his arm as he continued to direct the movements of his officers like the great Hans von Bülow himself, his men dancing to his tune. Finally, he realised we required his attention and with a slight rise of the hand, gestured for us to be patient. He yelled at two boys who were still in nightclothes as they neared the charred, damp remains of one corner of the building.

They scurried away. He let out a frustrated sigh and turned to us.

"What may I do for you gentlemen?"

"My name is Holmes, and my companion is Dr. Watson. We are up from London on business and have information as to what may have happened here."

"Is that so? Perhaps you should explain yourself, Mr. Holmes?"

"Indeed." Holmes missed the suspicion in the man's tone. "I am a consulting detective, having worked with Scotland Yard on numerous occasions. We are here in Newcastle trying to find the whereabouts of an Indian performer, a mystic named Nayar—"

"Performers are at the Royal, not the inn," the sergeant said in a weary tone.

"Not so. The mystic cancelled this evening's performance, sir," Holmes said, smoothly. "We have reason to believe he was alerted to our presence and this fire is nothing more than an attempt to keep us occupied so he might escape the city."

"Why on earth would he do that?"

"We believe he is involved in a complex and deadly case that has its origins in London." Holmes now had the man's attention. "As it was, we were attacked on the train this very afternoon which your confederates in York may confirm for you. We are of the opinion that Nayar's accomplice was behind that particular assault, and that word of our arrival was sent ahead, directing the man to flee."

"Well, I'll be…" the sergeant began.

"We believe," Holmes said pointedly, "that this fire was a second attack on our persons within twenty-four hours, and the third since we have begun our investigation."

"How so?"

"My companion had only a few hours since secured us board

in this very inn, and, if I am not mistaken, the fire originated there." Holmes pointed up at one of the windows, which, I realised sickeningly, was our room. The man nodded his agreement. "Watson, are those our rooms?" I nodded, weakly.

"You have my attention, Mr. Holmes."

"My intention is to apprehend Nayar, and with your help, take him into custody."

"Nayar... the Indian fakir who's been performing at the Theatre Royal?"

"The very same," I confirmed.

"As I said," Holmes continued, "he cancelled his final performances, but I am rather hoping our arrival took him by surprise and caused him to move with unexpected haste. With a little fortune, he may well have been forced to leave his possessions behind at either the theatre or his lodging house."

"Let's go take a look, shall we?"

The theatre was just a few short streets away across Grainger Town. It was dark, presumably because Nayar had cancelled his performance. We passed five huge columns that dominated the building's façade and turned left onto a narrow side street, which led to the stage door.

The police sergeant, who had finally given us his name as Harmony, rapped a large-knuckled hand on the door. It took a moment before a custodian, a thin, old man, unlocked it, and it was apparent that the two men knew one another. He let us in, and Holmes fidgeted in the carpeted passageway as Sergeant Harmony exchanged pleasantries with the man, whom he addressed as Mr. Rose. Finally the conversation drifted to the reason of our visit, and Rose agreed to take us to the dressing room recently vacated by Nayar, away down a dusty corridor.

There was an eerie yellowish glow to the room that had been assigned to the fakir, and as Holmes had surmised, it was obvious he had left in great haste. From the doorway I could see robes in exotic colours and unfamiliar fabrics scattered atop a steamer trunk while the dressing table was festooned with bracelets, makeup, and half a dozen purple feathers, the use for which baffled me. Harmony moved to enter the room, no doubt with the intention of poking around through the fakir's belongings, but Holmes held up a hand. "Sir, if you would be so kind as to stay outside and permit me to examine things in situ first, we might save a considerable amount of time."

"Won't you be wanting to see if we can find his boat tickets and such like?" the sergeant asked.

"We will get to all that in due time, my good man. But first, I must study things as they are. I will learn far more from that than from turning the place over. I have, you might say, a facility for observation and deduction." These were words I had heard him use time and again since we first took rooms together in March. There was no trace of modesty in them, merely the truth.

Harmony remained unconvinced, and crossed his arms with some impatience.

"You see, Sergeant Harmony," Holmes continued, "I have made a study of crime. On several occasions I have steered Scotland Yard clear of making colossal errors."

"Is that so," Harmony said, his voice laced with the heavy scepticism I had come to expect from those who had not encountered my companion before.

"Indeed it is," Holmes said, oblivious. "It all comes down to a finite set of rules regarding deduction. For example, in the short time we have been acquainted, I have discerned you smoke cigarettes and have for some years, along with at least three cups of tea a day. Additionally, you are unmarried and live on your own. Finally, you had white fish, cod I think, and spinach for your supper."

"How in the blue blazes could you know all that? Have you been following me?" Harmony demanded.

Holmes shook his head. "It is really quite simple, actually. Your teeth have a yellowish cast to them, something that comes with the consumption of tea. Based on the shade, I can surmise the quantity you drink daily. There is a similar discolouration between your index and middle fingers of your right hand. That implies tobacco, but the staining is slight enough to suggest the thinner cigarette rather than the cigar. You live alone and therefore do your own ironing, which explains the wrinkles in your shirt and trousers. On the other hand, without a wife to occupy your time, you take extra care to polish your shoes, which are extremely carefully maintained. I would estimate you ritually polish and brush them every evening."

"Uncanny," Harmony muttered. The man had turned a bright shade of red, more out of embarrassment than anger, and Mr. Rose was chuckling.

"As for your dinner. There is a fish bone stuck to your sleeve and a morsel of spinach between your top left canine and incisor. I would surmise you were dining when you were summoned to the fire and left in haste."

"Don't deny it," I told Harmony. "He does this to me and everyone he meets. It is disconcerting, but it also makes him the single best detective in England."

"You better be detecting then," he said, waving his hand toward the dressing room, indicating Holmes had won for now.

Holmes entered the room and withdrew his magnifying glass from his inside coat pocket. He began examining not the things on the dressing table, but the table itself, the chair and even the floor. He used a pencil to poke at the rubbish in the metal basket beneath the table. He then settled his inspection on the steamer trunk, poking at its contents with his pencil, moving things back and forth. Finally, he reached under a pair of shoes more befitting a child than a man and withdrew several small pieces of paper. With the glass, he looked beneath the shoes once more then rose to his feet.

"Indian stage magic is rather different than what you might see from local talent. For example, they tend to do more with ropes and knots," Holmes explained. "I have even heard, but not yet seen, something involving stiffening a rope and actually climbing up it."

"I'd pay to see that," Harmony said, and I agreed.

"There is cut rope here, debris from his stage tricks," Holmes said, gesturing toward neatly sliced lengths of thick, twisted rope. "Perhaps the most well-known magician from the land is Mohammed Chhel, who mixes the spiritual with stage craft. He is quite well known for confounding train conductors by making a cascade of tickets seemingly pour from his chin.

"Nayar has apparently been travelling around the country, largely by train. As a result, he has a stack of ticket receipts. He may well have studied under Chhel but left his materials behind in his hurry. This is a benefit to us as we may now correlate these with his appearances. Given how many of these appear to be to or from London, I would conclude he made extra trips to meet with his true employers. Similarly, he received a telegram recently, which is why he cancelled the performance. The wastebasket has the remains of a hastily burned note but there is enough unburned paper to confirm it is the same stock used for telegrams, further proof that contrary to our belief we did not lose our spy back in London. I cannot make out the content of the message, but can presume it was a warning.

"He also left behind his stage costumes and other gadgets, but there are no weapons or items of a personal nature here. It is safe to say he does not intend to return."

"Where has he gone?" Sergeant Harmony asked, his tone considerably more deferential than before. Now he was hanging on Holmes's every word.

"Mr. Rose, could you take us to the manager's office? We need to see Nayar's complete itinerary."

Rose nodded and reached into his baggy pockets and withdrew a sizeable key ring with more than a dozen keys of varying size and colour. We followed him to an office and, once the gas had been lit, Holmes began rifling through drawers and cabinets, making quick work of the records of the Theatre Royal. Sergeant Harmony, Mr. Rose and myself remained outside. We loitered in the hall, speaking quietly among ourselves, Harmony still marvelling over Holmes's observations about his person.

After some time, Holmes came out holding several sheets of paper, all in the same handwriting. At my questioning expression he explained they were travel records. "Confirmation," he said. "As we suspected, Nayar was engaged to perform here only in the last few months. Previously, he was kept close and available to his masters."

"I'm not sure I follow," Harmony interrupted Holmes, who was most excited with his discovery.

"Never you mind, Sergeant Harmony," Holmes assured him.

"This case is complex and I have no time to explain all its intricacies. We must hurry now to Jesmond."

"What the devil is in Jesmond?" Harmony inquired, struggling to keep up with Holmes as he strode back the way we had come, towards the stage door.

"Where the devil *is* Jesmond?" I inquired, totally at a loss.

"An area of the city, less than two miles from here. According to this receipt–" Holmes flourished a scrap of paper under my nose "–the management made a booking for Nayar in a rooming house there. We must perform a similarly thorough investigation of his lodgings." Harmony merely nodded at the obvious logic of the demand. I wanted my own lodgings, more precisely my bed therein, but given that it was now firewood and Holmes was bristling with energy, obviously ready to go through the night, I did not think I would be sleeping for quite some time.

We emerged onto Grey Street and the sergeant summoned a cab with a shrill whistle that carried into the quiet evening air. Harmony thanked Mr. Rose for his assistance and then insisted he would come with us to make certain all was done right and the citizens of Newcastle were well protected. My personal suspicion was that he had seen enough of the fire and our investigation promised to be far more interesting than sifting through debris.

Jesmond, a mere fifteen minutes away, was a picturesque area to the north of the city that might once have been its own village but was now in the process of being consumed by urban expansion. It was quiet and the streets were deserted and only a few houses had lights in their windows. I admired what I could discern of the homes; there was an air of wealth to the place that was missing from the city centre.

"We're in Brandling Village now," Harmony explained. It was

too dark for me to make out much, but I nodded in agreement. Eventually the cab came to a stop at a small house, and Harmony threw open the door for us before the driver could dismount. He asked the driver to wait for us, as we'd be returning within the hour. I hoped he was right.

"Allow me, Mr. Holmes," Harmony said, taking long strides to the front door and striking it with his large fist three times. A woman of maybe fifty opened the door, a shawl around her shoulders despite the summer warmth, glasses perched on her aquiline nose. She looked astonished to see a uniformed man at her door.

"May I help you?"

"Indeed, ma'am. I'm Sergeant Harmony with the Newcastle upon Tyne Borough Police and I have two gentlemen from London looking for one of your boarders. An Indian, goes by the name of Nayar?"

She recognised the name and shook her head first up and down then to the sides. "Well, officer, he has been staying with us, but his tour ends tomorrow and I gather his travel plans changed because he left with considerable haste earlier this evening."

"May we see the room?" Holmes inquired.

She looked uncertain at the prospect of allowing her home to be invaded at an inappropriate hour, but then nodded and stepped back. It was a small place, with three bedrooms at the top of the stairs and faded flowered wallpaper. The floors were hardwood with carpeted runners so our heavy footfalls were somewhat muffled. I hoped we did not disturb the other tenants.

Harmony deferred to Holmes, swinging the door open for my companion and holding a lantern high so its pale light could illuminate the space beyond, while Holmes stood framed in the doorway. When I was allowed a glimpse, I saw a small, unmade bed, a narrow chest of drawers and a short rack to hang clothing. There was a washbasin atop a thin-legged table, a stiff-looking sitting chair and little else. I did not spot a single scrap of paper, hunk of rope, or other potential piece of evidence save a pair of dark trousers and a white shirt, both thoroughly unremarkable.

Eventually Holmes entered the room and moved carefully around its perimeter, holding his lantern low, letting the light play along the baseboards, wainscoting, and cracking paint. After one circuit, he walked it a second time, this time holding the light higher and examining the upper reaches of the furniture. He pulled open the drawers, one at a time, peering closely then returning them to their closed position. He finally stood over the bed and examined the pillow, withdrew the blanket and felt along the surface of the mattress. He held the lantern out in my direction, a silent command to hold it so as to free his other hand, which I did. With practised ease, he ran his fingers under the mattress and finally hefted it up. I leaned close, letting the light reach underneath.

We both gasped at the same moment. Holmes swiftly plucked an object out from under the mattress and held it up before his face, where it glittered in the light.

"Is that a diamond?" Harmony asked in a loud, incredulous voice. He had remained in the doorway, the room being too small for three grown men to go prowling about.

"Indeed," Holmes confirmed, holding it between his thumb and forefinger as he examined it closely. "I would venture to say it is approximately a quarter carat in size, but we will need an expert to determine that for us."

"There's no chance he was paid in diamonds for stage mummery," Harmony said.

"I quite agree. It is more likely his true masters paid him in diamonds, easier to transport back home to India," Holmes declared. "Our man is not long gone, but at this late stage hours might as well be weeks; we will not find him here. I daresay he has left little to indicate the direction of his flight, either. Watson, we go back to London tomorrow and hope the trail has not run cold."

He pocketed the diamond.

Twelve

Mining in Pretoria

I was never more thankful of climbing into bed as I was that evening. Thankfully, Sergeant Harmony knew of another inn where we might lodge for the remainder of the night without raising suspicion or risking the wrath of our pyromaniac fakir. I slept deeply, but not long. We were up and ready for the earliest departure back home. In part our venture north had been the most futile of excursions—we had not caught up with Nayar, as had been our intent. But we had been subjected to two attacks, which were clues in themselves. And perhaps the diamond would prove to be the missing piece of evidence we needed to link all the parts of our investigation together? But I was fretful it would be a case of third time lucky. And I was sure I would not be able to sleep a wink on the train.

Holmes was determined to return to London with all haste having abandoned the notion we might intercept Nayar trying to flee the country. Now he was focused on the diamond, intending to have it analysed by a contact in Hatton Garden.

He was in the most foul of moods when we met for breakfast, a hasty affair of soggy toast and runny eggs, made by someone clearly unfamiliar with proper cooking. It made me miss Mrs. Hudson. Holmes glowered at the local paper, exasperated that nothing about last night's fire had made the deadline. It would no doubt be picked up in the evening edition. Although he had asked Sergeant Harmony to keep him informed, there had been no word from the policeman. No doubt he was still asleep in bed, which is where I would have been given the choice.

"It may be just as well," Holmes finally admitted. "He will almost certainly have nothing new to offer, and it would only prove to be a distraction from what must be our primary course."

We entered Newcastle Central Station through the grander of the two entrances, and I confess were on the lookout for Indians though we did not see any. Starlings nested in the ironworks above us, adding a constant rustle of movement to the other sounds of the station. We purchased one-way tickets to London and boarded a train, pleased to see that it was due to leave on schedule.

We settled into our seats having carefully scoured the faces of the other passengers and seen none with either a threatening or remarkable appearance. Nor did we see Holmes's villainous compatriot Bennett, which was perfectly fine with me.

For the first portion of the ride down as far as York, I wrote in my journal, noting the most recent developments to make certain I recorded the facts while they were fresh in my mind. Holmes, for his part, seemed to brood in silence, refusing to engage in any semblance of conversation.

His silence was finally broken when the train paused its passage for our half-hour luncheon. There, he uttered a single word, "Tea", and resumed his thinking. Now that we were deep into the case, I knew his consumption would shrink to almost nil, conserving his blood for brain activity in favour of digestion. I ate my fill while his drink went untouched. Once back aboard the train, Holmes continued his silent meditations while I felt myself beginning to nod off, but I could not allow myself the luxury of additional sleep, so instead I took out the notebook I had been using during my interviews with Miss Burdett and the *Dido* engineer Raskill, and began to pen something entirely different to my usual case notes: a draft of a letter to Mrs. Wynter, detailing all we had discovered about her son thus far. It took time, each word needing to be weighed carefully, because each one would truly count when finally read by the person they were intended for. I wanted the letter to be perfect but even after several hours at it I was not content.

As it was too late to call upon the jewellers once the train returned us to King's Cross, we returned to 221B Baker Street without any obvious persons following behind us, for which I was most grateful. Mrs. Hudson was all too glad to see us, offering us both a cold supper. Holmes went right up to our rooms with nary a word and was no doubt asleep in minutes. I elected to stay in our landlady's warm kitchen, enjoying some chicken and soup. She knew better than to ask for details of an ongoing case, though she did offer up a running commentary that was a mixture of gossip and local news, none of which I found very interesting, but I admit after the relative silence of the train journey I enjoyed the simple pleasure of human company with actual conversation. She also had a message for me, which had arrived during our sojourn in Newcastle. It was from one of the contacts given to me by Miss Burdett: Lieutenant Louis Dodge, a comrade of Norbert Wynter aboard the *Dido*, inviting me to pay him a visit. Given the nature of our case, which appeared to have quickened, I hoped I would have the time.

The following morning, Holmes and I were better rested, and in better moods. Holmes was done with silent contemplation. Indeed, he was quite the mockingbird that morning, expanding on the subject of diamonds and how often his past cases had involved the expensive baubles. When the clock struck ten, he declared it was time we were on our way. Within minutes we were on the street corner, Holmes flagging down a cab to have us on our way to Hatton Garden.

Antoine Pintard & Sons was a small operation, tucked in between a gold seller and another of the countless jewellers who operated within the old garden, which had become a centre for gold, silver, jewels, and other finery. The shop had a two-tiered display case in its narrow window to the right of the door. Signs proclaiming they sold only the finest of diamonds straight from the Pretoria mines caught my attention: another connection to the Boer conflict.

Within stood a man of about seventy years, grey hair ringing a bald scalp, side whiskers in need of a trim, and a pair of bifocals resting upon his large nose. His attire was modest in black and white, a splash of red around his neck. His eyes met Holmes's and his grim countenance brightened considerably.

"Sherlock," he exclaimed, clearly delighted.

"Good morning, Antoine," Holmes replied. "I trust you are well."

"I cannot complain, especially with someone in my shop, making me look prosperous." The man's eyes twinkled like the diamonds he traded in.

"This is my associate, Dr. Watson," said Holmes. Pintard reached out and we shook hands.

I took in my surroundings, noting the displays: rings, brooches, earrings, and necklaces, most set with diamonds, but some with rubies, emeralds, and topaz. There was more wealth in this small shop than I could have hoped to acquire in a lifetime's honest toil. That realisation only served to help me appreciate their breadth, variety and beauty all the more.

"So, what brings you to my door? Something for a lady this time? Hmm?"

I detected the traces of a French accent in the man's voice and no doubt Holmes would have used that to tell me everything I could possibly need to know about Pintard and more, but the jeweller's English was excellent and that told me enough.

"Not today, thank you, Antoine. No, I have a diamond I need identified."

"Identified? Hmm." Pintard withdrew a loupe from a cubby in the worktable behind the counter, placed a small black velvet mat on the latter, and waited for my companion to produce the gem. Holmes reached into his waistcoat pocket and the small, glittering stone appeared, shining in the well-lit establishment.

"There is no setting, so what do you expect from me?"

"As before, Antoine, I will take all you can glean from the diamond itself," Holmes said, and gave him an encouraging smile. "I do not expect miracles, only your expertise."

Pintard nodded then fell silent and grew entirely focused on the diamond. He took out a small measuring stick and jotted down some numbers, then he placed it on a scale and noted its weight. With practised elegance, he examined it from all angles and at some length. I did note that contrary to the sign out front, there was no son to be seen nor were there any other customers to wait upon. No wonder he appreciated the appearance of business.

After a considerable period, Pintard put down his loupe, consulting his scrawled figures and looked first at me then Holmes, who had silently observed the jeweller at work. "Do you know a lot about diamonds, Doctor?"

"Can't say that I do," I admitted.

"Diamonds are mined and then hand cut to shape for sale. We often receive rough-cut stones that we handcraft into whatever we desire. But, to sell them, we need to establish their size and weight along with other characteristics. For example, this diamond weighs just less than two one-thousandth ounce *avoirdupois*, which would make it approximately a quarter carat in size."

Holmes, as ever, proved himself right.

"Price obviously increases with the carat. This tiny gemstone would be a considerable possession for most people, but certainly not worth much to the wealthier mercantile and upper classes of this city. Then we look at the gem's clarity. That means the size and number of these little inclusions."

He handed me the diamond and his loupe, offering me a chance to better see and understand what he was referring to. Under the magnifying eyepiece the gem was beautiful, crystalline with facets and reflections that mesmerised me.

"Each inclusion is a blemish, the fewer the better, and this specimen, you will note, has quite a few. Therefore this diamond is worth something, but not as much as you would think. As in most walks of life, there is a price for beauty and if something is considered flawless people are willing to pay great sums of money for that perfection." I nodded my understanding. "Then you have what we call colour, which is the most subjective element in the entire transaction. Some stones have a yellow or pink cast to them and some women in certain circles currently find that appealing. This one is a tad muddy, tinged slightly brown." I nodded again, seeing it. "But, generally, especially in a shop like mine where our clientele has more... affordable tastes, the less colour to the gem the better."

I handled the gem in my palm and tried to imagine its worth based on the few facts I had been given. Even with this brief lesson, having been alerted to its flaws, I was at a loss. My only real thought was that however much it cost, it was more than I could currently afford to spend, although perhaps not out of my reach.

Holmes interrupted my thoughts. "Is it possible to differentiate possible territories where this particular stone might have been mined?"

"I believe so, yes. This appears to be one of the newer diamonds. You see the crown, Sherlock? It's smaller than the traditional cut. That's one of the vital differences between the diamonds mined in India and the ones coming by the tonne from Africa. They each have the same small tables and deep pavilions, but Indian diamonds have the heavier crown. This also strikes me as unfinished, or a rejected cut, because the cutlets are very uneven."

I had little idea about these technical terms, but Holmes nodded in agreement and I understood that his identification of this stone as being from Africa was another damning clue, tying Nayar to the Boers and Norbert Wynter. The assassination attempts on Holmes along with the death of the South African solicitor Lewis and presumed murder of Disraeli formed another strong series of strands to the web of intrigue, with the Indian and his wretched allies in the centre.

"I had hoped you would confirm my suspicion, Antoine. I too noticed the crown was smaller but being such a small gem compared with the ones I have previously studied I wanted an expert's opinion to bolster my own conclusion."

"You knew this was from Africa?" I asked, struck by the comment.

"I have made it abundantly clear, Watson, that I have made a great study of crime. One might reasonably deduce that that would mean I need to know the value of things thieves may seek to acquire, no? Diamonds certainly rank high on that list. In this particular case, I believe our Indian friend was paid in a currency that is lightweight and accepted everywhere. Given the relatively low quality and size of this stone, I would further suggest he was paid in easy to dispose of quantities and qualities once he returned home. Luckily for us, it also increased the likelihood of one such stone being left behind as there were so many."

"Do you need anything further?" Pintard asked.

"No, not at all. Thank you for the help, Antoine. It has been invaluable." With that, Holmes turned on his heel and left the shop. I shook the man's hand, said my own farewells, and chased Holmes out into the street.

"So, Holmes, now that we have more damning evidence, what is our next step? Nayar cannot be found and we need to link him to the men of the East India Club."

"Quite true, Watson. Now that we know for a fact this stone and its companions all came from a South African mine, we need to learn more about those mines. That requires some additional research."

"I daresay Lomax will be wanting to charge us rent at the library."

"For once, it might be well worth the investment to ensure our discretion when dealing with sensitive research."

We had—or rather I had—a brief meal before making our way to the London Library and my friend Lomax. He was good enough to once more find us some private space where we were able to conduct our research into mining in and around Pretoria.

The discovery of diamonds in the south of Africa had triggered a rush similar to that which had taken place in California. The first diamond was found in 1867 near the Vaal River, nearly five hundred and fifty miles northeast of Cape Town. One account told of a young child, Erasmus Jacobs, finding a diamond measuring an unheard of twenty-two carats in the Vaal. When an eighty-three carat stone was unearthed in 1869, the world needed little convincing that there was money to be made. The resulting uproar was dubbed the "Scramble for Africa" as panhandlers, swindlers, claim jumpers, the hungry and the desperate sought their fortune. The small town of Kimberley swelled to over fifty thousand people in just five years.

The most lucrative of the mines were dug on a farm owned by two brothers, Diederik and Johannes De Beer, Vooruitzicht. The Kimberley Mine and De Beer Mine were dug out by all manner of people, both white and Negro, but as they went deeper into the earth, the costs began to rise. In short order, the smaller operators began selling out to larger concerns, including Barney Barnato who had recently formed the Barnato Diamond Mining Company and bought out claims from desperate men with cheap cigars and Alfred Beit undercut them by using heavy machinery for extraction.

It made for dark but fascinating reading, proving once more that the very rich were the only ones to profit from the back-breaking labours of the poor. What was the true cost of these diamonds?

What safety measures were in place? What corners were being cut in pursuit of the bottom line?

While I studied the history of the mines, across the desk, Holmes read British government reports and parliamentary minutes. I noted that he was taking notes in a pad that went into his coat pocket when he concluded his reading. Whatever its contents, he kept it to himself and would no doubt share it only when he needed to. As the hours dragged on, my companion seemed to grow increasingly intent on his studies, the hunch to his shoulders growing more pronounced and his silences lengthier in duration. Finally, he turned his solemn gaze towards me.

"It appears, Watson, that several British Army officers made reports stating their suspicions that illegal mining works had been established under cover of the war," he said.

"Profiting when others are dying," I said. It was much the same conclusion I had reached on my own. "How absolutely abhorrent. I find it galling that their suspicions may never be investigated."

"It falls to us to make sure that does not happen, Watson."

It was still several hours before dusk when we left the London Library, but the bright blue sky was already changing to deeper shades by degree. The warmth of the day reminded me we were still in the grip of summer. Perspiration began to form almost immediately on my neck and run slowly down my back, making for an uncomfortable walk.

Out of a newly developed habit, I studied the streets and forced my ears to detect patterns. It was quiet and that in itself was odd given the last few days.

"Since we returned from Newcastle, there has been no evidence of Hampton's men trailing our steps," said I.

"I suspect, Watson, Hampton knows we are back in town but since we are doing nothing that appears to threaten the Admiralty, he's leaving us alone. For now, that allows us to move about freely."

"What now, Holmes?" I inquired as we worked our way back towards Baker Street.

"I believe I will need the evening to plot out our next course of action," Holmes admitted. "There are so many threads to this investigation and I fear we could go in one of several directions that would take us away from our ultimate goal, so I shall need to be absolutely certain we go towards that which will afford us the most useful information and greatest chance of success."

So taken with the possibility of illegal mining being mixed up with everything else we had learned over the past few days was I, that I was entirely unaware of my surroundings. My feet knew the way home through these familiar streets, so I allowed my mind to work harder than usual on the minutiae of the case, hoping to come up with a useful suggestion for Holmes that he might not have considered. As a result of that concentration, I entirely missed the flash of an arm cross in front of me, streaking from out of an alley. My companion, though, was far more alert and reached with his walking cane to block the attack.

I collected my wits and realised that we were both under assault, and catching a glimpse of our attacker, knew immediately that it could be none other than Nayar the fakir. Standing just within the alley opening, he was covered mostly in shadow, his dark brown skin blending into the shadows. He wielded that deadly tiger claw in his right hand, which made a horrid noise as the five blades cut through the humid night air between us. He was clad in a light, loose shirt and trousers that afforded a great freedom of movement, and some sort of sandals on his feet that gave him a degree of flexibility that Holmes and I lacked in our more appropriate attire. Nayar regained his balance, adjusting from his misjudged attack, and stepped back, reaching into a trouser pocket to withdraw a curved blade, which he now held in his left hand.

My medical training certainly taught me where a man might feel the most intense pain and my military experience included learning how to fire a weapon. I was therefore no stranger to combat, but nothing this intimate. I could feel adrenaline pumping through my veins, energising me, but I lacked the knowledge of how to fight him, and could only hope to defend myself. Holmes, on the other hand, was quite the experienced fighter, trained in a great many fighting styles. Still, he was confronted by a well-armed fighter and lacked the resources to even the odds.

As it turned out, I was mistaken, as Holmes raised his walking stick once more, brandishing it horizontally before him, gripped in both hands like a quarterstaff. He twirled it first one way then the other, gaining speed and keeping it as a barrier between him and Nayar. The Indian lunged, his knife hand raised. Holmes's natural balance was a match for the full-frontal assault. The walking stick smacked directly into the Indian's rib cage, driving him into the wall of the alley. Holmes held the stick vertically, rocking back on his heels, then lunged forward to ram one end down on our foe's left foot forcefully enough, surely, to break the bones through those soft sandals. The pain must have been excruciating, but Nayar betrayed no sense of pain. His cruel features remained fixed on Holmes, studying his prey, circling him as best the tight confines allowed.

Their two bodies clashed, the wooden stick becoming entangled in four arms, Holmes desperately trying to keep either the tiger claw or the knife from penetrating his hide. They slammed up against the stone wall, cannoning off of it, spinning about, grappling as they crashed once more into the hard surface. Nayar drove his forehead into Holmes's face, finally breaking them apart as the detective staggered backwards, dazed and confused. The Indian followed that with a vicious kick to the stomach, which sent the air from Holmes's lungs and forced him several feet back. I thought for sure he was a goner as the space between them allowed the Indian to gather his strength and rush forward, the tiger claw poised for the kill.

At the very moment I feared all five blades would slice into his flesh, Holmes twisted his torso, somehow evading the wicked claws, and rammed an elbow downward on Nayar's shoulder, changing his momentum and forcing the mystic to his knees. Holmes slammed the stick in his left hand down onto Nayar's hand, driving it open. The knife dropped free. Holmes went to kick it away, but even as he did Nayar swept his own leg in a semi-circle and knocked my friend off his feet.

Nayar leapt atop Holmes, using his knees to pin his arms. I feared Holmes was surely done for as the Indian raised back his right arm, ready to strike a killing blow. I sprang forward, intending to throw myself at his attacker, but before I could reach them Holmes bucked at the hips once, wriggling frantically beneath the assassin, then a second time, bringing his legs up hard enough that his knees dug into Nayar's back, distracting him for a precious few seconds from making that fatal swing. Holmes then twisted to his left, and raised his legs, which now gripped Nayar between them, and used the momentum of that turn to dislodge the man.

Still grasping his walking stick, Holmes raised it and began to savagely beat blow after blow on Nayar's body, never relinquishing the leg lock he had pinned the man with. The beating continued for fully half a minute until the Indian sagged. At that point, I felt free to rush to the pair and using my belt, looped it around the limp man's arms, binding him. Holmes then released Nayar and snatched at the tiger claw, tearing it from the man's hand.

Winded and breathing hard, Holmes sat with his back against the wall. Given the hour, people walked past the alley's entrance although precious few offered our fracas so much as a sideways glance. I took a position over the now harmless Indian and glowered down at him, rather amazed to note that neither man had drawn blood.

"Now then," Holmes began, standing over his bound opponent, his voice raspy from the exertion. "You know I am Sherlock Holmes and I know you are Nayar, an Indian performer who has been rather busy in London and beyond." Holmes drew in a deep breath, presumably gathering his wits. "I would very much like to know who your employers are. Do not waste your breath on lies. I already have my suspicions and am merely seeking confirmation."

Nayar said nothing, his eyes half-closed. A look of contempt crossed his face.

"Am I not making myself clear? All I seek is some information before we summon the constables. Or do you do nothing without compensation?"

There was still silence.

"Could it be, Watson, that the man does not know English?"

"I should think not," I offered. "After all, he has worked in this country without a translator in tow."

"Indeed, and his correspondence was all in English. Look closely, his eyes betray him. They demonstrate comprehension. I take that to mean that he chooses not to share what he knows, which is unfortunate."

Nayar stared, glowering menacingly up at us, though he didn't try to move. I guess that Holmes's blows had cracked a rib or two.

"Let me tell you what I know. You are free to add or, in the rare instance I might have misconstrued the facts, correct me." Nayar said nothing. "You and a ring of compatriots were hired to come to London and most likely Africa, to perform acts of murder on a number of people. So as not to call attention to yourselves, you used silent but still deadly means such as the poisonous extract of castor beans. For a reason I have yet to fully deduce, you hastened the death of Benjamin Disraeli. A compatriot of yours also killed a solicitor involved in the preparation of the treaty that should draw to a conclusion the conflict with the Boers, and is to be signed next week. I'd very much like you to tell me how any of this relates to an officer of the Royal Navy, a man by the name of Norbert Wynter. Now it is your turn to speak." I was so caught up with Holmes's summation that I was slow to react when Nayar finally stirred.

He sprung to his feet and threw himself forward, impaling himself on the tiger claw which Holmes had tossed aside, wriggling atop it before we could reach him.

Each of the five blades had pierced his abdomen, shredding skin, veins, and organs, creating a mess of blood and viscera.

We pulled him off the weapon, but even with only a cursory inspection, I could see more damage than any surgeon could possibly repair. Nayar would bleed to death before we could summon a cab to get us to the nearest hospital. Blood oozed from the wounds, bubbling between Holmes's fingers as he sought to staunch the flow, and still Nayar did not emit a single sound. Holmes knelt over him, a silent sentinel, watching as I checked the dying mystic's pulse, studied his eyes, which were already glazing over, and realised I was helpless. Our quarry would die in a dingy alleyway in the heart of London and there was nothing either of us could do about it but watch in horrified silence.

With no policeman in sight, we dragged the mystic's corpse further into the alley so he would not be easily visible in the fading daylight. From there, we decided it made the most sense to report the crime at the nearest police station.

There was little knowing at that moment that Nayar would not be the final victim in this sordid affair. He would not even be the final victim that day.

Thirteen

❧

A Summons from Gregson

The remainder of the evening was a sombre affair.

It took us some time to make our way to the nearest police station, and then considerably more time to convince the officer on duty that we were serious about a dead body. By the time we returned to the alley with a constable in tow, Nayar's corpse had grown cold. The constable accepted my medical credentials and therefore allowed me to dictate the findings for his report. We mentioned nothing of our case or that we knew Nayar's identity, allowing the officer to conclude that our attacker's motive must have been robbery. Neither of us desired to correct him as it suited our needs for that to remain the official word on the subject.

We returned to Baker Street without much appetite for supper. Both of us went to our rooms in silence.

The following morning dawned without a clear notion of how we should proceed. Nayar was dead, but I was sure that the signing of the peace treaty was still in jeopardy. We had little information to make a convincing case that it should be delayed or relocated, and an overwhelming fear that our enemies were bold enough to stage an attack to get their own way, even if that meant stepping finally from the shadows.

As I sat down to breakfast there was a sharp rapping on the street door below. It was followed by the sound of shuffling feet and the lock disengaging as Mrs. Hudson greeted someone. I could not hear the exchange, but the timbre of our landlady's voice led me to infer that it was an unexpected guest. I knocked lightly on Holmes's door, alerting him to the impending arrival of a visitor. He emerged within moments, eyes red from lack of sleep and the tension of the last few days. I was pleased to see that he was dressed, until I realised he was still wearing the same clothes he had been wearing the day before.

I was about to point this out when there was a ringing of the bell and Mrs. Hudson ushered in a young constable.

"Begging your pardon, but I am seeking Mr. Sherlock Holmes?" He looked from Holmes to me and back again. "Which one of you gentlemen might that be?"

"I am Holmes."

"I have been asked to bring you to, well, not to put too fine a point on it, the scene of a murder," the young man said. He was in his early twenties, sunburned cheeks and curly hair, brimming with nervousness.

"We know all about the murder," Holmes said, a look of confusion on his weary countenance. "After all, we are the ones who reported it."

Now the young constable seemed confused. He inclined his head slightly, trying to process this new information which obviously did not sit well with what he had been told. "You are?"

"Yes. We went to the Police Station yesterday evening and gave a full report."

"Last night?"

"Young man, you are in the exceedingly poor habit of repeating things I say. That is a habit you must be broken of. As someone who has been on the force for two years, you should know how to comport yourself."

"How the devil do you know how long...?"

"Is that really what's important?" Holmes said, his voice growing irritable. "Your police issue boots have two years' wear on them. The average London constable will require a new pair every three years. You are not old enough to have been on the force for five years, therefore you are wearing your first pair. I discounted the possibility that you are a new recruit with second-hand shoes because your hair is at least three weeks past regulation length. You have been with the force long enough to grow lax in your habits. Now, are we required to provide additional information about the Indian?"

"Indian?" The constable looked utterly perplexed now.

"Yes, the dead Indian. Your colleague's report will show that he is believed to have been intending to rob us, but during the fight he fell on his own weapon and died."

"I'm sorry, Mr. Holmes, but I believe there has been a mistake," the young man said. "He is... I mean... the murder victim is not an Indian."

"Why am I being summoned then? Who wants me and where?"

"Inspector Gregson asked me to come and bring you in, sir. He told me to tell you that he would be ever so grateful if you could see your way clear to coming and lending him your eyes."

"We are at cross purposes and talking about an entirely different dead man," I said. "Holmes, can we really afford the time to consult with Scotland Yard on another matter? We have a pressing concern of our own to tend to."

"Indeed we do, Watson, but it might well be time to consult with Scotland Yard, which has the international reach we lack and Gregson may be of some use to us. I am happy to exchange my services for his," Holmes replied.

And that is how we found ourselves accompanying the young constable, who was named Shaw, in a police carriage to the scene of a very different crime.

We rolled past Piccadilly Circus and Whitehall and continued toward the less savoury part of London, down by the water on the east side where illegal activity was rife and life appeared to be incredibly cheap.

Shaw escorted us into a dark red brick building that lacked name or number. I noted that its windows were boarded up, and there were signs of fire damage. Everything about the place spoke of sin and degradation, illegal activity under the guise of anonymity. Constable Shaw took us up a flight of stairs and down to the end of a narrow hallway, where a single candle burned, throwing a pallid cast onto a door.

The young policeman held open the door and we entered a room that was blinding in its brilliant colours. There were red shades over several lanterns, casting the room in a bright scarlet hue. The walls were a wild pattern of many florid colours. It was most definitely a wallpaper that one would never hang in a proper home. This, though, was far from a proper home. It looked to be exactly what it was: a house of ill repute that catered to a quiet clientele. As an army doctor, I had treated more than a few soldiers suffering from the diseases of vice. I had always felt rather sorry for the young women who were the vectors of such complaints, but I am not sure they would have appreciated my sympathy.

While I had never partaken of such services, I knew enough to recognise a brothel when I saw one and from the quality of the furniture, it was apparent that we were in an expensive establishment, despite the sordid building which housed it. As I scanned our surroundings, my eyes fell on two still figures under white sheets, one in the centre of the room, one lying on a divan, and realised that this was not just one death but two. Death had come to this part of the city with a vengeance last night.

Standing over the bodies was Tobias Gregson, an inspector with the Yard whom I had not seen since the Jefferson Hope case. Holmes considered Gregson and his colleague Lestrade the best of a bad lot, but I had a certain fondness for the tall, tow-headed man.

"Holmes, I am glad to have you here," the inspector said by way of greeting. He turned to me and smiled. "Dr. Watson, good to see you again. I have been enjoying your accounts of Mr. Holmes's exploits."

"You are too kind," I said, shaking the man's outstretched hand.

"How may we be of service, Inspector?" Holmes said abruptly. "We are working on a case of our own and the need for us to bring it to a satisfactory resolution is pressing."

"Very well, then," Gregson said. "We have taken down all the details, but before we move the bodies I would very much appreciate you taking a look around. You have an eye for this sort of thing others do not." He bent low and drew back one side of the white sheet that covered the body in the centre of the room, revealing the corpse of a young woman, not more than twenty. Her face was covered in smeared makeup, and her brown eyes were open; it seemed to me that there was an expression of abject terror in them. Her neck was ringed with dark bruises, several oval spots revealing where strong fingers had squeezed the life out of her.

Gregson then moved to the body that lay on the divan and repeated the action, pulling back the sheet to reveal a corpulent man of middle age, the lower half of his face almost obscured by a thick, greying moustache. I did not recognise him but Holmes let out his breath in a sharp hiss.

"Inspector, do you know who this man is?"

"I should hope so, Holmes. His name is Patrick Chatterton-Smythe, a Member of Parliament. His identity is the reason I am here rather than the City of London police. Once his body was identified, Scotland Yard was alerted and I was dispatched to investigate. Did you know Chatterton-Smythe?"

"We never met, at least not to be introduced, but I knew who he was. As it happens, Inspector, Chatterton-Smythe is directly connected to the very case I mentioned. His death adds an entirely new dimension to our investigation."

"I look forward to the details, but first, let us look at Mr. Chatterton-Smythe."

Holmes knelt to inspect the corpse without touching it. Rigor mortis had clearly set in, locking the dead man's muscles tight. This allowed me to estimate the time of death as some time during the night, the very night Nayar tried to kill Holmes and me. It was too striking a coincidence to ignore.

Holmes pulled down the man's collar, but there was no bruising like that on the girl. He then examined the man's hands, his wrists, and finally forced open the mouth, peering inside with his magnifying glass. Finally he rose, nodding at some conclusion that was beyond me.

"You should know, Holmes, one of those muckrakers from Fleet Street is already sniffing around and the papers will be full of this before too long," Gregson said. "A sitting Member of Parliament dead is bad enough, but to die in a place like this... there will be a scandal, mark my words. Not to mention the man had a wife and children."

Holmes nodded again. "And what shall you tell his family?"

"Why, it seems obvious to me what has happened here, although I asked you to come in case there was some more innocent solution I've missed." Gregson strode over to the corpse of the woman and pointed at her bruised neck. "See here, Chatterton-Smythe strangled this girl, no doubt a quarrel over payment. Then he made his way over to the divan and had some sort of apoplexy or suffered a failure of the heart, the result of shock or exertion. Look at the size of the man. And there's not a mark on him. I'm sure the doctor will agree."

I crossed over to the corpse of Chatterton-Smythe and made my own examination. The fleshy face was engorged with blood, the eyes popping from the head; such symptoms could be a sign of heart failure. I could see no obvious marks of violence, and said as much to Holmes. However, my companion shook his head.

"I'm afraid, Inspector, that these events are more nefarious than you suspected. The girl was indeed strangled, but not by Chatterton-Smythe. Observe the marks on her neck, clearly made by a man's hands, not by a ligature. Now look at our MP's hands."

I did so, and immediately saw what Holmes was talking about. "He's wearing a signet ring!"

"Exactly, Watson. Now would a man in the throes of a violent argument think to take off his signet ring before strangling his victim, and then calmly put it back on his finger? See, the ring has a small opal set into its face. Had it been worn by the girl's attacker, her skin would have been torn, and yet it has not."

Gregson nodded at this, but did not look completely convinced. "Then who killed her, and how did Chatterton-Smythe die? Are you saying he was also murdered? But how? Some kind of untraceable poison?"

I had had enough of untraceable poisons for one case, and so was relieved when Holmes laughed and shook his head.

"No, Inspector. Not this time. Both our victims died of the same cause, but in different ways. Come–" He beckoned to us both, and we crowded around the body of the dead MP. "Here, Watson, bring that lantern and raise it to the face." I did so, and Holmes pulled down the jaw, stiff from rigor. "See, Inspector. Note the bruising on the nose, practically obscured by the reddening of the skin. And what do you observe in the man's mouth?"

Gregson peered closer, his face intent. "See? I see nothing, Mr. Holmes."

"Look at the man's molars."

It was a moment before Gregson spoke. "Is that thread?" He drew back and I took his place. Sure enough, with the aid of Holmes's magnifying glass, I could see several strands of black fibre caught between Chatterton-Smythe's back teeth.

"Yes indeed, Inspector," said Holmes. He seemed more animated than I had seen him for some considerable time.

"And what is the significance?"

"Really, Inspector, is it not obvious?"

"Come now, Holmes," I said. We did not have the time for my companion to play games.

"Well, let us look at the evidence. We have an unknown woman, clearly strangled by a powerful man, given the size of the finger marks on her neck. But not by the man who lies dead in the same room, as he wears a ring that would have cut into her skin. Both their faces are engorged with blood, a sign both of strangulation and apoplexy. I say that both victims died as the result of their breath being stopped by an unknown hand. Chatterton-Smythe has bruising around his nose and black fibres caught in the back of his mouth. From that we can deduce that his nostrils were held shut and a wad of black material was pushed into his mouth, resulting in suffocation." Holmes swept his arm to encompass our surroundings. "Yet there is no such material in this room, so clearly the murderer took it with him, or rather them, as surely this must have been the work of more than one villain, to subdue the woman and to also hold the man down while another stopped his breath."

Gregson's expression was one of revulsion. "So what was the motive? A robbery gone awry?"

Holmes shook his head. "No, Inspector. This was nothing short of cold-blooded murder designed to besmirch Chatterton-Smythe's reputation."

"And the murderers?" Gregson insisted.

"That, Inspector, is something I endeavour to discover, and discover quickly. If my suspicions are accurate, the situation has grown even more dangerous than I first suspected."

"You said before Chatterton-Smythe was involved in your most current case. Can you give me the details?"

"I can and will be happy to share them. In exchange, I may need Scotland Yard to help me to intercede on England's behalf to stop more murders being committed before this investigation has run its course. But first, I suggest you dispatch a constable to locate the body of an Indian man called Nayar, and arrange for it to be sent to whichever morgue these two bodies are destined for.

Watson and I reported the death to officers from the local Police Station, and I believe it has a bearing on these murders. That victim is connected with the larger matter and having all three bodies in one place may prove valuable."

"A third body?"

"Yes, Gregson. The mortal remains of an assassin that very nearly made victims of Watson and me. It was that very body I thought to be the reason for young Shaw seeking me out this morning."

Gregson looked somewhat overwhelmed, but he nodded in agreement. "I need to make my report to the government; seeing as the victim was an MP, the Yard is treading lightly. Why don't you accompany me and give me your story on the ride?"

"That would be agreeable," Holmes said. "Come, Watson."

I stepped over the corpse that still lay on the floor, feeling great pity for the young woman, who was most certainly a victim–if not entirely an innocent one–in a much bigger affair. I hoped that her name would be discovered and that she would not go into an unmarked pauper's grave. I would treat her as fairly as possible when writing up the account of the case.

The police carriage was not as comfortable as I had imagined it might be, luxury obviously spared, and with three of us within– Shaw rode atop with the driver–it made for close quarters. Holmes outlined what we had uncovered in a clipped manner, keeping to the facts and refraining from sharing his thoughts and observations. The Houses of Parliament loomed over us as we rounded a corner and Gregson did not look at all pleased to be there. I could not blame him. This was sad business, but now also a most dangerous one, and there were no procedures for such a case for him to follow. He was a dogged sort, and the more time I spent in his company the more I grew to like his earnest demeanour.

"What exactly will you tell the leadership?" I asked.

"I will tell them the facts and share your thoughts about what truly happened," Gregson said.

"Do not speak of the conspiracy or the diamonds," Holmes instructed.

"Why not? You cannot expect me to lie to the House?"

"Of course not, only to omit certain facts. If Chatterton-Smythe's compatriots learn we know as much as we do, I suspect they will go to ground and complicate the case. I need to return to the East India Club, where I last saw Chatterton-Smythe, and learn what I can from his surviving conspirators, Frobisher and Haldaine."

Gregson nodded in agreement, but the expression on his face told me he did not like it. Anyone with even the slightest interest in current affairs knew that the government was already dealing with pressing issues concerning Afghanistan, the absorption of the Boer region, and the constant matter of Ireland. A political scandal like this could bring it down. Holmes tried to reassure him. "Gregson, you have my word you will be informed of the facts and will be free to act accordingly, taking the credit for bringing down a criminal conspiracy, preserving the signing of a significant treaty and protecting the realm. That's all good for you and for Scotland Yard. I daresay it will be the making of an already fine career."

With that, we climbed down from the carriage and walked north, back towards Baker Street.

En route, Holmes outlined his intention of resuming his disguise as a footman at the East India Club. "Chatterton-Smythe's murder is likely a sign of a falling out between him and Frobisher and Haldaine. While I am thus engaged, I would have you track down Wiggins and the rest of the Irregulars. I need them to make themselves available for additional duties urgently."

We parted ways, Holmes on to Baker Street to prepare his disguise, I in the general direction Holmes thought I was likely to find the boys. It was only a matter of minutes before I spotted a pack of urchins. Not knowing their names, I wondered how to address them, but was relieved of the dilemma when Wiggins emerged from the group, walking toward me with a cockish swagger to his step, the others following behind him as baby ducks do their mother.

"Mornin', Doctor," said he brightly. "Mr. Holmes got some work for us, 'as he?"

"Looking for a good cracksman?" one boy chirped.

"Need us at a flash house?" another asked.

"Want us to recommend a ladybird?" a third added, getting a round of laughter from the others at my expense.

"Nothing of the sort, young man," I corrected. And then I paused, not entirely sure what Holmes had planned for the boys. I said as much. "I will be absolutely honest with you and say that I have no true notion of what Sherlock desires from you, only that he asked me to bring you to him."

"That's handy," Wiggins said. "I'd rather be doing something for 'im than be in the clink any day of the week. Follow me, gentlemen," he grinned and set off, leading the way. The rank he afforded the ruffians earned him another round of laughter as I and my strange entourage made our way to 221B. They waited on the street while I went upstairs to find Holmes.

Upon entering our rooms, my companion was already in his footman's attire. "Wiggins is here?"

"Indeed, along with his followers," I confirmed.

"Most excellent," Holmes said.

"Holmes, are you placing these boys in danger?"

"I would think not, Watson," said he. With that, he picked up his walking stick, the only weapon he allowed himself, and returned to the street.

"Look at the mobsman," one boy called as Holmes emerged from the front door.

"Ready to give up detecting to work for the swells?"

"Need us to knock over a toff?"

"Nothing of the sort," Holmes chided the youngest of the bunch, a boy of no more than ten, with very curly locks and bright freckles. "I don't know what you might think Wiggins does for me, but whatever tales he tells you, burglary is far from it."

"Would if you paid me," Wiggins offered with a grin.

"Thank you, no. Today, you and the boys will accompany me to the East India Club."

"Oooh, fancy."

Holmes ignored the interruption. "When I signal you, there will be two men who require following. Split into two groups, one for each man. Within your group, take turns to follow closest, to make certain you are not detected. This particular engagement will necessitate you moving throughout parts of town where young men like yourself would most likely be chased off by local policemen, so be watchful and do nothing to draw unwanted attention. It is imperative you keep these gentlemen in your sights at all times. I will require regular reports, so set up a relay system to ensure the information remains current."

"The usual arrangement?" Wiggins asked.

Holmes reached into his waistcoat pocket and withdrew a handful of coins. "A shilling each for the day's work should suffice. When I receive satisfactory information that proves helpful, a guinea for each."

The promise of additional pay energised the group of ruffians, who began dusting themselves off and running their grimy hands through tousled hair in a futile effort to improve their appearance. All thoughts to our dwindling financial resources were banished as I chuckled at their meagre efforts then turned to my companion.

"And me, Holmes? What would you have me do?"

"Today you rest, Watson. Take the time to consider all we have learned and all we still need to learn. Apply your own thinking to the matter and when I return, I daresay sometime this evening, we will compare notes."

This was perfectly acceptable to me given how tired the last few days had left me. But then I recalled the invitation to visit one of Norbert Wynter's comrades on the *Dido*, Lieutenant Louis Dodge. Much as I wanted to take my leisure, I forced myself once more into the streets.

I took a cab to the house of Louis Dodge, just two streets from Trafalgar Square. As I emerged from the cab, I noted the sun was still shining strongly but dark storm clouds were chasing it from the horizon. I feared more rain was to come.

It was an imposing house, and the front door was nicely polished with a brilliant bronze knocker that neatly fit my hand. It was a matter of moments before a butler answered and I presented my card.

"Are you expected?" he asked in a soft voice.

"I have been invited to see Lieutenant Dodge but we do not have an appointment. I just now had the free time to pay him a call," I said.

He nodded once, had me wait in the vestibule and went off to inform his master. Dodge, I knew from my research, was one of the three men listed as wounded during the battle at Majuba Hill. His wounds were serious enough for him to be discharged for medical reasons and this was the home of his parents.

I had been waiting for some minutes when I heard the heavy thump of canes against thick carpet and the shuffle of footsteps. Lieutenant Dodge was a young man, but he used two sticks to assist his walking. His face was handsome and clean-shaven with bright blue eyes and slicked back hair, and he gave me an easy grin as he approached; I felt myself exhaling in relief. He might have been physically damaged, but from all appearances his mind remained whole, which was no small blessing.

"Dr. Watson?"

"At your service," I replied. The butler ushered us into the drawing room where two high-backed chairs were arranged before a dormant fireplace. Dodge shuffled over and lowered himself heavily into one of them. I took the chair opposite.

"It's late enough in the afternoon, Markham. The single malt if you please." The butler nodded without comment and went to a side table where he filled two small glasses with amber liquid. Once they were delivered, he left us alone.

"You appear well enough," I allowed as Dodge took a sip from the glass.

"If I keep this up, they say I may need the one cane by Christmas," Dodge said in a cheery tone. "It's hard work."

"Are you in pain?"

"You know, doctors always want to know about pain first. I don't know why that is," Dodge said.

"Pain indicates whether you are healing."

"Good point," he said and sipped again. I took a companionable mouthful and found it to be quite good stuff, at least fifteen years old, with a deliciously smoky flavour. "Now, sir, how may I be of service?"

I explained my connection to Mrs. Wynter and at the mention of Norbert's name, Dodge's face brightened considerably.

"Ah, Bertie! What a chap he was. The kind of man you always want at your side in a pinch. I tell you, Doctor, he was the most punctual man I had ever met. Although he was particularly poor at cards," he chuckled at the memory, "he was one of the best darts players I ever lost a sovereign to. They wanted to turn him into a sharpshooter but he refused. Didn't like the gunpowder, he always said."

I began scribbling in my notebook. "Anything you can tell me about Lieutenant Wynter would be most helpful."

"Happy to oblige," Dodge replied. "He was particularly poor at telling jokes but loved hearing them, believe you me. Bertie was always going on about his girl, Caroline something."

"That would be Miss Caroline Burdett," I corrected.

"Yes, that's right. Lovely thing. Have you met her?"

"I recently had the pleasure."

"She as pretty as the picture or did he hire a model to fool us all?"

"She is a striking woman," I allowed.

Dodge let out a good-natured laugh. "Good for him. They were going to get married once he got back." At that, his features clouded over, much as the sky outside was filling with darkness. I continued to write, allowing him his thoughts.

"That was a rough day," Dodge finally said.

"The battle at Majuba Hill?"

He nodded. "Beaten by farmers we were. I watched one of

our sailors get it in the neck before they got my hip. Ogle–the lieutenant in charge of the naval brigade from the *Dido*–warned us it was going to be bad. He wasn't wrong, just underestimated how bad it was to be."

"Was Wynter with you?"

He shook his head and drained his glass. He stared at it a long moment and I rose, took it from him and gave him a liberal second helping.

"Bertie was with the others, mixed in with the men from the *Boadicea*. We all landed together that morning then were split into squads and sent around the damned hill. Last time I saw him he was marching as if we were on parade. He wasn't taking it too seriously."

"Do you know what happened to him?"

Dodge took a long pull of the Scotch. I noted his hands clenched and unclenched, likely working his way through the unwelcome memories. "He saluted me, gave me a daft grin and marched off. When the firing was over, I was carried back to the *Dido* to be patched up and was out of it for some time. When I came to and asked after the others, I heard there were casualties… and fatalities. Bertie never came to visit, never sent a note and it was days later before it dawned on me he must have been one of the dead."

Something nagged at me and I reviewed some of my earlier notes and then looked directly at Dodge, who met my gaze with clear eyes. He could clearly handle his liquor.

"You have a question, Doctor?"

"Mrs. Wynter had it intimated to her by the Admiralty that Norbert Wynter was not killed but may have turned coward and deserted…" Before I could finish the thought with a question, Dodge let out a shocked laugh that resembled a bark.

"Bertie a coward? Never, Doctor. Never and a day. He may not have been the smartest man on the ship or the best card player, but he was someone we could all count on. Someone we could trust, rank be damned. Did you know he volunteered to be part of the mission? Would a coward, with so much to lose, do that? Tell me who blackens his name and we will have words."

I hesitated, lacking a name to offer him.

"Tell me his name, Doctor!" Dodge's expression had turned into one of fury. "Whoever that dog is, he was not aboard the *Dido*. He was not a member of that crew or he'd know better!" Then he gulped the rest of his Scotch. "It was a rotten day all around. You know, they never told us what happened. How we got so badly beaten. But from what I overheard the surgeons say, it was worse, far worse than anyone let on. I can't believe it was just three dead and three wounded. Something's not adding up but I never did have a head for numbers."

His suspicions tallied with what I had already heard. Wynter might not have been the only man missing after the battle but no one was willing to admit as much.

There was little left to say so I politely finished my own glass and shook Dodge's hand and took my leave. A light rain began to fall, warm to the skin given the day's heat, as I emerged into the street. What he told me matched what I had already heard and a clearer picture of our missing man was forming in my mind. And yet, we still had no eyewitness account of what had befallen him.

The remainder of that dreary day passed with a great deal of tedium. I returned to Baker Street, and after straightening my own belongings, I tidied up our sitting room, careful not to disturb Holmes's ongoing chemical studies. Thankfully, Mrs. Hudson has learned through trial and error where she might and might not clean, which made my job easier as there were almost layers of control within the outright chaos. With those tasks accomplished, I settled into my chair and reviewed my notes. Everything his comrades had told me confirmed his mother's suspicions and firmed my resolve that Norbert Wynter was anything but a coward. The Admiralty was obfuscating his absence if not outright lying, in addition to trying to roughly put us off the investigation. Someone would have to answer for that when this sordid affair was over.

As the day progressed towards evening, I found myself neither making new discoveries nor drawing fresh conclusions of worth. Instead, I took a simple late lunch and enjoyed tea with Mrs. Hudson. I quickly grew restless, a testament to just how thoroughly my companion was rubbing off on me.

As night fell, I grew increasingly anxious for Holmes to return. If questioned, I would have said that I was eager for fresh news, which was only partially true. Given the events of the last few days I would have welcomed any word that assured me of his safety.

Finally, I heard his familiar footfalls on the stairs and I straightened up in my chair, journal in hand, ready for his report. Opening the door, he saw me in my chair and broke into a broad grin.

"Ah, Watson, still awake. Excellent," said Holmes, still looking every inch the perfect model of a footman.

"Any trouble at the club?"

"Not at all." He sank down into the seat across from me. "Several of the staff recognised me from my previous visit and assumed I was again covering for an absence. I merely occupied myself, succeeding in appearing busy despite the fact I only served our suspects."

"Both Frobisher and Haldaine were at the club?"

He nodded, then spied my journal and cocked an eyebrow at me. "More melodrama for the masses?"

I admit, I continued to chafe under his withering criticism of my stories since he would have preferred they read like university texts, dry and to the point. And deathly dull. I chose to inject an element of thrill to my accounts of the detection process, but I never embellished. The fact that he never forbade my literary endeavours was evidence that he enjoyed the small celebrity they gave him.

I said nothing.

"Oh, very well," Holmes said, divesting himself of a pair of white gloves one finger at a time. "I arrived and immediately determined that Frobisher was already present. Having had an ownership stake in the original East India Company the gentleman appears to revisit past glory by practically living at the club. I noted that he always maintains the same table and by way of preparation, suspect that he is in the habit of ordering the same meals. As a result, the staff like him because he rarely makes a fuss and his needs are easily met.

"I served him tea and later a small lunch. I noted quickly that he appeared out of sorts, agitated. He had several of the day's newspapers with him though he did not appear to read them. His manner spoke of having less than his normal amount of sleep and his body language spoke of great tension. Other than the basic pleasantries he said nothing to the other members of the club or the staff, myself included, which I am led to believe is most out of character.

"Finally, in the early afternoon, nearly half past one, our co-conspirator Haldaine arrived. I marked immediately that he appeared equally tense. The pair glowered at one another for a time, neither speaking. I offered them tea but Haldaine waved me away with a demand for whiskey despite the early hour. This encouraged me, knowing well that a man who imbibed that early will likely loosen his tongue sooner rather than later.

"So was my hope, but in fact the two men spoke little, instead flicking through the newspapers without much interest although he did make some odd margin notes in one paper, allowing me to finally obtain a sample of his handwriting. However, when another footman arrived with two copies of the latest edition of *The Times*, they devoured them like starving men."

"I haven't left our rooms for hours," I interrupted. "What did the papers say? Was it about Chatterton-Smythe?"

"Inspector Gregson appears to have been correct in his assumption that the journalists of Fleet Street would emphasise the lurid details."

"Which was only to be expected; it is a ripe story," I remarked.

"There was great speculation about how this would affect the Liberals and other political nonsense, to which I paid little heed. But once the news spread, it was almost the sole topic under discussion by other members of the club. While few knew him, all knew *of* him. And it was at this point that Haldaine finally said something that caught my attention. 'Things have gone too far. Maybe the time has come to shut down the entire operation.' As you might imagine, Frobisher was not best pleased by the prospect, which confirmed to me that we were skirting close to the very heart of the matter. It was clear that Frobisher at least and perhaps both men were behind Chatterton-Smythe's death. There was no surprise, they did not remark on the particulars of his death, merely on the fact that events had progressed too far. But that is hardly proof for the court."

"Or why, Holmes. There is no motive. Or rather, we do not know what it is."

"That's where you are wrong, my dear Watson," Holmes said. "Frobisher started talking about the money the operation has cost them to date, accounting for the funds expended on bringing in the foreign operatives, which I took to mean Nayar and his colleagues. He was most insistent that more revenue be generated in order to replenish their reserves. That set me to thinking about how Nayar was paid."

"In diamonds," said I, following my companion's chain of thought. "Diamonds from African mines."

Holmes nodded in agreement. "They want more diamonds from those self-same mines."

"But Haldaine wants to end things?"

"So it seems. And clearly he was not the only one, for he said 'Chatterton-Smythe was right. He saw that every passing day was bringing us closer to exposure.' Frobisher, though, disagreed. 'I will do nothing of the sort. We have invested years into this operation and need to bring it to a satisfactory, not a hasty, close. Just because a paper is signed on means everything changes, nothing changes. These things take time.'"

I was always amazed at my companion's power of recall. He could recount great tracts of conversation word for word while I often struggled to remember what I had had for breakfast that day.

"Haldaine seemed subdued and suggested that their efforts to derail the signing of the treaty might still work but he was clearly concerned," Holmes went on. "But by their own confession, the pair hired the Indian criminals to delay the treaty signing to benefit their mining scheme. We apparently did not dig deep enough into researching the mines, Watson, something we need to address tomorrow."

"Dig deeper? My god, Holmes, did you just make a pun?" Holmes glared at me, rather unamused.

"Quite unintentional, Watson, this is no time for jokes of any sort. We need to do more research into the mines in and around Pretoria. These are the final strands of the web, Watson. We are close to understanding everything."

"Back to Lomax and the stacks?" I asked.

"No, we need government documents, we need current maps, and ownership papers. I suggest you sleep as much as you can tonight so you are fresh for what promises to be a lengthy spell of dreariness."

I was about to rise and do as he suggested, when there was a banging at the street door. I could hear Mrs. Hudson exclaim, "This is no time to be making such a racket! There are proper people trying to sleep!" which brought a ghost of a smile to my companion's lips. Then the street door opened and someone came rushing up the stairs, taking them two or three at a time.

Wiggins burst into our rooms, Mrs. Hudson hot on his heels. "You just don't go barging into other people's homes, young man!"

"It's perfectly alright, Mrs. Hudson," Holmes assured her, rising from his chair. "Wiggins is always welcome at my door."

"Well, be that as it may, Mr. Holmes, there's a way of doing things, and banging on the door fit to raise the dead isn't it."

"My apologies, Mrs. Hudson. Wiggins, apologise to Mrs. Hudson."

The boy bowed deeply, almost folding himself in two as he begged her indulgence. His grin betrayed the fact he was far from serious, but it was good to see that the lad was none the worse for his exertions. He seemed bright-eyed and most excited about something. He looked fit to burst with information.

"Got some news you want to 'ear *tonight*, guv'nor," he said, loudly. "The two men you had us follow. The skinny one went over to the Lamb and Flag for some nasty business."

"Mrs. Hudson, would you be so kind as to bring young Wiggins some water? Thank you," Holmes said. To Wiggins he continued: "Have a seat and give us all the detail you can muster."

"This has got to be worth a guinea if not two," he said, taking Holmes's normal seat.

"The details first, if you please," Holmes said with a smile, clearly enjoying the ruffian's company and mercenary manner. "I will decide how much they are worth."

"Right you are. So, Tommy and Pig Boy followed the fat one…"

"Edward Haldaine is his name," Holmes filled in.

"Haldaine, right you are," Wiggins said. "Me and three of the others followed the skinny man…"

"William Francis Frobisher," Holmes corrected.

"Why they got so many names? They frightened they might lose some?"

"It is a sign of social status," my companion explained.

"A lot of hot air wasted if you ask me," Wiggins said, accepting the glass of water from a disapproving Mrs. Hudson. He at least had the wherewithal to give her proper thanks this time. The urchin, it appeared, was not totally without manners.

"Unsurprisingly, no one asked you, Master Wiggins," Holmes said. "Now, details, boy, where exactly did Frobisher go?"

"We thought he was just taking in the night air, but then we could tell he had a particular place in mind. He meandered a bit, like he thought he might be being followed, then with his head down hustled over to Covent Garden in maybe quarter of an hour. He went to Rose Street and stopped to watch the fights."

"That's not where a boy should be," I began to say, but stopped short of rebuking Wiggins when I received a stern look from Holmes. The Lamb and Flag, London's oldest pub by most accounts, had earned its nickname of the "Bucket of Blood" thanks to the bare-knuckle boxing bouts held there with great regularity. Word had it, the alley became the place to go to hire thugs, muggers, and killers.

"The skinny... that is, *Mr.* Frobisher, stood and watched for a few minutes, but Willy said he wasn't really watching the fights as he was watchin' the audience."

"An astute young man," Holmes said.

"When the loser was carried off, the skinny man walks over to a bunch of fellows and talks them up. We took turns gettin' close enough to overhear best we could. He pulled out a wad with more pounds in one place than I ever seen, and peeled a few right off. I wanted to practise my tooling skills, you know," said he, wiggling his fingers, demonstrating just how light they were. "But knew you'd be cross with me if I wound up gettin' pinched."

"More that you got caught than the fact you picked the man's pocket," Holmes assured him. Now it was my turn to give him a look.

"This huge fella, boxer's nose and bald as you like, took the money and they shook hands."

"Did you happen to hear who was being targeted for a beating?"

"Oh for sure I did. That's why I'm here, see."

"Go on," said Holmes.

"Get this, Mr. Holmes, 'twas the other one, the fat man... Haldaine."

My jaw dropped, but Holmes merely nodded as if he had expected as much.

"Interesting. Well done, Wiggins." To me he said, "First one or both conspire to kill Chatterton-Smythe when his resolve weakened, and now that Haldaine is showing the same second thoughts about this affair, his partner is ready to help him see the error of his way and keep him in line."

"Oh no, you've got that wrong, Mr. Holmes," Wiggins interrupted.

"How so?"

"The skinny man, Frobisher, ain't looking to keep Haldaine in line."

"No?"

"He wasn't paying for no beating, see. He wants the fat man killed, end of story."

Fourteen

ᄋᲱ

Locating the Mine

The rain poured down all that night and into the early morning, making a bad day even worse. But Holmes was adamant that we go to Parliament and obtain the vital records in search of the final pieces to connect the clues into a complete picture. Holmes had ordered Wiggins to continue with his surveillance of Frobisher and Haldaine; the attack on the latter could be thwarted now that we were aware it was imminent. I wasn't happy. This was dangerous work for children, but Holmes continued to reassure me these boys were in their own way more dangerous than the fighters at the Bucket of Blood. I was, needless to say, sceptical.

Donning our coats and hats, we tried with little success to hail a cab. We had to walk several streets to a busier thoroughfare before managing to obtain one. I decided that this was the time to tell him about my interviews with Wynter's comrades, the engineer Raskill and Lieutenant Dodge. I had not revealed these activities to my friend, thinking he would not understand my motivations.

"Holmes, I have spoken to men from the *Dido* and they raise some concerns that may or may not have a bearing on the case."

"Why did you seek them out?"

"I wanted to understand Norbert Wynter, see the sort of chap he was, see if there might be a clue to his disappearance."

"We have plenty of clues and are hunting them down," he said.

"But this appears to be one avenue we never considered exploring."

"What did you learn? What suspicions have been raised?" He displayed no interest in Wynter the man, just Wynter the case.

"As to his being a deserter, one told me he volunteered for the Naval Brigade that reinforced the 58th Regiment at Majuba Hill but neither man I spoke with saw what happened once he disembarked the *Dido*. But, both men did imply there was much not discussed after the battle. Secrets are being kept and not as well as the Admiralty may believe."

"All very interesting, Watson, but without detail, it raises more questions and I daresay we likely do not have time for them until we exhaust our current line of inquiry."

He fell silent, returning his gaze to the world beyond the carriage window and I was left to worry about what else was being kept from us.

It was only after we arrived at the Houses of Parliament that he expressed any interest in the machinations our investigation would demand. "Who shall we bother for this information, Watson?" I had wondered if he intended to do much the same as young Wiggins had last night and simply stand there banging on the door until someone came to answer, then barge his way into the House of Commons and declare his intent.

I offered an alternative course of action. "Based on my reading,

I believe we should start with Mr. Leonard Courtney."

"Who might he be?"

"The Undersecretary of State for the Colonies."

"And why not his master, the Secretary of State for the Colonies, John Wodehouse, 1st Earl of Kimberley?" Holmes asked. I was impressed he actually had bothered to learn the man's name but no doubt it came as a part of his investigation, needing to know who might be involved in an international affair such as this.

I explained how according to some of the articles I read yesterday, Wodehouse was already travelling. "Also, Courtney is on record as being quite concerned over expenditures in Africa and might be a willing ally in learning what has been happening over there, out of sight, but not out of mind."

"Good work, Watson. Let us seek out Mr. Courtney."

Holmes was not accustomed to the wheels of politics and did not fully grasp the difficulty of walking in to see such an important individual without an appointment or even letter of introduction. I had earlier suggested we bring Inspector Gregson with us to add some authority to our presence, but Holmes refused, stubbornly determined that this was still our investigation and a representative from Scotland Yard would only serve to prematurely connect our questions with Chatterton-Smythe's murder, an eventuality we wanted to delay for as long as possible.

Gamely, we found our way to the outer office of the Undersecretary and were met by a young man in a dark suit that was beginning to fray slightly around the trouser cuffs. Holmes introduced himself and expressed a desire to meet with Mr. Courtney. At that, the man laughed out loud, irritating my companion considerably.

"I am Gilbert Harries, the Undersecretary's private secretary.

Do you know how many members of the House want some time with the Undersecretary? If I allowed them all, we'd never get any work done."

"I know we do not have an appointment," I interrupted, smoothly, looking to see off an altercation before Holmes's ego could get the better of him and put an end to our hopes. "Our business, though, is of most vital and urgent importance."

"What does it concern?" Harries asked, still clearly amused at our temerity.

"A matter that should not be discussed before public ears," Holmes said, enigmatically. He stared intently at the man who actually withered a little under his gaze.

"This is Whitehall," the secretary declared as if we did not understand our whereabouts. "This may be as far from public as one could find." He laughed at his own humour although I did not find it quite so amusing. After all, those toiling here were to *serve* the public.

Holmes merely glared at the man, clearly unhappy with having his time wasted.

"Mr. Courtney is not in his chamber at present," Harries said, his smile finally fading.

"If you would be so kind as to intercede, I can explain what we need and perhaps you might be of some help?" Holmes said. He had dropped his voice to a low, deep tone, one I assumed he used to convey the importance of our presence.

"Well this could certainly be a diverting discussion," Harries said, and I finally understood what Holmes did not. He was a bored functionary, rarely asked to step out of his role and he appreciated this distraction. "Come with me."

Harries conducted us into the main office, a wood-panelled

room that spoke of age and importance, the room itself imbued with the gravitas of the building. On the Undersecretary's desk were maps and books, and a large world globe waited for study atop a pedestal. Once the door was closed behind us, he turned.

"Now we are more private, how may the Undersecretary's office assist you?"

"We are seeking the current maps and records of ownership for the diamond mines in the Boer territory," said Holmes. "It is our belief that something is happening in Africa that bodes ill for England."

Harries stared at Holmes incredulously. "You cannot be serious? Surely?"

Holmes merely stared back at him.

"Holmes you said your name was?" Harries asked, clearly hesitating to commit himself to a course of action he felt to be ludicrous in nature.

"Sherlock Holmes. If you would like someone to vouch for my veracity, I suggest you contact Scotland Yard and ask for Inspector Gregson. I am a consulting detective and have done him a number of services recently. He will assure you my request is both legitimate and worthy of your attention."

"Scotland Yard? Very well. I will need some time to verify your claim, of course, and even more time to obtain the Undersecretary's approval for the release of the information you have requested and to actually gather the documents you need," Harries said, making it obvious that we were in for a long wait.

"Since time is of the essence, may I suggest you assign these tasks to several underlings so all might be done at once?" Holmes said, the exasperation slowly creeping into his voice.

"You clearly have no understanding of how the government works, do you?"

"I have been acquainted with aspects which I find inefficient and distasteful, starting with the manner in which bureaucrats appear to delight in wasting people's time," Holmes said testily and I feared we would lose the man's much-needed cooperation.

Sure enough, he looked upset, so to ameliorate the matter, I interjected once more.

"Sir, I assure you that my friend Holmes here has the Crown's interests at heart," I said. "If he claims every second is precious, believe me, every second is precious. The very least you could do is send others to verify his identity and see if the Undersecretary would be so kind as to let us look at what must surely be public records in the meantime?"

"And you are...?" he asked.

"Dr. John Watson, late of Her Majesty's Army Medical Department, and now a doctor in civil practice and companion to Mr. Holmes," I informed him. I hoped my military service would reassure him that we were not lunatics intent on interrupting government business.

"A doctor and a detective? Why–"

"If you'd be so kind," I said. "We really are pressed for time and however Her Majesty's servants may assist us in our efforts to protect the realm would truly be a blessing."

Finally, the logic of our requests and the earnestness of our demeanour must have convinced Harries that our presence was serious and our business pressing. He asked us to be patient and we accompanied him back to his desk, where he wrote several notes.

"You know, gentlemen, being private secretary to the Undersecretary gives one certain privileges." There was a sense of pride in his voice now that he had committed himself to our assistance. He gave out a sharp yell and an even younger man in a cheap suit arrived to take and distribute the notes.

Clearly, Holmes had expected access to the records to be immediate, but I knew better. In order to keep him occupied, I suggested he take a stroll through the building and let me wait with Harries until the documents we needed arrived. He nodded his agreement and swiftly strode off, no doubt in search of mischief.

As one might imagine, gathering all the approvals and documents was a Sisyphean task that took a good part of the day, but Harries finally managed to obtain our requested materials and was kind enough to set us up in the Lords Library so that we might peruse them. Before all the papers were stacked on a table, Holmes was already unrolling maps and was examining them with his magnifying glass.

"Watson, would you be so kind as to begin determining the relevant mine ownerships, cross-referencing against shareholder documentation, and providing us with a list of suspects? I would rule out, of course, anyone who has sold out to either the Barnato Diamond Mining Company or the factors controlling the Kimberley and the old De Beer mines, most notably Cecil Rhodes and his partner C.D. Rudd, but anticipate that not all have done so."

His words made perfect sense but the detailed work he was asking for better suited the skills of a legal clerk than those I possessed as a doctor. It was very slow going, and I spent the remainder of the day sifting through dense reports, filings filled with most imprecise legal language, and ownership paperwork. Much of it was written in a variety of hasty hands as the paperwork made real the claims but they were a formality compared with the actual possession of the mines and division of their imagined wealth. I was aghast at how sloppy some of the documentation was, with missing or incomplete information that would have made pressing a claim difficult if not downright impossible in some cases. Clearly, no one had done an audit of these reports. I tried to imagine medical records—even on the front line—being allowed to be so disordered and how that might result in the difference between proper treatment and a patient's death.

Holmes, for his part, was dogged in his reading of maps, poring over every inch of them, taking documents from me to match to the various locations. He was hasty with the papers, making so much mess that I was forced periodically to pause my own investigations to re-order them.

After we had been at it several hours, Harries appeared to let us know that the library would soon be closing for the evening, and informed us that we would have to surrender the maps and documents to his safe keeping within the next half hour. Holmes tried to argue, but I laid a hand on his forearm, reminding him we were here only because of Harries's kindness, not duty, and he could easily rescind permission. We needed to maintain the private secretary's good will in case we had to return in the morning.

Holmes did not press the point, instead he instructed, "Look at this, Watson." He gestured with his magnifying glass at a map of Boer territories. With two fingers he traced the courses of the Buffels and Slang Rivers.

"The rivers form a junction at this formation of rock named Sorrow's Crown."

"What of it?" I peered closer, and saw an unfamiliar symbol next to the rock formation. "What is that?" I inquired.

"It appears on several other maps of the region, and denotes classified filings. Do you have anything for this area?"

I consulted my notes, realising that with haste and weariness, my handwriting had become almost indecipherable. I checked for any mention of Buffels, Slang, or Sorrow's Crown but found nothing.

Holmes was about to toss the map aside when something captured his attention and he paused, a long finger tracing one of the lines of longitude running across the map. He then slowly withdrew his notebook and thumbed back a few pages. With narrowing eyes, he studied something in his notebook and then the map. He snapped his notebook closed and replaced it in his pocket. Clearly he found something but would not voice it until we were alone.

"Ask Harries if we can access those files," Holmes instructed. "I would wager the clues we seek are there."

With more than a little trepidation, I approached Harries's desk. He was clearly ready for me to surrender the loaned papers. A look of disapproval crept across his face as he saw that I was empty-handed.

"Something else, Doctor?"

"Yes, actually and believe me, I do hesitate to ask at such a late hour."

"But you intend to ask anyway?"

I nodded. "On the maps there are symbols denoting classified files and Mr. Holmes asks if there is any possible way we could see those reports."

He shook his head slowly from side to side.

"I am afraid not, Doctor. Classified means they are secrets of Her Majesty and not mine to share. I suppose if Mr. Holmes were to draft an official request, detailing his reason for asking, the Undersecretary *might* see his way clear to share some of the information contained within them if it is not considered a threat to national security to do so. But, the files themselves could not be released. Now, it is time for me to lock up for the night, so I must ask you to bring me everything."

"Of course."

I walked slowly back to the library and Holmes, who gave me a questioning look, but quickly surmised the answer from the look on my face. His shoulders slumped. We bundled everything together, took them to back to Harries and bade our farewells.

Once on the damp streets of Westminster, Holmes took a deep breath of the summer air. The rain had stopped, but it would be several hours before the muck solidified. "The secrets we seek are in those files, Watson. If the government is keeping these secrets, then we can deduce that the government is somehow involved. We simply *must* get our hands on them." I shook my head. I couldn't see how it could be done, but Holmes was like a terrier with his teeth sunk deep into a bone. "There must be someone we can turn to for assistance? Someone we haven't thought of?"

"The only avenue open to us, I fear, is to take this to Scotland Yard. Although since the Yard answers to the government, it's only a slim chance. Now, Holmes, what was all that about with your notebook? Was there some connection with the map?"

"Indeed, Watson, a vital clue. I believe I have deciphered the numbers," said he.

I was trying to recall which numbers he meant when my thoughts were interrupted by the sound of fast-approaching footsteps. I turned and saw Petey, one of the Baker Street Irregulars, haring towards us pell-mell.

"However did you find us?" Holmes questioned the boy, as he gasped, hands on knees, gazing up at us.

"Well," he managed after a moment. "After the attack the other day, Wiggo decided one of us needed to keep an eye on you, Mr. Holmes."

"Very resourceful, our young Wiggins is," Holmes said. "Now, boy, what's the message?"

"The fat man dies tonight!"

Interlude

∿

This concludes the initial account as recorded by Dr. John Watson during the time of the events. What follows was written subsequently and was kept by Dr. Watson in a locked box, and found amongst his personal effects. The following chapters were written between six months and no more than a year after the events concluded.

These additional passages were discovered by the doctor's descendants and after a time, brought to Her Majesty's Government where they were reunited with another journal—that which contained the initial account above—pertaining to the Sorrow's Crown investigation, completing the full account of what happened in the summer of 1881.

This unified report is revealed for the first time.

Fifteen

Murder Most Foul

"Watson, it is imperative we keep Haldaine alive," Holmes instructed, as if there could ever have been any doubt. In the absence of government records, the man's knowledge was vital to any satisfactory resolution. It was imperative we do all we could to keep Haldaine alive.

"Where is this to happen?"

"Barton Street, where he lives," Petey answered.

"To Barton Street, hurry on, chaps, hurry on!" Holmes directed us. The young street Arab, having gathered his second wind, was off like a shot.

"I will summon Gregson," I said.

"Capital," Holmes said, and turned to follow the boy into the dimming night. They were gone before I could bat an eye.

I knew Gregson kept late hours, especially when working on an investigation, so I turned back towards Piccadilly and waited for the familiar sound of an approaching cab to transport me to Metropolitan Police Headquarters on the north side of Great

Scotland Yard. As I stood there in my impatience, I fancied the sense that I was being watched but as I scanned the streets I saw nothing and wrote it off as just nerves. The journey seemed interminable. I felt a deep gnawing anxiety that would not cease. Holmes, still recovering from his injuries, was going once more into battle, but this time I was not at his side. Not that my presence would have made much difference in the grand scheme of things, but there was no denying the fact that he had been fortunate to escape multiple attempts on his life and another such encounter might be more than the fickle gods of fate would favour.

Arriving at the station, I hastened through the doors, and was surprised at how busy it was, even as the evening was upon us. The main counter was bustling with activity. Men and women of all ages crowded in to speak with the desk sergeant on the opposite side. Behind him, a variety of uniformed and shirt-sleeved men moved back and forth. I tried to work a path through the throng to reach the sergeant in charge, intending to inquire if Gregson, or even Lestrade, were on the premises.

The din was disconcerting after hours spent in the relative silence of the Lords Library. It was an assault on my ears: people with lost dogs, stolen purses, battered or robbed in some fashion they wouldn't have wanted their spouses to learn about. Each and every one of them felt that they absolutely needed to present their case first and the exasperated desk sergeant waved his arms to order silence, but to little avail.

Deciding to adopt the same approach as those others present, I took a deep breath and bellowed: "My name is Dr. John Watson and it is vital I speak with Inspector Gregson!" My voice carried over the hubbub, and the desk sergeant's eyes met mine. "Is there some way you could determine if he is present?"

As I had hoped, my title caught his attention. He nodded. "Let me see if I can be of some help, Doctor."

He disappeared through a door behind the wooden counter.

I waited for more than a quarter-hour before Gregson finally emerged. He scanned the crowd of faces, no doubt looking for Holmes. Confused to see me alone, he came hurrying over. "Whatever is wrong, Dr. Watson?"

"I need you to accompany me to Barton Street, Inspector. Holmes has been informed a crime is being planned," I said. "It is imperative we make haste."

"What sort of crime?" But I was in no mood to stand there and explain myself. Every second was of the essence.

"Let us make haste. I will give you the details on the way: a murder is being planned and I need your help accessing several classified government files! But let us be on our way!" I turned towards the entrance, my action a signal, I hoped, that time was not to be wasted.

"I can help you with the former," Gregson said, on my heels. "But what do you mean classified files? I don't follow."

We reached the street, and he signalled to a constable to bring around a police carriage. "I believe we should bring some assistance if murder is under discussion," he said.

I was not of a mind to argue; there is a comfort in numbers, especially well-trained numbers of uniformed constables, although it did make me reluctant to fully detail everything to Gregson while others might overhear. As the carriage hurried towards Barton Street, I explained that Holmes had received intelligence regarding an attempt on Haldaine's life and his connection to Chatterton-Smythe, and how in turn that all connected to the dead Indian Nayar and our case.

Gregson absorbed the information slowly, gravely nodding his head every now and then.

"What's all this about classified files, man? How the devil does that connect with your investigation?"

"Let us discuss that aspect of the case once we have averted this heinous crime," I said, not wishing to reveal Holmes's reasoning until it was just us three.

The carriage made good progress to Barton Street, the horses moving at a brisk clip. The street was lined with large, older homes that spoke of wealth and pedigree. The streets were well lit in this part of town, but there were still shadows and places where mischief could be conducted aplenty. In fact, as we rounded a corner, we spotted a cluster of people and I feared the worst.

Instead, as we grew closer I recognised Holmes standing in front of one of the large houses, surrounded by eight ruffians. I marked Wiggins amongst them. Each boy brandished a billy club. Lying on the ground before them I saw a singular shape: a fallen man, extremely large in stature, with a bald head and a nose that had clearly been broken long before Wiggins and his fellows got their hands on him. I was sure it was the man Wiggins had described, the man Frobisher had hired at the Lamb and Flag. He was quite clearly unconscious, the butt of an extinguished cigar dangling from his slack mouth.

I emerged from the carriage and hastened to his side to check on his condition. His pulse was steady, as was his breathing, so I left him and rushed to Holmes's side.

The boys recognised me and let me through their cordon.

"Watson, whatever took you so long? Good evening, Inspector."

Gregson merely nodded at Holmes and studied the fallen man sprawled out across the pavement. Upon seeing that he was a man of the law, the boys quickly made their weapons vanish—into deep pockets, stuffed down trouser legs, and in one case, shoved under a cap—as they melted back to allow him through. Gregson chuckled to himself but made no move to chastise any of them.

Holmes spoke. "These boys alerted me to an assassination attempt on Edward Haldaine, so I came here to make sure that did not come to pass. As it was, we arrived at a most opportune moment, finding this bounder laying in wait for Haldaine. When I called him out, the fool tried to attack me, but as you can tell, it did not go well for him. I was more than protected." He looked around at Wiggins and the other boys. "They laid him out and then stood guard until you arrived."

Gregson turned to the two constables who had travelled with us. "Collect this unfortunate fellow and take him back to the Yard for questioning." They did as he instructed, lifting the fallen man and carrying him to the carriage. Gregson approached Holmes and looked about. "Where is Mr. Haldaine?"

"Safely inside his house," Holmes said.

Pulling out a notebook and pencil, Gregson looked intently at Holmes. "From the beginning, leave nothing out, Holmes, if you please. What happened here?"

"Very well, Inspector," Holmes began. "I tasked Wiggins and his compatriots to follow Mr. Haldaine from his place of business, as I had reason to believe that an attempt would be made on his life— they had previously overheard a business arrangement between the man you have taken into custody and an associate of Mr. Haldaine. However, they were not as subtle as they should have been, and Haldaine must have heard their footsteps, for once in sight of home he broke into a run, unaware it was actually Wiggins and his gang coming to his aid. By then, I had arrived on the street, in time to see his assailant step out of an alley to intercept him. I called out to the would-be murderer, and aimed my pistol at him, which stopped him in his tracks."

"I see," said Gregson.

"Haldaine continued running, not looking more than once in my direction. His attacker turned toward me, a mistake on his part, as it meant he was ill prepared for Wiggins and the boys, who arrived and beat him rather soundly."

Holmes took that moment to reach into a pocket, withdraw some coins and hand them to the Irregulars. "If this carries on, you will drain my coffers for good. But you have proved invaluable yet again."

"That's nice of you to say, guv'nor," said Wiggins.

"I think, though, that I will have no further need of your protection this evening. Inspector Gregson will be sufficient."

"If you say so, Mr. Holmes, but if you don't mind me saying, he might be an inspector and all, but he's just one and we're eight," Petey said, offering a wry dirt-smeared grin.

"One of him may well be worth the eight of you," I said. The street Arabs made derisive noises at that, and their scoffing earned them a look of distaste from the inspector. Having pocketed their pay, the gaggle of boys disappeared into the night.

I must admit, they were beginning to grow on me.

"Has Haldaine emerged since?" asked Gregson.

"No."

"I ought to have a word with him, let him know that everything here is well in hand," Gregson said. He rapped on the front door, eschewing the lion-headed knocker in favour of his tight fist. The sound reverberated through the darkness. I realised just how quiet it was.

A thin-faced butler opened the door. Gregson identified himself, asking to speak with Haldaine. The butler gestured for Gregson to enter, and the inspector nodded for us to follow, but Holmes shook his head. Gregson looked confused, then shrugged, and entered the house alone.

"Holmes, are you quite well?"

"I am indeed, Watson, why do you ask?"

"Over the past few days you have gone without food and sleep, been attacked twice and have been obsessing over this case, but now you are offered the opportunity to enter the house of one of our chief suspects you decline?"

"You have little to fear. I feel perfectly adequate, and most certainly able to see this through to its proper conclusion." With that matter settled to his satisfaction if not my own, he turned his gaze to me and inquired, "Have you asked the inspector about the files?"

"I mentioned them, yes, but he would like more information," I said.

"Very well," he said, and fell silent as we awaited Gregson's return.

When the inspector finally emerged, he looked thoughtful. "There is a public house just a few streets away. Why don't we repair there and share information?" Having gone most of the day without food, this seemed a capital idea to me. My stomach was of the opinion that my throat must have been cut.

"Holmes, I do think sharing information might be in order," I said. "There is much we don't know, and the inspector could well be the man to help fill those gaps in our knowledge."

We walked to the pub in silence. Within, the air was thick with smoke and stale beer. It was not the most salubrious of venues, neither was it the quietest. Both served our purpose well. I bought three pints from the bar, then joined Gregson and Holmes at a table, who sat opposite one another. Holmes leaned forward. "Let us begin this exchange with a frank account of what Haldaine just told you, if you please?"

If Gregson had expected to begin the questions he showed no sign of irritation or surprise. "He was scared out of his wits, Mr. Holmes. He claimed to have no idea what happened, or why. His version of events matches yours well enough."

"That is because it is what happened, and exactly as it happened," Holmes agreed.

"What I found interesting is that he didn't so much as ask who you were—even though he saw you point your weapon at the man lying in wait for him—or the man himself."

"Curious, indeed," I noted, but Holmes seemed less surprised.

"Of course not," Holmes said. "A police inspector asking questions might draw attention to Haldaine's other dealings. No doubt he knows all too well who ordered the attack: his partner in crime, William Francis Frobisher. Haldaine's life is very much at risk. The irony is he dare not so much as point an accusatory finger towards Frobisher for fear of exposing their crimes. He is tangled in the heart of his own web. I doubt he will rest tonight."

"That's just as well," I said.

"Now, Holmes," Gregson cut across our conversation, "I want to know what is going on here. I want to know all about these files you want and I want a solid reason why I should even attempt to get hold of them, should I actually be able to."

Holmes studied the inspector, then began telling a tale of murder, treachery and betrayal that spanned continents. "I am closing in on the secrets behind a series of murders, a line that stretches from here to Newcastle by way of India and South Africa."

"What happened in Newcastle?" Gregson asked, confused.

"Plenty," I said. "But most telling is the significance of the castor beans." The inspector looked at me blankly for a moment, but Holmes wore an expression of approval. He too had made the connection, presumably from the short article about the death of the clerk working on the treaty we had read on the train on the way to the wrong Newcastle. "Newcastle, in Africa, is where the peace treaty to end the Boer conflict is being prepared for signature in just a few days. Initially we had wrongly assumed it was Newcastle upon Tyne, convinced to pursue a line of thought by the import of castor beans and the touring schedule of the fakir. A quite different murder involving the extract of castor beans should have pointed us in the right direction much earlier," I admitted.

Gregson blinked twice at that and then folded his hands before him. "Continue."

I sat quietly, sipping my beer, as Holmes detailed what we knew and what we had learned since we last met. He began at the beginning, outlining how a mother's grief had brought us to the Admiralty and how we had been pushed from pillar to post in an attempt to deflect our inquiries. As the story unfolded, Gregson's demeanour changed, the inspector becoming intent. Holmes recounted our misapprehension and journey north to the wrong Newcastle, the attack on the train and our suspicions as to the identities of the attackers, including Nayar, and the discovery of his diamond, and how that had been confirmed to be a poor quality South African rough cut. As Holmes explained about the secret designations on the maps, he concluded with, "Gregson, there must be a reason the government has marked those portions of the map as secret, but without documentation connecting those locations to Frobisher, Haldaine, and the dead Chatterton-Smythe, we have no evidence for a judge and risk a murderer walking free."

"You make a compelling case, Holmes, but I must be truthful with you." Gregson shook his head, obviously struggling with all that we had told him. "I am not sure even Scotland Yard will be able to manage to get you those files. We serve at the government's pleasure. Worse, if you are wrong, and there is a legitimate reason that they have been classified, some matter of national security, it could mean trouble for all of us. I'd be putting my job on the line, Holmes. You do understand that, don't you? I can't afford for you to be wrong."

"I am not wrong," the detective said, absolutely sure of himself. "And I know you will endeavour to obtain those files for us." It wasn't a question.

"More fool me," Gregson said.

Sixteen

Declassified

The following morning was gloomy, which certainly befit our mood. We had scant evidence to link Frobisher with the attempt on Haldaine's life, only Wiggins's word that he had heard Frobisher hire the would-be assassin at the Lamb and Flag. The word of a street Arab would not hold up at the Old Bailey. We needed the arrested man to confess to the crime and implicate Frobisher, or for Frobisher himself to confess to ordering the death of the shipping magnate, both of which were unlikely eventualities as things stood. Even though we had Gregson's word he was going to try to access the classified papers, I did not think an inspector with so few years of service would be a match for parliamentary bureaucracy. I must confess I was not altogether hopeful. I sat in my chair, having updated my journal, mulling over what we had learned. Holmes played his violin for a while, but soon joined me in front of the fire.

"Do you expect Gregson to prove successful?" I inquired, more to break the silence between us than anything else.

"That remains to be seen, Watson," said he. "While the inspector is undeniably one of the best of a bad lot when it comes to the finer practices of detection, his skills with the machinations of government remain to be seen."

"What if the hoodlum does not confess to being hired to murder Haldaine?"

"He will, I think, with the right incentives. I would very much like to question him myself."

"What makes you so certain he will talk to you or anyone else?"

"I may not be able to break his resistance," Holmes observed, "but if he begins denying the obvious, who better to pierce his pretence and force a confession? In fact, rather than sit here waiting for Gregson, we should make haste to Scotland Yard and make it our duty to have a word with the blaggard."

Suddenly fired with ambition, Holmes was on his feet and reaching for his coat. Even before he had one arm into it he was dashing for the door. I hastily put on my own jacket and chased him down the stairs, out the door, and into the street. As chance would have it, there was a hansom at the kerb. Holmes was already pulling the door open as I closed the door to 221B.

Minutes later the cab was drawing up before the Yard. Holmes entered and strode to the wooden counter with great purpose, leaving me to pay the driver before I caught up with him. The desk sergeant recognised my companion.

"Mr. Holmes isn't it?"

"Indeed, Sergeant."

"And what can we do for you today, Mr. Holmes?"

"I would very much like to question the gentleman Inspector Gregson brought here yesterday evening. Picked up on Barton Street."

The sergeant grimaced. "I know you consult with Inspectors

Gregson and Lestrade, sir, and normally I would be happy to help you, but Inspector Gregson is currently out of the building. I can't let you see his collars without his say so."

"What of Lestrade? He should be interested in what the prisoner has to say."

The sergeant checked his desk register, nodded, and bade us wait for a moment as he disappeared into the bowels of the building. He was gone for several minutes, leaving us to study the desperate and the disenfranchised in the hall, until he emerged with Lestrade. He did not appear best pleased to see us.

The dark-eyed, hunch-shouldered inspector did not bother with greetings. He met my companion's eye and with a weary hand, gestured for us to follow him.

We trailed through narrow hallways and down a flight of stairs to the basement. Lestrade opened a door with a heavy key, then locked it again behind us, before leading us deeper still through a series of locking gates until we reached the interview room where our prisoner was being held.

Haldaine's attacker sat in a chair before a table, his hands cuffed. His face was badly bruised, no doubt the work of the Baker Street Irregulars and their billy clubs.

He looked almost as pleased to see us as Lestrade had.

"All we got so far is that his name is Alf, no surname," Lestrade said. "Ask your questions, Holmes. I will remain as witness."

"Very kind of you," Holmes said, and took a seat directly opposite the prisoner.

Alf was a surly-looking fellow to say the least. His teeth were chipped and black, and his bald head was coated with grime. He also smelled as if he had not seen or used soap in days. His clothing, all in dark fabric, was cheap and well worn.

"Alf," said Holmes, "can you tell me what brought you to Barton Street last night?"

"Taking an after-dinner constitutional, your lordship," said he, with a rough voice filled with contempt.

"Nonsense. You had no business being on Barton Street save to make mischief. Specifically, I put it to you, you were there to commit some act of bodily harm to a man named Edward Haldaine."

The bruiser shrugged, the handcuffs restricting his movement. "That's what you say. Don't make it true."

"It is more than that, Alf, it is what I *know*, and I promise you I shall prove it. When I do, you won't find yourself in prison, you'll be heading down Dead Man's Walk, waiting to swing by the neck."

"Won't happen," said Alf, cocksure and arrogant. "I was out walking and those brats took me down, attempting to mug *me*. That's how it happened. That's all there is to know."

"Stuff and nonsense," Holmes said.

"You ain't got nothin' to connect me to nothin', just words. I ain't afraid of no words," Alf said, so many negatives in his sentence I wasn't entirely sure if he was confessing or denying his part in the conspiracy to murder Haldaine.

"Oh, but that is where you are quite wrong," said Holmes, patiently. "You see, Alf, despite this pretence at familiarity, we do not really know one another. If we did, you would be aware that I am a consulting detective. The best in London."

The two eyed one another.

"You don't 'alf talk some tosh," the prisoner said, shaking his head.

Holmes continued. "You were seen with William Francis Frobisher in the Lamb and Flag, not two days ago. A witness overheard the deal being made, and money changing hands." I hoped neither Alf nor Lestrade would ask who the witness was.

Alf looked disconcerted at this, but bore up bravely. "Doesn't mean nothin'. A man can say what he likes, doesn't mean he'll do it."

Holmes smiled. "Then why did you appear at the home of Mr. Haldaine with a pistol in your possession? I had a chance to examine the weapon while you were taking your leisure on the pavement, Alf. It had not been recently fired, but it had been methodically cleaned and was primed and loaded, so you had obviously taken the time to prepare for the task ahead. That says premeditation, Alf. That says intent."

Alf grew silent. His fingers drummed out a tattoo on the table. He did not bother to disagree with anything Holmes had said.

"Confession is good for the soul," Lestrade said.

Alf's response was both rude and anatomically challenging, and for that earned the man the back of Lestrade's hand.

"Did you try and kill Haldaine?" Holmes pressed. It was a simple enough question, but the semantics of it allowed the man to deflect his inquiry.

"Try? No. You and those gutter rats stopped me. You can't arrest a man for thinking about somethin'."

"Your intent then was exactly as I surmised: you were on Barton Street with one purpose."

"Two," Alf contradicted.

"Two?" Holmes asked, sounding somewhat surprised, which I rather enjoyed for the rarity of it.

"To do as ordered and get paid. The fella who hired me said half on delivery," Alf said, as if Holmes was a fool. It was hard not to laugh.

"Now that we have ascertained you were there with the

intention of committing murder, let us consider the man who hired you. Was it Frobisher?"

"I don't know who you're talking about. I ain't got no clue who wanted the job done."

An incredulous Lestrade interrupted at this point. "You don't know who hired you?"

"That's not how we do things. He knew where to find me, I knew he'd be good for the price, didn't need to know nothin' more than that."

"He did not give you a name?" Holmes said.

"Would have been a fool to."

"But you would recognise him if you saw him again, I take it?"

"In exchange."

Lestrade moved closer. "What do you want?"

"Well, fer one, I ain't fond of the idea of hanging," Alf said, with a tight look in his eyes. "If I help you, I want to be sure I get off, see?"

"Unlike murder, conspiracy to murder is not a hanging offence," Lestrade informed him, "despite what Mr. Holmes would have you believe. But I know your sort, Alf; if I dig around enough I'm sure I'll turn up quite the history. Most of it will be petty stuff, no doubt, but it all adds up. We could see you in Newgate for quite a stretch. Help us and I can put in a word for you with the judge."

"Or you could just forget you ever saw me…"

"Impossible," Lestrade said. "The best I can do is to vouch for you."

"The inspector's word carries some weight," Holmes said to Alf. "No doubt it will go in your favour if he speaks up for you."

"But will it keep me out of Newgate?"

"Unlikely, but I would wager that it could not hurt your defence."

"Alright." Alf turned to Lestrade. "I have your word? You'll do that? You'll speak for me?" Lestrade nodded. "Right. So... he's a skinny one and comes from money. Got the bearing of an officer about him, you know the sort. He weren't at home in the Bucket of Blood. You stand him in front of me, I can tell you it's 'im or not."

Holmes rose and gave Lestrade a nod. The ferret-faced detective ushered Alf out of the door, cuffs clanking, leaving us alone in the dismal room.

"We need to bring in Frobisher and put him in front of Alf," I said. "And that being the case, we will need a charge to level against him. It won't work to simply lure him here."

"Indeed, and a charge his solicitor cannot refute," Holmes agreed.

"Which may be an easier thing to say than actually accomplish," I said. "I don't think that even the combined evidence of Alf and Wiggins will be enough to make a conspiracy charge against such a powerful man stand up in court."

We left the interview room and made our way upstairs to the ground floor of the police station. I immediately noticed an increased level of activity. The reception was filled with all manner of unsavoury types. Holmes glanced about, and seemed ready to leave the building, but stopped short. I followed the direction of his gaze and saw a neat man in a dark suit, who was cleaning a pair of glasses on a monogrammed handkerchief. He most certainly looked out of place among the throng of dragsmen and inebriates, an island amidst a sea of humanity.

Before I could make further study, I heard Holmes's name being called. Inspector Gregson emerged from behind the desk sergeant's counter and beckoned for us to follow him.

Gregson had a flushed, excited look on his face, which I took to mean he had had some success with our request. He very wisely did not say a word until we were secreted in the warren of cramped, tiny spaces where the inspectors had their desks. We stopped at his, tidier than most by some degree, which I took to be a reflection of both his mind and his methods. Upon it stood a tall stack of books. They appeared to be leather-bound ledgers, a uniform set, although the neat writing on the spines indicated they were from different times and places. Each bore an identical symbol—that which Harries had unwittingly confirmed denoted "classified"—just like the ones we had seen on the maps.

"Most excellent work, Gregson," Holmes said, a look of delight on his face. "Did you have trouble obtaining these?"

"You might say that, Holmes. I had to make promises, offer favours, and even forgive some debts in order to get my hands on these. As it is, I would wager some of the Civil Service mandarins are unaware the documents have left the premises so you do not have a great deal of time to review them." I had not thought about the connection until Gregson said it, but the very clerks who walked the corridors of both Houses owed their origins—and loyalty, one would hazard—to the East India Company. The notion of a permanent, unified and politically neutral administrative body was still relatively young, but for the best part of a century the Company had been schooling administrators in the Chinese manner to be at the beck and call of the government. The model was designed to eliminate corruption, but I feared, suddenly, that it had failed. Here we had officials trained by the Company, men who had risen well up the career ladder of the Service to positions of considerable influence during their years serving in Westminster. My mind raced. Who better to cover up the misdeeds of someone like William Francis Frobisher, one of the last vested shareholders of the East India Company? What price for loyalty like that? I understood, suddenly, how vital documentation could simply be made to disappear.

Gregson carried on speaking, "Unfortunately, I cannot let you leave the station with them. But I can set you up with a room and let you examine them in private. That is the best I can do."

"That should suffice," Holmes said.

We divided the stack of ledgers between us and followed Inspector Gregson to a quiet side room. There was a worn, round table that would barely be large enough for five men to conference at, but more than enough for we two. Gregson left us to our studies, closing and locking the door, ensuring our privacy but also, in his mind at least I am sure, guaranteeing we would not be making off with the ledgers. The lock, rudimentary as it was, would have offered no great challenge to my companion should he have set his mind to picking it, I'm sure.

"Now then, Watson, let us find out the secrets of government, shall we?" He withdrew a letter, one I previously saw in our rooms, recently delivered. Holmes withdrew a second sheet of paper, the one on which he had sketched the symbol while first looking at the East India Trading Company's business. "Look for this, Watson. I am fascinated to find out what it is they have been so determined to keep from us."

"Something worth killing for," said I, studying the mark.

"One would assume," Holmes agreed, and turned the first page.

Seventeen

Bringing Justice to Light

One man's tedium is another man's glory. While I revelled in my medical studies, I completely understand how the mechanisms of the human body could bore another man to tears. I was reminded of such sympathies when I cracked open the first of the main ledgers and began reading through the neat script it contained.

The contents were distinctly dry, being records of land sales in the Boer region of South Africa. Some were for small plots of land, barely ten acres, some for great swathes of territory. There was no obvious pattern, and at first I was sure that we had made a hideous mistake. The records were not indexed so Holmes and I were forced to sift through the volumes from beginning to end, calling out a name of a purchaser or buyer in the hope that the other would have found another record involving the same party, attempting to recreate a path of ownership in search of the telltale clue that would betray the hand holding it once and for all.

To some actuary in some dusty office this might conceivably

represent fascinating work, but for me, it was mind-numbingly tedious. I kept having to pause to refresh myself with the mark Holmes thought I should find replicated in these records. Holmes though, a voracious sponge for information, was far swifter when it came to absorbing the material and making sense out of it. Of course, he also has the amazing facility for "forgetting" the material deemed extraneous, so once this case concluded, no doubt all of this new information would simply vanish, knowing he could always research it afresh if by some miracle he was ever required to call upon it again.

Now and then, Holmes made notations, a look of grim satisfaction on his countenance. I dared not pause and inquire. When he was ready, he would share his newfound intelligence.

The hours ticked away. We were left to our own devices by Gregson and Lestrade, much to my relief. I was parched and my back ached, so I closed the volume before me and rose. I suggested that we take a break, but was rebuffed. He allowed that I could take my leisure, which I was tempted to do, but I did not want to appear less in his eyes, even if that is precisely what I was. I stretched, working the muscles in my shoulders slowly and thoroughly, paced three small circuits around the cramped room in three times as many strides, and then resumed my seat. I continued to read the tedious detail of land ownership in the southern regions of Africa, oblivious to what exactly was worth such secret classification thus far.

Holmes, however, seemed increasingly animated. By this time he had spread a map across one half of the table, and was marking points on it in pencil. He also had pulled various scraps of paper from his pockets, spreading them beside the ledgers. Eventually my curiosity got the better of me.

"Holmes, what are you about?"

"Is it not obvious, Watson? You have been reading the same material as me."

"Perhaps so, but I confess I cannot imagine why this information is considered worthy of such secrecy. Surely the buying and selling of land is a matter of public record?"

Holmes smiled. "Indeed, Watson, but what if someone wanted to prevent citizens such as ourselves from seeing a pattern in such mundane matters? See here–" he drew two ledgers towards him, and opened them at pages he had marked with scraps of paper "–several small landowners sold their claims to the Rotherfield Holdings Company in 1877. Nothing unusual in that, and the land was sold for very little. But see here, Rotherfield sold the combined land holdings to Messrs. Laverick and Chappell only three weeks later, who in turn sold it, together with other parcels of land bought from smaller concerns, to either Price & Cooper Incorporated or Wicks & Hook Limited. In the course of only a month, thirty small holdings were combined into two adjacent holdings." Here he took up his pencil and circled a great area on the map in front of him. "This sort of transaction appears to have taken place dozens of times. Several hundred square miles are all now under the control of either Price & Cooper or Wicks & Hook.

"Now, please note that against each transaction is the mark we have sought."

He swivelled one volume towards me and with a pencil, he stabbed at the very mark drawn on the paper in my hand. Page after page, he showed me the repeated mark.

"What does it mean, Holmes?"

"One of the street Arabs did me the service of seeking out the very real estate historian you suggested we needed. His return correspondence confirmed that the mark is to designate a specific family's holdings, used in rare circumstances. Frobisher's family is just one such that used this back when his family worked for the East India Company, similarly acquiring real estate holdings."

"Financed by family money," I ventured.

"I would surmise as much, yes," Holmes confirmed for me. "Though not in the same company as his fellows, but note those self-same marks appear next to acquisitions that have come to form the holdings of Price & Cooper or Wicks & Hook.

"Have you ever heard the name before, Watson? Surely we, as keen readers of the daily press, should at least have heard of such a monumental concern."

"I have not."

"Deep in these journals exist the board of directors for both concerns and would it surprise you to learn that they are identical? A trio of directors as it were."

"Frobisher, Haldaine, and Chatterton-Smythe," I said slowly.

Holmes nodded. "They were clever, using two corporations to obscure they were the same owners rather than competing concerns."

"Do you mean that Chatterton-Smythe orchestrated a mass buy-out of small landowners? How did he force them to part with their land so willingly? And how did he get the funds?"

"Yes, I believe it was Chatterton-Smythe who fronted the land purchases but also used the Frobisher family mark to further mask his hand in affairs. As to the funds, I suspect that is where Frobisher, with his familial wealth and military history, and Haldaine with his commercial interests across the world, come into play. And those who sold the land? That is darker business, Watson. I also suspect that those companies in the middle of the chain, such as Rotherfield Holdings, are nothing more than fabrications. Our criminals have been buying and selling to themselves, to hide the fact that they were amassing more land than any unelected body should hold."

"So you conclude that Chatterton-Smythe managed to have these ledgers declared classified to prevent anyone from seeing what they were about? Is that possible, Holmes?"

"You know full well, Watson, that once we gather all the facts, even the seemingly impossible can be proved to be the truth."

I scratched at my temple and shook my head in disbelief. "It seems that Frobisher and Haldaine are not the only ones who have things to explain," I said.

I rose and knocked on the door loudly enough to be heard above the din of routine police work on the other side. After a time, a constable unlocked the door and escorted us to Gregson's desk. The inspector had rolled up his shirtsleeves and was writing a report. When we approached, he put down his pen and looked at us.

"You two look quite the sight. Have either of you had anything to eat?"

"No, our mission was too vital to be put on hold," Holmes said, earning him a look of mild rebuke from Gregson. "Now we have what we need, I believe, to present our case. For that, I suggest you arrange to have Edward Haldaine and William Frobisher brought to the station forthwith, Inspector. It will be far more convenient for you to arrest them here—"

"Arrest them? One of the city's pre-eminent businessmen and a decorated war hero? Are you out of your mind, Mr. Holmes?"

"We are talking at the very least about the murder of a peer of the realm, Inspector. I am most definitely in my right mind. Once the evidence has been laid out I trust you will see it is the only course of action available to us. With our friend Alf already present to make the formal identification of Frobisher, bringing the pair here offers the most expeditious use of time." Gregson was dumbstruck. He merely nodded, clearly trusting that Holmes wasn't about to light the touch paper that would send his promising career up in smoke. "Once that is done, I am in no doubt you will be convinced that we need to contact Mr. Leonard Courtney, Undersecretary of State for the Colonies, and have him send urgent word to Pretoria to ensure the signing of the peace treaty with the Boers is preserved."

At that bold statement, Gregson's mouth literally fell open and he blinked, unable to muster a word.

One look into Holmes's eyes more than convinced him of the sincerity and urgency of the request.

He came alive in that moment, the policeman within taking the reins. Gregson snapped his fingers, summoning a constable, who waited while the inspector wrote his orders.

"Holmes, it will be a while before both men are here," said Gregson. "I strongly suggest you both fortify yourselves with some food and drink. If your accusations prove incorrect, your stay here will be much longer and we will not be feeding you." He wasn't smiling.

I pulled on Holmes's sleeve and led him through the reception and out onto the street, where the sun had already lowered itself behind the tallest buildings, casting deep shadows. We rounded the corner and found the first restaurant we could, a small establishment where we had plates of fish from Billingsgate. I ate like a starving man, while Holmes merely picked at his haddock and pushed potatoes around his plate.

* * *

We took a slower pace back to Scotland Yard and were preoccupied with the summer heat making us drowsy so I missed the figure emerging from the doorway. Holmes, though, reacted more quickly and shoved me out of the way as I heard the whoosh of air near my ear. My eyes sought the cause of the sound and my blood ran cold when I saw one of the deadly tiger claws. The figure was off balance and Holmes managed to grab the back of his dark shirt and use the man's momentum to hurl him into the brick of the nearest building.

This stunned the attacker, who staggered backward. He looked very much like Nayar, but not quite. His face was broader and his skin a touch darker but they were clearly of the same lineage, as with the attacker on the train, a brother or first cousin perhaps. Whoever he was, the man recovered his balance and with a snarl, swung towards Holmes, who backpedalled away from the steel claw. Once the arm was fully extended, Holmes grabbed it with both hands and drew the man forward with irresistible force, raising a knee that stiffly met the solar plexus.

The air expelled from his lungs, the Indian was stalled in his attack. He still possessed his weapon while neither of us had any such device. We were also far enough from Scotland Yard that the hope of uniformed officers interceding was unlikely. The Indian recovered quickly and stalked Holmes, ignoring me entirely, and I was most uncertain how best to intercede and improve our odds.

The Indian crouched, preparing to launch himself at Holmes when a rock struck his head, injuring him and allowing Holmes the opportunity to grab the man's steel-clad hand and bend it backwards, forcing the fingers to open, depriving him of the dangerous leverage he previously possessed.

As Holmes forced the claw from the man's fingers, I stole a glance at the direction the rock came from and met the eyes of Petey, handling a slingshot in his right hand, saluting me with his left, a winning grin on his face. Our youthful shadow proved providential and I swore I would not begrudge that rabble another coin. They had earned it with their timely appearance and bravery.

Holmes possessed the claw by the time I looked back at the two, still bending the wrist, threatening to break bone. The Indian tried to kick Holmes's knee so he could break free. Instead, my companion delivered two quick jabs that appeared to take the fight out of the would-be killer.

The man fell to the ground where I straddled him in an attempt to pin him down, suddenly aware we had attracted much attention from the passers-by. Holmes was asking one to summon the police while we stood watch. The Indian lay supine and silent, hatred clouding his eyes.

"You and Nayar are related, are you not?" Holmes asked him.

"The devil with you," was all he would say, but that seemed to confirm our suspicions. I took a closer look at his face. I realised he did not merely resemble our attacker on the train, it *was* him.

"Holmes, this is the same fellow who tried to do for us on the train," I said. "How on earth did he escape custody in York?"

"A question we may be certain Gregson can find out for us," Holmes said. By then, a policeman arrived and took custody of the man. Holmes instructed him to have the inspector join us for the interview as if he were the commanding officer.

We returned to Scotland Yard and Gregson rose upon seeing us. "Are you two fine?"

"He certainly had the worst of it," Holmes said. "I believe this is the man who tried to kill us on the train and is related to the dead mystic Nayar. I think, if you can get him to talk, we will learn they are family."

"How do you make that out?"

"While this one is darker, they possess the same wide-set eyes, bone structure, and nearly identical crooked teeth. The resemblance is painfully obvious, but that's not important, it merely confirms they are linked in this and working together for the gentlemen we've been studying."

"Why the attack now?"

"We need to learn how he escaped custody, but once he realised his brother was dead, desire for revenge against his killer surfaced: me. It was only a matter of time to him and now we have him and perhaps he, like Alf, can help identify the men behind all of this."

Gregson then confirmed that both Frobisher and Haldaine had been sent for and would be presently among us. He had also ordered a constable to track down the whereabouts of the Undersecretary that evening in case his services would be required. Holmes smiled, satisfied with the efficiency and forethought.

Haldaine was the first to arrive and happened to be brought to the very same room where we had interrogated Alf earlier in the day. I rather wondered if he would have appreciated the symmetry of it, had he but known.

"Mr. Haldaine, I trust you are recovered from last night's unpleasantness?" Gregson said by way of introduction.

"I am, yes. I take it I am here regarding that criminal?"

"In part," Gregson admitted.

"Do you need me to identify him? I did not get a good look at him in the darkness, and then those boys intervened. I am not sure how reliable my account will be, I'm afraid."

"That won't be necessary," Gregson assured him. "The man has confessed his intent."

"Then what do you need me for? Surely you can just charge him and be done with it? The man tried to kill me," Haldaine blustered.

"You are here, Mr. Haldaine, because we now have evidence to prove you were part of a criminal conspiracy—" Holmes himself was interrupted at that very moment by a sharp knock on the door. Without waiting for permission to enter, the door swung open, and a man in a black suit stood in the doorway. I realised I had seen him before. He was the man whom we had seen in the reception area, the man who had seemed so out of place.

"Good evening," he said with a pleasant voice.

"This is an official interview, you have no business here," Gregson declared, his anger at the intrusion obvious.

Before answering, the man reached into his coat pocket and withdrew a leather case. He unbound the tie and opened it, revealing a document. He silently handed this to Gregson who read it once, and then read it a second time. Without a word, he replaced it in the leather case and returned it to the man.

There was absolutely nothing remarkable about the intruder. His features were bland: a fine, thin nose, eyes a little widely set apart and ears that stuck out slightly from his head, but none of these characteristics were noteworthy. I'd forget him after a glance, which I came to realise was the desired effect.

Holmes watched the exchange and once the man had pocketed what I presumed were his credentials, he said, "You are with Her Majesty's Government, I presume." It was not a question.

The intruder did not answer directly. Instead he said, "I have arranged transportation. Would you all be so kind as to accompany me to Westminster?" It might have been couched as a request, but

I felt sure that we had little choice in the matter. I rose, followed by Haldaine, Gregson, and finally, Holmes.

As we left through the main portion of the first floor, Haldaine stumbled at one point and Holmes gestured for me to follow his gaze. Directly before the shipping magnate was Nayar's relative and the stumble was clearly because he recognised the figure, a silent conviction that thrilled my heart.

Two carriages, entirely nondescript in appearance, awaited us on the street. I noted that both drivers were attired all in black, both with incredibly well-polished shoes reflecting the evening lamps. I glimpsed Frobisher in one of the carriages, beside him a man nearly identical to our as-yet unidentified visitor. We climbed into the other carriage and rode in silence until we reached the Palace of Westminster.

We were taken down a set of narrow winding stairs to a level below ground, and into a room with windows that overlooked the gently lapping waters of the Thames. In the centre of the room stood a table and matching chairs. On the table lay several rolled-up maps.

Frobisher and Haldaine glared at one another, but neither made a move in the other's direction, though the tension was obvious.

Our silent host positioned them opposite one another at the table, while he gestured for a curious Gregson to take the seat across from Haldaine. I was invited to sit to the unknown man's right and Holmes to his left. The man himself sat with his back close to the door, a guardian to keep us from being disturbed or a warder to prevent us from attempting to leave.

"Mr. Holmes," he said, once we had taken our seats, "if you would be so kind. Outline for everyone what it is you believe you know."

Holmes nodded at the request and folded his hands before him.

"Very well. This is the situation as I am aware of it. The late Patrick Chatterton-Smythe used his position as a Member of Parliament to learn of new diamond seams in the Boer region of Africa."

"How would he know of such discoveries?" Gregson asked.

"Since he is no longer available to answer that I will conjecture that he learned of it from one of the undersecretaries, perhaps someone he knew outside of government. It is not particularly relevant how he found out, merely that he did," Holmes said.

"Representatives of Her Majesty's Government, as well as private concerns, have been mapping the area for many years, and all potential sites are logged and reports sent back to London. He used his influence to have the documentation of the finds expunged from the official record, merely adding a coded sigil to indicate he altered records, and also to direct confederates to a private set of documents, detailing promising territories near a rock formation known as Sorrow's Crown. He needed capital to obtain the lands and therefore sought out others—Mr. Frobisher here providing much of the aforesaid capital—to pool their resources to buy the land upon which the seams were found, seeking to keep the original owners in the dark as to the value of their property. These parcels of land were combined and passed through the hands of a number of false companies and corporations, until finally ending up in the ownership of Price & Cooper and Wicks & Hook, concerns created and controlled by Mr. Chatterton-Smythe and his confederates, Edward Haldaine and William Frobisher, the three who happen to serve on the boards of both companies."

Haldaine began to say something in protest, but a look from the man in black silenced him.

"The plan was to then dig illegal mines on the land and extract the gems, without the knowledge of the British government or the native Boers, thereby avoiding unnecessary taxation or regulation. Mr. Haldaine's shipping interests offered the perfect means of import, enabling them to circumvent customs."

Frobisher and Haldaine exchanged concerned looks.

"They had not reckoned with the tenacity of one woman, Mrs. Hermione Frances Sara Wynter, whose dogged determination to find out the truth about her son has been their undoing." Both then stared at Holmes. Gregson was silent while the still unidentified man nodded once, confirmation that Holmes was indeed on the right track.

"I am entirely uncertain as to how, but Chatterton-Smythe made a deal with Mr. Frobisher here, a decorated officer with familial shareholdings in the East India Company. Mr. Frobisher has a vast network of contacts and resources across the Empire, and yes, the funds with which to successfully mount an illegal mining operation in the region. With Chatterton-Smythe obfuscating the official records with the help of a high-placed civil servant trained at the East India College before it closed its doors in '58, and helping speed through fraudulent companies' charters, he created a series of false companies to hide the true owners of the land. Mr. Haldaine here was recruited to the enterprise for his shipping empire, specifically his access to vessels both legally registered and unknown to any government authority. Chatterton-Smythe also used the Frobisher family mark to annotate the land transactions as a key to his partners as to which properties were under their control.

"However, it was impossible to keep their mining activities completely secret. It seems likely that those small-scale miners and landowners who had sold their property cheap—not knowing what it was worth because the reports of new seams were never made public—began to bring claims against the fraudulent companies which had bought their land, citing unfair practice. It was at this point that the triumvirate recognised they would need some form of physical presence in South Africa. Rather than turn to London's criminal community, they reached out through the remnants of the network that had been the East India Company to the subcontinent and found a fakir, Nayar, and his kin. I still need to ascertain the vital links, but suspect Nayar first used his ricin extract from castor beans on those claimants."

A sudden thought exploded in my mind, a final link made between stray threads. I pushed my chair back, standing, and exclaimed, "That is exactly what happened!"

All eyes turned to me. Holmes cocked an amused eyebrow in my direction while Frobisher and Haldaine shifted uncomfortably in their chairs.

"When you asked me to read up on castor beans and their deadly extract," I explained, "there was a report of two men, miners if I recall, who died after supposedly eating castor beans, which were found among their supplies. It was believed that the men committed suicide, for the beans are known to be poisonous if eaten whole. No, I see now that the Indians must have poisoned the men with ricin and then planted the beans in their belongings to hide their murder."

"Well done, Watson," Holmes said. He paused a moment before continuing his discourse. I sank back down into my seat.

"These men were not the last to be extinguished in this manner. I believe that there are likely many others whose deaths were falsely attributed to illness, and whose demises were never reported.

"This operation endured for several years," Holmes went on, "until the Boer conflict broke out. This was no doubt welcomed by our triumvirate; war is an excellent cover for illegal activities.

One might consider whether they played any part in its beginning or continuation…" At this Holmes paused, clearly thinking of yet another avenue of possible investigation. "In March, however, when the ceasefire was ordered and a treaty seemed inevitable, our men began to panic. There was vast wealth still untapped. A treaty would mean the region would be granted its independence as suzerainty to the Crown and British officials would be crawling over their lands. Our trio, fearing exposure, wanted to conclude their operations as quickly as possible, but the treaty was due to be signed in August, far too soon. As a result, they sought ways to slow down the peace process and once more called on Nayar."

"Are you suggesting Nayar was the one who killed Disraeli?" I asked, earning me astonished looks from almost everyone in the room.

"Why kill Disraeli and not Gladstone, who was sitting PM at the time?" Gregson asked.

"While Prime Minister Gladstone wanted peace, Benjamin Disraeli saw things differently. But he was already a weak man, and could not be relied upon to oppose the treaty with any great strength. Therefore they decided to kill him. His death—they hoped—would create a national sensation. There'd be great outpourings of both grief and affection and the political machinery would inevitably slow down, perhaps delaying the signing of the treaty. It was a vain hope, but they were desperate."

"How could an Indian get so close to Disraeli when he was already ill?" Gregson asked, genuinely distressed by the notion.

"Among the odds and ends left behind in Newcastle were clothes that upon reflection could have been used to pass Nayar off as a house servant. As you know, Inspector, servants tend to be overlooked, little seen and heard less. Nayar could easily have disguised himself, gained access and managed to slip the oil extract into his food, tea, or even medicines. No doubt with all the comings and goings of doctors and messengers and well wishers, one more servant would never have raised suspicion, especially with Disraeli's secretary out of the country."

Gregson uttered an oath and looked sharply at Frobisher and Haldaine. Both men refused to meet his eyes. He turned to me and I gave him silent confirmation that yes, this reached the top of government and involved a dearly loved figure. He was obviously aghast. Holmes's voice never wavered during all this, sounding sure and strong as he ticked his way through the narrative, outlining all of our suspicions.

"Nayar appears to be more resourceful than I imagined," said I.

"Think of it, Watson. Nayar was a performing magician, travelling around England and performing his tricks. Suppose he was one of several such magicians, all free to roam at whim. If we check with South African authorities, I suspect a confederate of his was performing there when the poor solicitor died. If true, he should be apprehended and interrogated to see how far this ring went."

The dark-suited man withdrew a small book from his pocket and made a note, clearly receiving the message from Holmes.

"What solicitor is this?" Gregson inquired, clearly befuddled by the international intrigue.

"While all this was happening in England, work on the treaty progressed in South Africa, and Nayar was called into action, using the ricin extract to kill a solicitor by the name of Charles Lewis. Lewis was part of the Boer contingent working on the treaty, and for all we know others were also dispatched. The news of Lewis's death only made it as far as the British papers because of his relative status in the Boer community. Who knows how many others died in these villains' attempts to upset the peace?

"Here in London, Chatterton-Smythe grew scared, no doubt after hearing–through his connections at the Admiralty–of Dr. Watson and my investigations into goings-on in South Africa. In fact at the time we were ignorant of the scale of the affair. We were only making inquiries at the behest of a mother seeking news of her son. Nayar was sent to dispatch me to my maker, though as luck would have it, he failed. A second attempt was made by another member of his gang on a northbound train, and a third, Nayar himself once again, back here in London. It was during that encounter that the fakir met his end.

"By this time Chatterton-Smythe had become a risk his partners could not stomach, and they called upon Nayar's underlings. They must have had at least three other individuals in their employ. I say this because they staged a death for Chatterton-Smythe that would have required several pairs of hands. Nayar's kin was in custody during this time, indicating there is at least one other man at large. They sought to create a scandal, making it appear that a member of the House of Commons had died after murdering a woman of easy virtue.

"Mr. Haldaine here was growing concerned, but had yet to break faith with his partner in crime. Mr. Frobisher, however, no doubt the one of the three with the most capital invested in the scheme, decided to be rid of Haldaine and take the remainder of what the mines would produce for himself. A crude falling-out amongst thieves. Rather than go back to the Indians, who might betray him to Haldaine, he decided to engage local talent, a certain gentleman of the name of Alf, recruited from that well-known den of iniquity, the Lamb and Flag. He was dispatched to Barton Street with every intention of killing Haldaine, no doubt planning to disguise the murder as a robbery gone awry."

At this Frobisher stirred in his seat, mouth opening, clearly uncertain what he wanted to say or do. Haldaine had begun examining the floor rather than appear a part of this most unusual interrogation.

"Today, I asked Inspector Gregson to bring me the documentation that Chatterton-Smythe had seen classified, as I believed it would help me unravel the web of land transactions and confirm our suspicions. It was the final piece of the puzzle."

There was complete silence as Holmes's narration concluded and the enormity of what had been revealed settled over the room's occupants.

"That's incredible," Gregson said finally, breaking the uncomfortable quiet. "I will have to place these two men under arrest and sort this all out so they may be tried for their many crimes. I will need a medical examiner and an accountant and a barrister…"

He started to rise but Holmes gestured that he remain in place. "There is more," said he.

Gregson's eyes went wide with surprise. "What more could there possibly be?"

"We must not forget what brought us into this investigation in the first place: the fate of one Lieutenant Norbert Wynter." All eyes were on Holmes. "I lack the specific information needed to be certain, but in reading carefully, there appears to be some secret and horrifying event which happened to part of the Naval Brigade from HMS *Dido* near a region known locally as Sorrow's Crown earlier this year, which was covered up by someone in the government."

"Sorrow's Crown is one of the spots owned by this cabal," I said.

"Yes, at the juncture of the Buffels and Slang Rivers," Holmes confirmed.

"How did you figure that out?"

"The notations in the records, the seeming jumble of numbers I found in Haldaine's handwriting at the East India Club. I kept assuming they were a cypher of some sort, the randomness of 33, 27, 50, 20, 59, and 10. It took me some time to realise these were coordinates, longitude and latitude for that exact spot. I finally determined their meaning when perusing the South Africa maps yesterday."

"Anyone could have written those numbers," Gregson said. "How do we tie a scrap of paper to Haldaine?"

"True, Inspector, but there is a distinctive loop to the threes and the seven is reversed, matching Haldaine's hand." Holmes withdrew one of the scraps he had gathered at the East India Club and showed it first to me, then Gregson. "It matches those ledgers, once you can compare them. That is, if we're allowed to prove our case."

All eyes now turned to the dark-suited man, who had merely listened without nodding once in any direction to accept or refute the claims Holmes had laid before the group. He sat still, without betraying a single emotion, until finally, Frobisher spoke up.

"Is it true?"

The man in black nodded once.

Eighteen

The Man in Black

"What remains here, Mr. Holmes, is very much the provenance of the government of Great Britain, not her subjects," the man said as he rose from his chair. He turned to direct his attention toward Gregson and added, "You have more than enough work to do, Inspector. First, we will cable South Africa and increase the security of all involved in the execution of the treaty. Now that we know what threats we face, it should be relatively easy to neutralise them."

He then turned his back on the rest of us and reached for the door handle. As his hand touched the knob Holmes's walking stick snapped against the wood, just above his knuckles.

"Your turn," said he.

I held my breath, not sure how the official would react to Holmes's temerity.

"Inspector Gregson, may I have a private word with Mr. Holmes and Dr. Watson?"

Gregson blinked once then rose and hoisted Frobisher and

Haldaine to their feet. He rapped his knuckles once on the door to summon assistance and a moment later the door opened. A constable helped the inspector escort the two once-powerful men out of the room. As it closed, the man in black resumed his seat, seemingly unperturbed by Holmes's demand.

"You come across like a very proper gentleman," said Holmes. "But your accent reveals you were raised in Leeds and your mannerisms speak of someone forcing himself to behave in a particular manner, going against your more rough-and-tumble upbringing. The cut of your suit is a season or two out of date indicating you are well paid but do not refresh your wardrobe to remain fashionable. All we are meant to see is a nondescript figure in a black suit, inviting no further scrutiny. I, on the eye, look past that veneer. I see someone rescued from poverty and trained first at Oxford, as noted by your cufflinks, and now working for some arm of Her Majesty's Government. The occasional flexing of your hands shows you would rather have administered a royal thrashing to these felons, but remain loyal to your masters."

The unnamed man let out a single laugh and sat back. "Lord, Mycroft has you described to a T," said he.

I did not recognise the name, but if its mention was meant to get a reaction out of Holmes, it failed, although there was a momentary flash in his eyes which I suspect I was the only one to catch.

"I suppose Her Majesty owes you some form of an explanation," he continued. "Your family has done much for Queen and country and might need your services in the future so let us consider this the beginning of a dialogue." He reached across the table to one of the map cases, opened and then unrolled it to reveal a map of the region where the fighting between the British and the Boers had occurred.

"There were four major conflicts in this brief war," the man said. I nodded, recalling the rushed history lesson we had received only days earlier from Professor West. "That is to say there were four battles that were reported. There were, in fact, five."

Holmes nodded, but I am sure I gaped at the man. A fifth unknown battle seemed impossible. How could such a conflict have evaded public attention? He continued with his lecture, tapping a finger at a symbol labelled "Majuba Hill".

"We offered peace on February 21st and the Transvaal independence was guaranteed. Paul Kruger agreed and President Brand of the Orange Free State endorsed the deal. That is the known history. The problem lay in the fact that Major-General Colley was slow to relay the news. The Majuba Hill battle took place, which delayed the peace timetable until March 4th this year, when the negotiations began at O'Neil's Cottage. That was enough of a black eye to the Crown so when another battle took place, another humiliating defeat I should say, it was kept quiet.

"This fifth battle was joined between Schuinshoogte and Majuba Hill as Colley's successor in command sought refuge at Mount Prospect. He was without the cavalry, and lacked sufficient ammunition. The ground was too steep, making it impossible for the twelve hundred men to successfully protect their flank. This area became a killing zone as the advancing British infantry were exposed to Boer fire from both the front and right flank. It was ugly, Mr. Holmes. None of our men made it closer than maybe fifty yards from the Boer positions, and they made a rather disorderly withdrawal under intense fire. What followed was a massacre."

I stared at the man, unable to believe what he was saying.

"Given the location, this event became known as the Sorrow's Crown Massacre. A small portion of the Naval Brigade that had fought at Majuba, some twenty naval troops from HMS *Dido* and HMS *Boadicea* joined their army brethren amongst the dead. There was only one poor man who survived the attack and he was horribly injured. He lasted long enough to make a full report. Once it reached the Admiralty and then Her Majesty, it was determined not to publicise a defeat sustained in a battle that occurred when everyone believed a ceasefire was in place. It would not have looked good for us, needless to say, and might have jeopardised the peace. As a result, the Queen herself insisted the report be classified, never to be revealed. The files of those men lost were 'adjusted', erasing any trace of evidence that the battle had ever taken place. The surviving officers are subject to a set of secret laws and should anyone so much as mention the Battle of Sorrow's Crown, they will be arrested and tried for treason."

I sat stunned, unable to formulate a proper response to the revelation of such a heinous action. How could this be my country? My mind drifted back to Mrs. Wynter, desperate to believe her son was anything but a deserter. We had the proof of the matter, but could we ever tell her?

"Now, I have a question for you, Mr. Holmes. How did you find that which we had worked so hard to ensure no longer existed?"

"There is always a trail of connections, seen and unseen, sir. One simply needs to know how to interpret the signs. I believe, were one to exhume the graves of Mount Prospect Cemetery near Majuba Hill one would find more bodies than the official records from the February 27th battle could account for. Dr. Watson here interviewed comrades of our missing man, who confirmed that he never returned to the *Dido*. Inquiries into his whereabouts met with lies and obfuscation. I believe that is where he lies, along with several of his fellows who were likewise listed as deserters."

"So, you divined a secret battle and an international conspiracy, simply because you were looking for one missing sailor," the man said. It was not a question.

"Yes," Holmes agreed. "Now, in the spirit of free and frank exchange, I have a question for you, my unnamed friend. Given your presence here and knowledge of our activities, you clearly represent some covert arm of the government. I desire to know how you became aware of my investigation."

"Ah, that's easy enough to answer, Mr. Holmes. We, like the late Mr. Chatterton-Smythe, have ears at the Admiralty. We already knew that a certain Mrs. Wynter had been making inquiries into the disappearance of her son. But you proved far more successful. I began studying you and following your actions from afar. Had you needed help at any point we would have come to your aid, but you seem to have a fondness for younger, and less law-abiding assistance."

I chuckled out loud at the idea that the government allowed the street urchins to do their dirty work. On the other hand, I was getting quite perturbed at the number of people who had been following our trail. Hampton's men, Nayar or his kin, the Irregulars, and now it seemed some secret branch of the government. This provoked a chill down my spine.

"Actually, sir," said I, interrupting the exchange. "A little assistance might have been welcome when Hampton's men were stalking and attacking us."

Holmes tightened his lips at that and we eyed the dark-suited man. "Again, you seemed to take it well and those unauthorised attacks occurred early in your investigation. Had they continued, we might have stepped in."

"What of Hampton? He's got to pay for sending those blokes after us," said I.

"I suggest you check Mr. Hampton's accounts," said Holmes. "We were informed that Wynter had been paid through July, but if he died in February, who received those funds? I suggest to you that it was arranged as a sort of retainer for Hampton, funds he could use to recruit his men when necessary."

Ah, yes, I nodded in agreement. It was all getting tidied up now.

"True. Be assured that within a day or two, Mr. Hampton will no longer serve in Her Majesty's Navy and finding employment should also prove difficult. As for the men, to actually do his bidding they were following orders so I will see that their advancement opportunities are now curtailed."

I made a noise to indicate my overall dissatisfaction with the plan but saw little else that could be done.

"Let me put it another way: why do you exist?" Holmes asked flatly.

I stared at the man, not at all expecting any sort of a satisfactory answer, but curious to see how he deflected Holmes from his course.

"Great Britain has enemies, Mr. Holmes. Powerful enemies. We are here to serve in our own way."

There was another lengthy silence as the unspoken prospects filled the air.

"Now, gentlemen, I have work to do, so I need to know, before we open that door, if you will agree to keep every word of what you have discovered, from the true nature of Disraeli's death to the events at Sorrow's Crown, a secret? I cannot cut out your tongues, which would solve my problem most expeditiously." He laughed, although I was not entirely sure he was joking. "But I know more than a little about you both. You are of good character and have done much good work in your own way. As it stands, Her Majesty owes you a debt for exposing the illegal mining and the deeds of those three men, but before I can allow you to leave this room she needs your promise of discretion."

He paused, letting the words fill the air and settle around us. I knew my own answer, but could not be sure that Holmes would acquiesce.

"Let me speak plainly—we are all men of the world here. If you disagree, or at some later date say something inappropriate, we will have little choice but to destroy you."

It was a cold threat, but one I knew he could and would keep, which unleashed a chill shiver and set it to running from the nape of my neck all the way down to the base of my spine.

"You owe us a debt," Holmes said. I closed my eyes, dreading the next words to leave my companion's mouth. "It is one I am minded to have you pay immediately. Dr. Watson and I will agree to your terms but only on one condition."

"Name it," the man in black said.

"As we have said, this all began with the search for the whereabouts of Lieutenant Norbert Wynter, late of the *Dido*, one of the casualties of Sorrow's Crown. Someone not only did him the disservice of listing him as Missing in Action, but went so far as to besmirch his name with whispers of desertion."

"While I have a great many powers, raising the dead is not among them."

"You may though, possess the ability to bring a measure of peace to his widowed mother," Holmes countered. "I want his record restored, his reputation burnished, and his mother properly accommodated for not only losing her son, but for her long months of uncertainty and anguish." The man nodded.

"I will go one better. When you return home, you should find a receipt for your next two months' rent already paid."

I gaped at his knowledge of our financial straits but chose to remain silent, lest I jinx our good fortune. A man with that many resources at his disposal was not to be trifled with and I admit knowing he had such easy access to our intimate doings was most disquieting.

The deal was done swiftly and within a heartbeat, the case was closed. Holmes had once more done the seemingly impossible.

The man knocked twice on the door and within moments, two identically dressed men presented themselves. They flanked Holmes and me. Our host said, "Now, Doctor, I would appreciate you turning in your journal. I am afraid I must insist that no published record of any aspects of this case be revealed. While I appreciate that you are a man of your word, and your character is unimpeachable, the Crown would feel more comfortable if it was in safe keeping. This is not a request, Doctor."

I had rarely felt so menaced in such a calm manner. The mere presence of these men, so close to me, was not comfortable, nor was the dead, cold stare of the man in black for all his mild manners. He walked forward, hand outstretched. I wanted to argue but knew my words would be ignored.

Rather than waste my breath on a futile argument, I reached into my coat and withdrew the journal. The man took it from me, flipped the cover open to verify I was handing over the appropriate volume, and then pocketed it. I thought of the notebook in which I had transcribed the interviews with Wynter's comrades and Miss Caroline Burdett, no doubt sitting in plain sight in our sitting room in Baker Street, and hoped he would not ask whether I had any other writings the Crown would prefer remain hidden. I did not think I could lie convincingly to this man.

"Thank you, Dr. Watson," he said. "I truly have enjoyed your stories of Mr. Holmes's other cases, and genuinely regret that I will not be able to enjoy your account of this adventure." He nodded once in our direction and then turned on his well-polished heel and strode out of the room with his comrades.

Holmes and I were suddenly alone for the first time in I could not recall how long, and I was feeling a broiling mixture of emotions, uncertain of which one to let out. As their footsteps receded, a feeling of exhaustion came over me and I knew all I wanted was to return to Baker Street and sleep.

"That was underhanded, Holmes," I finally said.

"Indeed, but all very legal it appears," he said.

"Are you not bothered by these secrets? Nearly two dozen dead men with wives, parents, siblings, and children all ignorant of what became of them!"

"Of course I am, Watson, but I am sanguine enough to realise there are things we can control, and things that are beyond our purview. I am not at all interested in being engaged in politics and state secrets. We are more useful employed helping people like Mrs. Wynter. The sum of our employment was to find the truth about Norbert Wynter and that we have done, and done admirably well. Strip away everything else we have experienced and learned, and take pride in the fact that we have accomplished what we set out to do. Mrs. Wynter's son's reputation and memory will be returned to her."

He was not wrong, but then he so rarely was.

Nineteen

Peace

For all my tiredness, I could not sleep.

We returned to Baker Street, stopping on the way so that Holmes could place an order with his street Arabs to procure a batch of cigars due in from Nicaragua on the morning tide. I had no idea how my companion could be so aware of the comings and goings at Custom House.

While Holmes sat in his chair by the fire, no doubt fussing over the cigars, I sat at the table in our sitting room, paper and pen in hand, completing the composition of my letter to Mrs. Wynter. I opened the notebook which contained the interviews with Miss Burdett, George Raskill, and Louis Dodge, and sifted through it one more time to see what his friends and lover had to say about him. There was no doubt more to the man than I would ever know but I knew enough to confirm once and for all that he was anything but a deserter.

He was in love. He was a poor gambler. He was an excellent dart player. He could not tell jokes. He *volunteered* for the mission that had cost him his life. Lieutenant Norbert Wynter was a man like any other with foibles and accomplishments but no one could call him a deserter.

I began twice before finding the proper way to compose my biographical sketch; my letter was to be a fitting eulogy for the son who did not come home from war. It was difficult to write about a man I had never met and barely knew, even from the interviews I had conducted. I kept at it, though, and was thoroughly ignored by Holmes, who only stirred when an Irregular arrived with a package that smelled strongly of tobacco. He then sat smoking, keeping his own counsel. He had never shown any curiosity about Wynter the man. Holmes saw him as an object to be found, not a man to be understood.

That fell to me and clarified in my own mind what qualities I brought to our partnership. His keen intellect could never be matched but his understanding of human nature, the human condition, that was something I knew all too well. I could continue reminding him of the personal price exacted by the very act of living.

With that in mind, I proceeded deliberately, conjuring forth the words I needed to bring Norbert Wynter to life one final time. The letter covered three sheets of paper, each in the best possible penmanship I could muster. I let the ink dry, reread it and declared the missive as proper as I could manage. I signed it, placed it in an envelope, and slipped the letter into my jacket pocket.

I waited until Holmes retired to his room, then ventured out. I had a place I needed to be. Whilst I could not tell Mrs. Wynter the particulars of her son's death, I could set her mind at ease and offer her the testimonies of his comrades, and in some small way, perhaps, finally bring him home to her.

About the Authors

Steven Savile is the author of over thirty novels, including *Inheritance* and *Vampire Wars*, and won the L. Ron Hubbard Writers of the Future Award in 2002. He was nominated for the International Media Tie-In Writer's SCRIBE Award in 2007 for *Slaine: The Exile* and was runner-up in the British Fantasy Awards in 2011. He has written extensively for *Star Wars*, *Warhammer* (Black Library), *Doctor Who* and *Torchwood*.

Robert Greenberger held senior editorial roles at both Marvel and DC Comics before becoming a freelance writer and editor. He has written many books, both fiction and non-fiction, including *The Essential Batman Encyclopedia*, *The DC Comics Encyclopedia*, as well as novels for *Batman*, *Hellboy*, *Predator* and *Star Trek*.

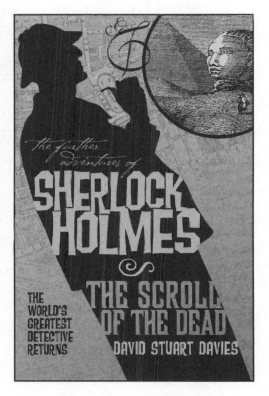

THE FURTHER ADVENTURES
OF SHERLOCK HOLMES

THE SCROLL OF THE DEAD

David Stuart Davies

In this fast-paced adventure, Sherlock Holmes attends a seance to unmask
an impostor posing as a medium. His foe, Sebastian Melmoth is a man hell-
bent on discovering a mysterious Egyptian papyrus that may hold the key
to immortality. It is up to Holmes and Watson to use their deductive skills
to stop him or face disaster.

ISBN: 9781848564930

AVAILABLE NOW!

THE FURTHER ADVENTURES
OF SHERLOCK HOLMES
THE VEILED DETECTIVE

David Stuart Davies

It is 1880, and a young Sherlock Holmes arrives in London to pursue a career as a private detective. He soon attracts the attention of criminal mastermind Professor James Moriarty, who is driven by his desire to control this fledgling genius. Enter Dr John H. Watson, soon to make history as Holmes' famous companion.

ISBN: 9781848564909

AVAILABLE NOW!

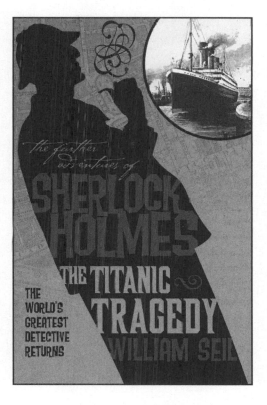

THE FURTHER ADVENTURES
OF SHERLOCK HOLMES

THE TITANIC TRAGEDY

William Seil

Holmes and Watson board the Titanic in 1912, where Holmes is to carry out a secret government mission. Soon after departure, highly important submarine plans for the U.S. navy are stolen. Holmes and Watson work through a list of suspects which includes Colonel James Moriarty, brother to the late Professor Moriarty—will they find the culprit before tragedy strikes?

ISBN: 9780857687104

AVAILABLE NOW!

THE FURTHER ADVENTURES
OF SHERLOCK HOLMES

THE WEB WEAVER

Sam Siciliano

A mysterious gypsy places a cruel curse on the guests at a ball. When
a series of terrible misfortunes affects those who attended, Mr. Donald
Wheelwright engages Sherlock Holmes to find out what really happened
that night. Can he save Wheelwright and his beautiful wife Violet from
the devastating curse?

ISBN: 9780857686985

AVAILABLE NOW!